PERIPHAGE BLUES

Chuck Boeheim

Lampworks Publishing

COPYRIGHT

ISBN (ebook): 979-8-9927954-0-0
ISBN (print): 979-8-9927954-1-7

CONTENTS

THE COLOR OF AIR

SHE HAD A CHESHIRE SMILE.

It was meant for me and no one else in the crowded room. It made the bar lights dim in existential despair. It was a smile that kept secrets.

She sat down beside me on a miraculously open stool. The working girls at the end of the bar wilted visibly; several looked like they were considering a career change. The bartender started over, but she looked dismissively away; he ceased to exist though his body continued for a time to do bartenderly things.

"Nice entrance. Was it holography? A glamour? Pheromones?" I knocked back my 80 proof antidote and hoped the zombie behind the bar could still recognize an empty glass.

"Anything wrong with old-fashioned style and grace?" Her voice was low and rich, with harmonics that made the auditory nerves swoon with pleasure. My suspicion went up another notch. A telepath?

"I never knew those to be in fashion in this port," I replied. "Buy you a drink?"

"Thank you, Captain Whitt, but I don't drink anything they serve here. But please go ahead." She raised a finger and a fresh glass appeared in front of me. That speed was going to put a blip in the bar's service stats for weeks.

I took a sip, along with a moment to study her. She wore a simple dress that fell from one shoulder, which accented her graceful body without concealing it. She moved within its veil like a glimpsed shadow, and I could tell that wisp was all she wore. She had flawless cinnamon skin, pale wheaten eyes and hair, and sensuous, deep chocolate lips. She almost seemed like a photographic negative.

"So you know my name. If you're looking for passage, all the berths are full." They weren't, but the one that was had paid handsomely for their privacy.

"I was more interested in making your acquaintance," she said. My finger tightened on the needle gun in my pocket. Inquisitive folks are seldom good news in my line of work.

"Care to elaborate on that interest?"

"I have heard that you are the only man to have slept with a Medusa and live. Tell me, is it true?"

I shuddered a bit at that. "Let me put it this way: I'm alive because the only thing I *didn't* do that night is sleep. What's your interest in that?"

"I wanted someone with ... experience," she breathed into my ear.

"I don't think you would enjoy Medusa foreplay ... wait, that's not it, is it? You want to know how to defeat a Medusa."

"I thought we might join forces." She freighted the last two words with enough innuendo to form its own event horizon.

"I have a full agenda for the foreseeable future. Why would I be interested?"

"I happen to know that there is a valuable piece of art with a ready buyer, which belongs to a particularly possessive Medusan. If you want to know more, we should go somewhere more private. Say, your quarters?"

"We wouldn't want any witnesses, would we?" This bar was too public for good sex or for the discreet disposal of an inconvenient body – though both had happened here. I was leaning towards the latter, with the mention of the Medusa and the private piece of unfinished business I had with it.

We made our way to the lift. My new acquaintance preceded me as we stepped on the platform with an alluring sway. I decided a little horizontal encounter might be a welcome diversion before I dumped her. As the doors closed, I asked, "Somehow you know my name. How about yours?"

"In your language, it would be translated as Color of Air."

"How does it sound in your language?"

She pressed herself against me and lightly touched my lips with hers. Flavors of purple mint danced across my palate, with a tenor of red pepper and a downbeat of lilac at the end. She drew back and smiled her secret smile. "That's how we 'say' it in my language."

"Well, that's rather novel. Not very good for long-distance communication, is it?"

"No, it's not. My people live to touch."

"I look forward to our negotiations."

The lift door opened at the .7G level, my habitual compromise between comfortable sleeping and not chasing stray items in the smallest breeze. My room was a half span spinward, giving me time to observe her as we walked. She was a very good actor, but her eyes flicked to the door an instant before I turned to open it. She knew which one was mine; she had scouted me very thoroughly.

Inside, she turned to me, eyes downcast seductively. She touched her right fingers to her right shoulder, the wisp fell away, leaving her naked before me. Naked? That implies a certain vulnerability, and she still wore a confidence that was magnificent enough for a royal court.

I found myself with an armful of warm fragrant woman, teaching me new words in her language. I especially liked the one with tones of raspberry and cocoa that used black pepper for punctuation. I wondered what the translation was.

She pushed my jacket back over my shoulders, then stepped around behind me to ease it down my arms. She reached around from behind and began unbuttoning my shirt while nibbling artfully on my ear. Another pair of hands undid the clasp on my belt. Another slid within my shirt to explore the smooth muscles there, while another began to work its way under my waistband ...

Too many hands. She must have had an accomplice waiting in my cabin. I whirled, going for the throats. My left hand closed on air, my right on ...

I held a many-armed, three-breasted goddess who could have presided over an ancient fertility temple. She gently loosened my grip with two hands, placed one hand against my cheek, and continued, well, other things with the rest.

"This is the form I prefer, but it's just *so* hard to buy clothes for."

"It might have been safer to have given me some warning."

"I never felt unsafe." She opened a hand containing the clip from my needle gun and another hand holding the empty weapon.

This was my kind of woman. The kind that kept you wondering if you were going to get out alive. She efficiently plucked away the rest of my clothes and enfolded me in a many-armed embrace.

"At first, I was thinking genetically modified human, but now my money's on nonhuman," I said while trying to figure out how to return that embrace without getting tangled.

" 'What's in a name? A rose by any other name would smell as sweet.' I have always felt that was a profound insight since, to me, the scent of the rose is its true name."

"What's my true name, then?"

"It's more complicated with sentient beings. I taste desire, caution, confidence, and the lamb curry you had for lunch. I think we had better let that wear off, or I would name you 'Confident Garlic.'"

I chuckled. She was good with a one-liner. I was stroking her back, ostensibly in foreplay, but also noticing the multiple shoulder joints down her back and deciding which one would be easiest to dislocate in a fight. Actually, it's all foreplay. She moaned in basil-scented approval.

She pushed me down on the bed and climbed on top. What followed was frenzied and breathless and perhaps too soon concluded, though the anticipation of a second round made that more of a promise than a regret. I lay bathed in basil satisfaction amid her ever-present purple mint, red pepper, and lilac. A scent like evergreens in the wind entered her smile.

"We should conclude our negotiations now," she said.

"We haven't even begun them."

"We've been talking this entire time in my language. I've learned everything I need to know."

I wondered what the color/scent equivalent of a raised eyebrow was. "And what have you learned?"

She bent to kiss me deeply. A tang of citrus and sugar was an unfamiliar answer. Then, before my eyes, her outline softened and flowed. Her body became a thick liquid that poured down to cover me from head to toe. It was more intensely pleasurable than anything that had gone before but also scared the hell out of me. I thrashed but couldn't break free. I couldn't breathe. The fluid filled my mouth and nose. I tried reaching for the knife I had hidden under the pillow, but I was held in soft bands that were as strong as steel. I could feel those bands tightening, driving the air from my lungs. As blackness covered my vision, I could hear my bones breaking. The darkness had the scent of hickory smoke.

I hadn't expected the afterlife to have ocean breezes, scents of kelp and barnacles, tastes of papaya and banana accented with cloves. I hadn't expected an afterlife at all. There was no time. No rhythms to count. Nowhere to be and no way to get there. I had lost the sense of a beginning and an end and the habit of measuring how long it had been or was to be. I was vaguely aware that this was unlike my accustomed state. Existence should be coupled with events, but those were curiously lacking.

Light was returning now along with patterns of darkness. Lines. Objects. An eye was open. I could see my cabin. My viewpoint rose, lurching slightly, and moved towards the bathroom. I had no sensation that I was in control of that motion. The interior of the bathroom came into view, a mirror. I saw a humanform blob, glistening, smooth and featureless. It was lumpy, as if there were larger pieces concealed deep inside. Pieces like parts of a body in the process of digestion. I needed to retch, but I had no stomach. I needed to scream, but I had no mouth. When I read that story, I never expected to need that line.

Color of Air was a Shapestealer. I had heard whispered tales of such beings but not from anyone who had ever seen one. Always by someone who knew someone who knew someone now dead, alas. They were reputed to be without feeling, but no mention had ever been made that their diet consisted of starship captains.

The figure in the mirror sat on the toilet and excreted a large quantity of mass. I have disposed of bodies before, but this had to be nearly untraceable. The form slimmed down until it was an unremarkable humanform of average size, which described either me or Color of Air to first order. It stood and inspected itself intently with an eyeless gaze. It melted and ran like a wax figurine in a reactor core.

The shoulders broadened, the waist narrowed; it took on my proportions. Features appeared on the face, briefly those of Color of Air, but then flowing into my own. The Shapestealer was impersonating me. Worse than that, it was *becoming* me, stealing my face and probably my life.

The Shapestealer contemplated me in the mirror, adjusting minor details until even I wasn't sure of the image that had faced me on prior mornings. Had that mole been precisely *there*? Or had it been a half-inch higher? And what did it matter, in that location that no one would see?

Now she was practicing my facial expressions: the jaunty grin, the poker face, the roguish smile, the thunderous frown, the look of absolute innocence (reserved for customs officers). Some of these Color of Air wouldn't have seen in our brief acquaintance. Was she reading them from muscle memory?

After she had refined an image that I wouldn't have given a second glance in the mirror, she turned back to the bedroom. Vertigo struck hard at the sensation of watching my body move without my will. In a panic, I employed all the hindbrain commands that had worked without fail every day of my life (not counting some bouts with illicit substances). Not only did I fail to stop, turn aside, grab onto a doorway, or collapse on the bed, I couldn't even feel my body doing the things I saw it doing. No scuff of carpet on the feet, no sense of fabric as she handled my discarded clothes. I was a disembodied passenger in my own body.

Color of Air decided that the clothes I had worn yesterday weren't suitable and reached for my luggage. I felt a prickle that would have been sweat if I could still operate my glands. I didn't want to die again.

I heard the frown in the Shapestealer's tone as she muttered in my voice, "I should know this combination now. Maybe it's in muscle memory." She placed my hand on the keypad; the fingers began to trace out the opening engram. She did have my muscle memory. And that was very dangerous.

"STOP! IT'S BOOBY TRAPPED!" I shouted as loudly as I could.

Color of Air stepped back and glanced around the room. She was clearly surprised but kept her wits. My needle gun appeared in her hand. "Did you have an assistant AI?" she said out loud. She sounded like me.

She heard me. Somehow, she heard me. I tried again. "Don't touch the luggage! It will kill you … me … us." No words disturbed the air in the room, but Color of Air heard me. She sat down heavily on the bed.

«You're in my head,» she said. «That shouldn't happen.» She didn't speak out loud, but I could "hear" her all the same. The voice in my head sounded like the woman from the bar last night.

«What is supposed to happen?» I demanded. «Let me guess, you get all my memories and skills but you digest the person.»

«Crudely put, but something like that.»

10

«*But you're surprised, so something didn't work as you expected.*»

«*Tell me how to open the luggage.*»

She wasn't going to get sidetracked, but odds were that her plan was off the rails.

«*I'm not going to tell you anything. You want to know how to defeat a Medusa, I'm going to need some information. You want my ship, I'm going to need some assurances that you don't kill me. You see where I'm going with this?*»

«*How did you know I want your ship?*»

«*I read the clues, made the deduction,*» I told her. It had been a bluff that paid off, in truth. «*You don't just need my memories, you need my street smarts.*» I felt like I was bidding on a job I didn't want — passenger in my own head — but I wanted even less to be dead. I clung to the hope that there was a way out. For that, I had to stall for time.

«*What do you want in return?*»

«*I want my body back.*»

«*That's not possible now.*»

«*Then I want to at least continue to not be dead.*»

«*That's not what I want.*»

Color of Air arose, wearing a body that looked like mine. She walked into the bathroom, stood in the bathtub, and carefully plugged the drain. Then she melted into a puddle.

I lost vision and hearing, though I continued to "hear" her thoughts. Touch and smell came to the fore, unnoticed until now, as we sank into the basin and sloshed viscously in the bottom. It tasted of the chemicals of the cleaner's art, fragrances that distracted from but utterly failed to cover the residues of past inhabitants. Skin cells human and avian, scales of reptiloids, the choke of a silicomorph. All of these had completely escaped my notice as a human. I could feel churning and sloshing along with the thoughts of her plan to dislodge me somehow. It made me want to hang on as if I were on a bareback toadsteed from Canyonrim (that had been quite a ride), but I had no hands to hang on with and nothing to hang on to. All I could do was muster a determination not to be bucked off.

I finally felt a rising sensation, and my vision returned. A young female human was forming in the mirror, dusky of skin, dark of hair, pretty in a youthful, athletic way. Was this her original form?

«*I'm still here,*» I told her. «*Now can we talk about some mutually beneficial arrangement?*»

Color of Air didn't answer me. She strode out of the bedroom. I had pegged her as willful and accustomed to getting her way from the moment she walked into the bar. Then I wondered how safe I could be interpreting human body language in such an alien being. She must put on mannerisms as easily as skin. I felt safe in the willfulness assessment anyway, no matter the body language.

She started donning the clothes I had worn last evening. From glimpses of my body, I could see that she had resumed a form that would fit them, presumably mine. The hands and feet looked tolerably familiar. When she exited the room, she took my uniID card and needle gun.

She didn't go far. A short walk spinward, she entered a cabin she appeared to have rented. I really wanted to know what face she had used with the front desk. I saw my hands opening a drawer, pulling out a package, and fanning a deck of uniID cards. I had paid dearly for a couple of fake cards, which were supposed to have unbreakable encryption and all sorts of guarantees of identity verification. She had at least twenty-five. I would have whistled if I still had lips.

She selected a card with a hologram of a fairly average-looking male with pale hair and skin much lighter than mine. As she headed out the door, I caught a passing reflection of that face wearing my clothes. It was maddening to only see myself when she happened to pass a mirrored surface; she didn't seem to feel any need to check her own appearance. I only saw what she saw.

We "ascended" hubward into a lighter gravity region. The lift had the scent of sunshine and grass that had been cut the day before. «There's a Blue on the station», she said to herself. A smugness like fresh cream colored the thought, making me think she was showing off her perception for my benefit. But the giraffe-like quadrupeds didn't travel far from their homeworld, so this was indeed interesting. I had never sensed their native smell before.

Just outside the lift on level 6.32 was the entrance to the hospital. But she turned into an unoccupied side corridor just short of the shimmerdoor marked Admissions. She raised her leg to chest height, knee bent, put her left forearm around the knee, and efficiently broke her arm with a sharp pull.

I yelped at the sharp snap, expecting a blast of pain, but nothing came. I guessed a Shapestealer didn't feel pain that way. For that matter, why break it when she could just make it any shape she wanted?

Color of Air walked back around the corner and through the semi-solid air of the shimmerdoor. The stiff air pressed her clothes — *my* clothes, I reminded myself — against her body in a brief tingle as she passed through. The sensation was a tickle like the scent of dill. Her senses were definitely syncopated.

The receptionist at the front desk looked up and then dropped the tablet he held as he took in the forearm dangling crookedly in the breeze. "What happened to you?"

"It got slammed when some cargo shifted," Color of Air said through convincingly gritted teeth.

"Sit down. I'll send a medic with a gurney right away. Do you have your uniID with you?"

Color of Air passed over the card that matched her current face. The receptionist scanned it, then pushed over a standard DNApad with its microscopic needle. Color of

Air pulled her hand back. "I must decline. I have a privacy lock on my DNA due to some proprietary sequences I carry." This must not be unheard-of, since the receptionist merely switched it for a fingerprint scanner. Mighty convenient excuse for someone who might not even have DNA.

The medic rushed in, pushing a nullGrav gurney. She prodded the break with delicate fingers, then ran a sensor wand over the fracture. "We can set this for you and give you an injection of bonegrow to fuse it together. I want a better image, though, so we'll take you to Imaging first." Now I understood why she had taken the trouble of an authentic fracture.

"Thank you. Not my first break, so I know the drill." Color of Air was affecting a tough nonchalance that went with the body she was wearing. "I don't need the floater; I can walk."

The medic escorted us out of the reception area, waving a hand at the interior shimmerdoor to make it depolarize momentarily to let us pass. Color of Air affected a slight stagger, and the medic moved closer to take her elbow (the unbroken one) and prop her up. (I had pronoun dissonance, still thinking of Color of Air as the female I first saw even though she was now wearing a male body.) Color of Air took the medic's hand, warm and vanilla fragrant. I could feel the cinnamon-sharp whorls of fingerprint patterns silently transfer into Color of Air's hand.

In Imaging, we were handed off to the technician on duty. But as soon as the technician, a small woman with mouse-colored hair, turned away after issuing instructions to remove our shirt, Color of Air pulled the needle gun and shot her in the back of the neck. The technician slumped to the floor. I hoped it had been set to stun.

Color of Air stripped off her clothes and turned the control panel so she could reach it from the imaging table. As she climbed on the bed, I got glimpses of dark limbs and breasts, so she seemed to have reverted to the form I had seen after she had attempted to flush me out in the bathtub.

She set the scan for full body and let herself go boneless on the table. Literally. I felt like a humanform sack of gelatin. She triggered the scan with a hand that looked more like a pseudopod and waited for the result. The results came in. X-rays: a smooth sheet of protoplasm, with no visible structure. Infrared: the same. Ultrasound: a blank dark sheet.

By now, Color of Air was fuming. «Where are you?» she muttered. I was unable to and uninterested in enlightening her. She removed a panel from the machine and changed a void-your-warranty setting inside that would allow the machine to scan a silicomorph turtle or cook anything with lesser integuments.

«Wait!» I said. «Move the technician into the shielded room.

You'll kill her at that setting if she stays there.»

I felt a deep iron tang of skepticism. *«Why do you care?»*

«She's a living being, innocent of any involvement in this. Have some compassion.»

«I don't expect compassion from solids. They are filled with fear and self-interest.» Nonetheless, she firmed up her body enough to get off the table and drag the technician into the shielded booth. Then she returned to the table.

«Satisfied?»

«Thank you.»

«Now you can die with a clear conscience.» She triggered the machine.

After five minutes she turned it off with a slight tremble in her finger. After another minute of resting, she pulled her body upright and tried to make it assume a coherent form. It objected and slumped back down. She had taken enough radiation to kill any lifeform I knew about, even the quartz-based ones. She hurt, like a sunburn from a close orbit around Sirius-A, more like carbon charring than a tan. She healed in minutes; she knew her limits.

«I hate to tell you, but I'm still here. It didn't even hurt.»

She firmed up into the slender form that seemed to be her baseline. From that vantage point, she bared her teeth at me on the shiny control screen. It wasn't a happy smile —it had sharp teeth and dagger eyes. Then she shifted into the form that matched her current uniID, dressed hurriedly, and headed for the door.

«*Wait!*»

She stopped. Impatience was capsaicin-sharp. «*What?*»

«*If you leave the machine on that setting, the next patient will be injured or killed.*»

«*Why do you care?*»

«*It's the right thing to do. Protect innocent people. Besides, right now, they'll shrug this off as a minor mystery disappearance. You don't want it to become sabotage or murder.*»

«*Fine.*» She went back to the console, restored it to normal parameters, and replaced the panel. Then she left with a set to her shoulders that said she wouldn't be stopped again.

At the first intersection, she started to turn right, towards the entrance. I said, «*No, go left. Use the medic's fingerprints you lifted.*»

«*Too clever,*» she said. I didn't know if she meant me or my plan, but she turned left.

I guided her through a few more turns, with the incongruity of the tall man's body and the petite medic's hand to wave at the shimmerdoors. We came to the receiving department (for supplies, not living beings), which had a prosaic and functional exit into a freight corridor. Color of Air seemed to know how to navigate this network and made her way to a connecting door near our two cabins.

I remarked that she might not want to wear the face that the hospital could connect with an assault on the technician. Color of Air snapped, «*Don't tell me my business!*» I saw in a brief reflection that she had put on a face that was so generic that it might have belonged to an android or a video star.

Safe in my quarters again, Color of Air sat in the chair and eyed the crouching luggage. I wished for the bottle of whiskey on the table beside it, but my host made no move toward it. After a while she asked me, «*Why did you help me in the hospital?*»

«*I didn't want anyone else to get hurt, so I got you out the back way.*»

«*Everything I have heard about you says that you are self-interested, calculating, and avaricious. That doesn't sound like someone who would be concerned with the welfare of others.*»

«*Look at you, wearing other people's faces. What do any of them tell me about who's inside?*»

Color of Air made no reply. When she spoke again, it was a different topic.

«*I don't want you in my head, but I can't get rid of you and I can't assimilate you. You're most persistent at both surviving and offering help. What am I going to do with you? What do you want?*»

«*I didn't want this, any more than you did. We just have to make the best of our situation. I have skills and a ship. You have an interest in purloining something valuable. That sounds like the basis of a partnership to me. I want an equal share.*» What I really wanted was another shot at the Medusa. This body I was riding in might tilt the odds in my favor this time.

«*I don't understand you. Aren't you angry?*»

I looked inside. Of course I was angry. Spitting gamma rays like a breached core angry. My life had been hijacked, my body destroyed. I was reduced to a voice in a box in the dark, looking out through someone else's eyes. I hadn't noticed. Why?

I had been totally preoccupied with survival since my breath had been cut off and my bones broken. I was more than a little fascinated to see the capabilities of this being. More than that, I didn't have a heart to pound, a stomach to churn, or cortisol-laden anxiety to sicken my blood. Without these symptoms, there had been nothing to call that anger to my attention. Who knew?

«*I am angry that you didn't ask for my partnership before stealing it, but anger isn't going to accomplish anything useful. I just have to make the best of the hand I've been dealt.*» In that moment, the seeds of revenge stirred in the darkness. My life *had* been stolen, and it would be sweet to get it back.

«*What do you propose? I can get where I need to go by other ships, and I have abilities to infiltrate any vault. You'll need to be persuasive …*»

The cabin shimmerdoor, which had been set to complete privacy, abruptly opened, surprising us both. The man who filled the doorway was broad, with a sleeveless vest that left no doubt that his arms were powerful enough to throw me across the room. His face had been gruesomely scarred on one side, a defect that could be repaired except that the owner liked the effect. Oh shit.

"I told you to come meet me this morning, Whitt. Where have you been?"

"I think you have the wrong person. That's not my name," said Color of Air. I winced.

"Don't play games with me. I figured that was an alias, and I don't much care what your real name is. I'll ask you one more time. Where have you been?" He advanced menacingly into the cabin.

"At the hospital," I heard my voice say coolly. "I had food poisoning."

«Gee, thanks,» I snorted.

"Whitt, a woman was looking for you yesterday. Word was that it might be a Periphage. You've got two seconds before I assume that you've been eaten and vaporize you."

«He doesn't make empty threats. If he says it, he can do it. Let me speak to him, right now!»

I felt a sudden connection being made, like a mic going live. I didn't have time to experiment. I just hoped it worked.

"Easy, Magid. It was just a joke. I'm still feeling a little off-color."

The pun was unintentional, I swear.

"Prove to me you were at the hospital this morning."

"I can't. I erased all my records when I checked out. Those are the skills you're hiring me for, remember?"

«*Palms open, raise my hands and make a small shrug.*» Did it look like my shrug? I couldn't tell, but I hoped Magid couldn't either.

"You're making me nervous, Whitt."

"You're always nervous, Magid. We're going to leave on time tomorrow morning. Don't worry."

"I don't worry, I just take out insurance." With a lightning-fast move he clapped a bracelet on my wrist. "Once we are in hyperspace, I take that off. If you take it off or don't show up, you get ionized. It will also save you from being eaten by a Periphage. It will blow you up before it eats you. Same to you, but it's a better death."

"What the hell is a Periphage? I've never heard of such a thing."

"You wouldn't have. They're rare, never show themselves, and the authorities keep mum. Don't want to panic people. Some call them Shapestealers."

"And you know about them because… ?"

He showed some crooked teeth. Again, fixable, and again, part of the image. "I want to capture one. Tame it. Can you imagine a spy that can look like your rival for a bit of blackmail, or look like someone with clearance for confidential information? Or be my stand-in if someone has a hit out on me?"

«*Nod slowly, look thoughtful,*» I told Color of Air.

«*I'll kill him!*»

«*No! The bracelet will kill us first. Just nod.*»

"That would be quite handy," I said when I felt the nod. "I'm not sure if I believe these things exist without more proof."

"You always did have a skeptical mind," Magid said in rough approval. "I suggest that you not test that bracelet, though. Don't be late tomorrow." He turned and left.

«*This is all your fault!*» shrieked Color of Air as the door closed. The shriek was violet ghost pepper laced with turpentine. That's exactly as unpleasant as it sounds. «*We have to get this bracelet off, we have to get off this station! They know I'm here.*»

«*Don't try to shapeshift,*» I warned. «*That will set it off and vaporize everything in this cabin. You won't get away. Just play along. We get on board the ship, take Magid to his destination, he removes the bracelet. We talk about how to take on your Medusa.*»

I felt hickory caution. «*You're willing to help with that. After all this?*»

«*I play the ball where it lies, even when the ball turns out to be a landmine. If I'm going to live inside your head, I have to make the best of it.*» And find your weakness, I added silently.

«*What are you offering? And asking?*»

«*With my cooperation, you have a ship, contacts in most ports, and considerable financial resources. I want a voice in setting the agenda. I have some goals and interests that are important to me. Basically, I'll help you if you help me.*»

«*Since I can't be rid of you, we can see how it goes.*» Hardly the spirit in which it was offered. Or maybe it was. «*Tell me how we can ditch this Magid and scram.*»

«*We can't. He's a fixer for the Syndicate, untouchable short of a full-out war. You don't back out of a deal with him unless you want to be shut out of all action on the stations in this sector, probably for life or what little remains. The fastest way out of this is spending three days taking Magid to his destination.*»

«*I don't like this man who knows too much, I don't like getting dragged off on something that isn't my business, and I don't like being confined by* this.*»* She gestured towards the offending bracelet.

«*What would you have done before you had a passenger?*»

«*I would have killed him right then. I probably wouldn't eat him. He wouldn't taste good. Maybe wrap myself around him and detonate the bracelet. I would have put myself together in a few hours. He wouldn't.*»

I shuddered (figuratively) at the bloody-mindedness of those tactics. I liked dangerous women, but this was taking it to a new level. It did give me an insight into her abilities if she thought she could survive a blast like that. The question was, would I? It sounded like her consciousness was distributed throughout her substance like a hologram. Was I a hologram now, too?

«*Is that what you are? A Periphage?*»

«*Someone's made-up name. I call myself (scent of hibiscus, a bay laurel tree in the sun, and warm yeast bread). The closest you could come to that in your language is 'Arilune.'*»

«Are there many Arilune?»

«There is one, but a few leave the one to travel the currents of space.»

That didn't make a lot of sense. It had an oblique koan-like quality to it. A one-hand-clapping sort of thing.

Color of Air seemed unwilling to discuss the matter any further and fell silent. We had seventeen hours until departure and nothing that needed to be done. Nothing that we could agree on, that is. Many other beings would have paced, but she sank into a motionless trance. I didn't think she was sleeping, but I could detect no thoughts. After a while, I realized I could also detect neither breathing nor heartbeat. It was the quietest time I had ever experienced. Also one of the most boring. I could only wait and think through my plans.

THE COLOR OF SPACE

TWO HOURS BEFORE DEPARTURE, Color of Air finally stirred. She didn't stretch, or yawn, or rub her eyes. None of those appeared necessary for an amorphous blob, even when wearing a form that would have done those things.

«*Right,*» she said, «*what clothes would you usually wear?"*

«*Slacks and a turtleneck for a routine departure like this one. They're in the luggage."*

«*Open it.*»

«*Give me control so I can make sure the sequence is correct.*»

«*No.*»

«*You might blow yourself up if you do it wrong.*»

«Then tell me how to do it right.»

I sighed. My plan hinged on getting some trust and cooperation. During Magid's visit yesterday, Color of Air relinquished the ability to speak to me. I had hoped to chip away at her distrust to allow me control a little bit at a time. I would have to take it slow.

«Very well,» I said. *«Hold your first two fingers and your last two fingers together, and spread them and your thumb apart. Now place your hand on the side panel of the luggage and say, "Live long and prosper, but don't infringe any copyrights."»*

Color of Air was skeptical but did as I said. The hand salute was absurdly easy for her, though many people struggled with it. The luggage opened, showing some clothes and some moderately illegal hand weapons. Just enough to allay suspicions. I had given guest access with that passphrase, which kept the most lethal properties of the case unrevealed. It also reset the passphrase so it couldn't be used next time.

Color of Air removed the outfit I had indicated and put it on. She packed the clothes I had been wearing, as well as the wispy little dress she had worn when we met. She closed it and started to lift it, but I hurriedly said, *«Wait!»*

«What now?»

«I don't carry my own luggage. It would look suspicious. Say: "Return to the ship."»

She repeated the phrase and watched skeptically as the luggage arose on four articulated legs and marched out the door. From its sedate pace, you couldn't tell that it was capable of a top speed of 90 kph and was armored like a tank.

«Now, we should go to the main lock. It will be waiting for us in my cabin.»

Color of Air sighed, and we departed the cabin. Given that she didn't breathe, that had to be a learned behavior, intentionally employed. I smiled. I was getting under her skin. Then I sobered at the unintended literal meaning.

Twenty minutes later, we reached the docks at the hub and walked with magnetized slow steps down the zero-G corridor to my ship. Color of Air placed a palm on the access plate. It chirped happily at the palm print match. Impressive, considering my custom access plate had a resolution an order of magnitude finer than the merely industrial-grade units she'd fooled in the hospital. However, the door didn't open.

«I told you it would be easier if you let me drive.«

«No. You navigate, I drive.»

Magid ghosted in from a side corridor, not bothering with magsoles in freefall. He looked even more menacing, swimming in the air like the shark that he was. "Is there a problem, Captain? I'd hate to be delayed because you hadn't paid your docking fees."

"No problem. Just checking the security logs. Can't be too careful."

"Well, let's go."

»*Ah, Whitt?*»

«*Let me drive.*»

Purple sage annoyance. «*Ugh. Just for a moment.*»

The welcome feeling of control over this familiar yet alien body would have staggered me had I not been standing in zero G. I placed my hand on the palm scanner one more time and said, "Permission to come aboard?"

The hatch slid open, and the ship's voice said, "Permission granted, Captain. Welcome aboard the *Rapier Whitt*, passenger. Please provide a name or pseudonym for me to use during our voyage."

"Just Magid," growled the fixer. "Show me to my cabin and talk to me as little as possible."

"Please follow my avatar to your quarters," said the ship. A hologram of a demure girl in a kimono appeared in the gangway, gesturing deferentially for Magid to follow her.

"No holograms! I get twitchy when people appear out of thin air."

"As you wish." The avatar was replaced by a glowing wisp hanging in the air. The grumbling passenger followed it deeper into the ship. Before he turned the corner, he yelled back over his shoulder.

"Don't leave before my assistant gets here."

«*You didn't mention another passenger,*» said Color of Air accusingly.

«*That's because he failed to mention it to me. Typical Magid move to keep people off balance. I'll wager that his assistant's job description includes bodyguard and assassin.»*

«Captain Whitt... did you really name your ship the Rapier Whitt?*»*

«Couldn't resist. Of course, she's just Rapier to her friends.»

I started to walk towards the bridge, but my feet didn't move. Color of Air had taken back control. Oh, well. One step at a time. I told her which way to go.

The bridge was uncluttered, just a chair before a large screen. In truth, I could have done this from my cabin, but I liked the tradition. Besides, Station rules required a person on the bridge. I wondered if I still qualified.

Color of Air sat in my command chair and said, "Begin departure checklist."

«Confident, aren't you?»

«I've acquired the knowledge to pilot a starship.»

I wondered at the choice of the word "acquired." Predictably (to me), nothing happened.

«She likes being addressed by name. Say: "Rapier, please begin the departure checklist."»

Color of Air rephrased her question properly and was rewarded by the image of Rapier's avatar on the screen along with the checklist. Rapier tied the sleeves of her kimono back with a cord to indicate that she was ready to go to work. Color of Air wrinkled her nose in disdain at the image but began plowing through the checklist. (Yes, it felt strange for someone else to wrinkle *my* nose to show *their* disdain.) After twenty minutes, the preflight checklist was complete.

"I'm sorry, Captain, but the hyperspace condenser needs maintenance," said Rapier. "I have placed a service call. This will delay our departure by twelve hours."

"What! I didn't see any faults."

«If you'll allow me, I believe I can expedite our departure,» I interceded.

«Go ahead,» she said shortly.

"Good job, Rapier. That was just a systems check. Override code alpha-nine-gamma. Proceed."

"Well, look at that, Boss, there's nothing wrong with the hyperspace condenser after all. You had me worried for a moment."

"Carry on. You can complete the rest of the sequence on your own."

Color of Air was silent for a moment. *«I just stepped in one of your booby traps, didn't I?»*

«Yep. If I don't do two particular steps out of order during the checklist, Rapier takes that as a signal to insert a trumped-up delay.» Without extracting more concessions, I wouldn't tell her which steps to swap. *«How about you just let me pilot us out from the station while you watch over my shoulder?»*

«Very well. Any tricks, and you're going back in your box.»

"Captain, the other passenger has arrived and has been assigned the cabin next to the one who declined to give his name. You should be apprised that she is heavily armed."

"I would expect no less. Tell Station Control that we're ready to leave."

"Undocking now."

The *Rapier Whitt* fell away from the Station, moving out one thousand kilometers on a gently rolling wave of pseudogravity. The ship had the same shape as all her hyperdrive brethren, approximately that of an egg. The rounded shape with the somewhat pointed tail conformed to the shape of the field needed to move her through hyperspace in a way that had once been explained to me but had left me in no way enlightened.

"Go for hyperspace. Set destination for Amyrium. Engage." I added, under my breath like a benediction, "Run fast, run straight, until the stars return." It was from an old poem.

The stars on all sides began to redden and recede as we fell down a deep hole at right angles to all four of our standard dimensions. As their color passed crimson and faded towards embers, they stretched out into long streaks radiating in all directions. Finally, they dimmed and vanished, and we were alone in the sea of hyperspace.

«*That little poem was another failsafe code for you and your ship, wasn't it? How many more were there in the entire departure sequence?*»

«*There were a few more. I won't say how many. And they're different every time, so you can't repeat what I did.*»

«*Amazing. It's as if you were planning for this.*»

«Planning for kidnapping, mutiny, being boarded by customs agents and real pirates. I can't be too careful.»

«I admire your paranoia. It is a beautiful thing.»

She rose and headed for my cabin. She seemed to know where it was. I was getting a picture that she was very good at thoroughly researching physical details, but the softer nuances escaped her. I put that away to use for my advantage later.

We descended from the flight deck to the living quarters but were intercepted as we crossed the common area in the center of the ship. A compact woman dressed in skintight black entered from the passenger section. Presumably, this was Magid's assistant. She was sharp-featured, ice blond, with skin like milk. She walked with assurance in the .7 G, muscles rippling under her onepiece.

«I'd like to have that body,» said Color of Air.

Strange thing to hear from someone who could take any shape she wanted. I filed that away under personality traits of Shapestealers.

"I am Spanov," said our passenger. She had a lovely accent. "Magid instructed me to relieve you of your bracelet. You have fulfilled his conditions for release. Allow me." She extended a small electronic key and tapped it to a corresponding spot on the bracelet. The band fell apart, and she plucked it from our wrist. Her hand lingered for a second longer than necessary. The warmth sank under the skin like rosemary smoke.

"Thank you," said Color of Air. "I appreciate his promptness. What was that all about, if I may ask? I've never heard of these ShapeStealers he's so worried about."

"I do not know … he does not tell me these things."

"I was just going to have a cup of coffee. Would you care to join me?" Color of Air gestured toward the seats at one side.

«*What are you playing at?*» I asked.

«*Gathering information.*»

«*Be careful. If you make her suspicious, we'll be right back in that bracelet. She may be prettier than Magid, but she's just as deadly.*»

«*Don't worry.*»

"I would very much like a coffee, thank you. Can you make a Turkish coffee?"

Rapier's avatar appeared in the galley. "Yes, I can make that for you."

"Perfect, thank you." Spanov added with a mischievous twinkle, "Dark as sin, and twice as sweet."

Rapier's avatar began measuring coffee beans into a grinder. Color of Air guided Spanov to a seat.

"I'm sorry I didn't have a chance to greet you personally when you came aboard. I was occupied with pre-launch duties when you arrived. I trust that Rapier did an adequate job?"

"Yes, I find her charming. Did you base her on someone you know, or did you purchase a designer personality?"

"I … I'll tell you the story sometime when there's time to do it justice."

"I look forward to hearing it," said Spanov.

«*If you want to help,*» said Color of Air, «*you can supply background like that so I can better impersonate you. I usually get a host's memories when I absorb them, but yours are walled off from me.*»

That was probably keeping me alive. «*The degree of cooperation I give you will depend on the degree of freedom I enjoy in this enterprise.*»

Rapier announced that the coffee was ready. There was an awkward pause until I prompted, «*Rapier is just a hologram. She can't carry the cups to the table.*»

Color of Air rose to get the two coffees, covering her lapse with a rueful smile. «*How did she make the coffee, then?*»

«*She has manipulators in the galley and med bay, but in most places she doesn't have any hands.*»

We returned with a pair of steaming cups, small and pungent. Color of Air placed one in front of Spanov, then lifted our own cup to inhale the aroma. The first sip went down like a mournful bassoon note with the roll of a great Japanese *taiko* drum in the background. Coffee was an entirely different experience with ShapeStealer synesthesia.

Spanov sampled her own cup. "Black, as promised. And sweet. But sin … it could be even sweeter than this, no?" She ran her finger slowly around the rim of the cup, then brought her finger to her lips.

"I like to keep that bitter edge."

"Magid did say you lived dangerously."

"You have no idea."

Her eyes went to a painting on the wall. It was meant to draw attention — not only the only painting on the ship, but mesmerizing in its intensity. It showed a red, rocky desert under a distant sunset, the horizon lit as if on fire behind crystalline outcroppings.

"Is that your painting?" she asked.

«*Ug. Whitt, you answer this.*» I felt Color of Air yield vocal control.

"No, I can't paint. My sister painted that. It's one of the few things I have left from her."

"She is gone?"

"She and her ship disappeared on a survey expedition a few years ago. She gave me that painting just before departure. I've been looking for others she might have given away or sold, but no luck. And I'm still chasing any clue to what happened to her. It was her first command. Nothing's ever turned up."

Spanov knocked back the remainder of her dark brew before standing. "This will be an interesting voyage. Rapier told me that there's an exercise deck on board. I would like to use it to keep up my training during our voyage if I may."

Color of Air took back vocal control.

"Certainly. May I ask what you'll be training in?"

"Martial arts." Spanov's coy smile all but invited the response.

"If you'd like a sparring partner, I would enjoy the opportunity for a workout." Color of Air had certainly mastered the art of double entendre.

"I would like that. Tomorrow, say? A good workout before breakfast."

"Tomorrow it is. Enjoy your voyage, Spanov."

"You may call me Grigoreva, Captain."

"Off duty, please call me Sam."

«*Noooo! Never Sam! Only Samuel!*»

"-uel. Samuel."

Spanov departed, slightly puzzled at the hiccup in the middle of "Samuel."

Color of Air wasn't very communicative after that. She found her way to my quarters, undressed, and sank into one of her periods of utter stillness. I wondered if this was her version of sleep or if it served a different function. Unfortunately, I didn't need to sleep after my transformation to become a passenger in her head, so I could only wait and plan. Perhaps I was a bad dream to disturb her sleep.

In the morning, Color of Air again made her abrupt transition from sleeping to waking. No stretching or rubbing of eyes to ease into motion. She stood in front of the mirror and willed a change. She first flowed into the dusky, athletic female form that seemed to be her base but then turned transparent. I faced a mannequin made of water or clear gel, slightly bluish in tinge. At first, I thought it was featureless, but then I saw tiny bright motes distributed throughout the form. They were moving, streaming from the center to extremities and back again. There were knots and whorls, but nothing looked like stable organs or networks. «*That is beautiful,*» I said. I felt a slight pulse of pleasure in answer.

"Captain! What has happened to you?" Rapier's avatar was suddenly by our side. "Are you the Captain? You looked like him until a minute ago."

«*Whitt, calm your ship!*» Color of Air gave me voice control, simultaneously shifting back into my form.

"It's ok, Rapier. VIP protocol, code of silence. This is just between us for now, understand?"

"Yes, Captain. Can you explain?"

«*Shift back to your form.*» I saw the young female form reappear in the mirror. "Rapier, this is my new partner, Color of Air. We'll be traveling together. She can assume whatever form she wants. You are not to take that as unusual. Please give her full privileges on the ship." I followed this with the authorization code. I didn't mention to Color of Air that "full privileges" was code for "full guest privileges," excluding all command functions.

"But you can take any form?" asked Rapier dubiously.

"Just about. Run through your repertoire, Color of Air, so

that Rapier will recognize them."

She started with the dark beauty who had accosted me in the bar, then the many-armed goddess of the bedroom, several men and women of average appearance. There were a lot, all nude. I saw male equipment, female, mixed, one hermaphrodite, a sexless reptiloid with shimmering scales, avian, and more. I thought there was a good chance she was holding some back in case she needed a surprise. I would.

"All right, I'm getting dizzy," said Rapier. "How do I know it's really the Captain?"

"When the Melanesse Ambassador was on board for a week, she shed so much fur that I had to clean all the air filters afterwards, three times."

"Served you right. She shed most of it in *your* cabin. Very well, it seems to be you. Welcome aboard, Color of Air." Rapier's image took a step closer. She was suddenly wearing a tengu mask and clutching a sheathed katana in her left hand. "I just want you to know I'm *very* protective of my Captain. I'll be watching you." She vanished.

«*Your ship has quite an attitude. I like her.*»

«*Her mother was a ship's navigation system and her father was a military-grade firewall. The personality is custom-designed. We suit each other.*»

We went down to the exercise deck and found Spanov waiting for us. She was dressed in a brief two-piece outfit that didn't look like it would contain her for long. Seventy-two hours ago, as a human male, I would have already been at a disadvantage, but Color of Air just looked her over coolly. We were wearing my body, of course. As Color of Air slipped off my robe to stand dressed only in thigh-length tights, I felt her enhancing the definition of our muscles and tightening our abs. I felt slightly insulted that she needed to embellish what I had already worked so hard on.

"Good morning, Grigoreva. I trust you slept well?"

"Yes, Samuel. And you as well?"

"A trifle restless. Some exercise should help that."

«*You were restless? You didn't move.*»

«*I was speaking for you. I could feel your activity. You would have paced if you could.*»

"I will try not to bruise you too much then." She wore a smile that belied that promise.

"What gravity level would you like?"

"Variable."

Color of Air and I were in agreement with a raised eyebrow response. Only the most expert martial artists elected variable gravity.

"Rapier, please initiate variable gravity mode, hyperbolic curve. You may officiate."

We squared off. At Rapier's signal, Spanov launched herself at me. We grappled momentarily, then Color of Air hooked an ankle and threw her down. Spanov planted a foot in our sternum and tossed us over her head as she rolled. Gravity was declining; better not get thrown when it was increasing. That was a good way to break some bones.

Color of Air miscalculated the landing because we didn't fall as fast in lower gravity. Spanov recovered and reached us before we had our footing again. Spanov tried to get us in an arm lock, but Color of Air added enough flexibility to our joints to eel away from the hold. We were approaching the moment of zero-G.

Color of Air was good but relied on her unique talents to even the field. I knew I was a better fighter. «*Let me take over. I am sure that I can beat her or at least draw.*»

«*No. Winning isn't the goal.*»

What did that mean?

Gravity reached zero, simulating the moment when a ballistic vessel stops its ascent before starting its tumble back to earth. Spanov launched herself into the air. What was she doing? She would be helpless, swimming in the middle of the room until the gravity returned on the other side.

As Spanov soared into the air, she flipped around and coiled. She had taken off with more force than I thought; she would reach the ceiling. She launched straight back at us the moment her feet touched the ceiling. With no weight, we had no traction and no way to evade her rush. I felt Color of Air's admiration for that maneuver and her rising lust for the hunt.

Color of Air slapped our feet on the deck, where they acquired a tacky texture that adhered as strongly as magnetic boots. She stretched up to snag Spanov's hands, which had been spread to grapple with us, then converted Spanov's momentum into a roll. Gravity returned, ramping up as we skidded across the floor.

We were on top, pressing Spanov down with our returning weight. This was the first time I had touched another person since Color of Air had assimilated me. It was electric. Every point of contact thrilled with warmth and life. When Color of Air said her species lived to touch, she wasn't kidding. Spanov was sweet citrus and plums, dark wine, and a burst of cloves. My head spun (or would have if I had a head) with the overwhelming senses of touch, smell, and color.

Increasing gravity pushed us down into Spanov, who was as solid as a slab of oak despite the appearance of feminine curves. She struggled to breathe while Color of Air simulated the same. That brought our faces close to each other. Her eyes studied ours frankly.

"I thought ... you were my type," she got out, shallowly.

The gravity reached maximum and lightened again. Our weight advantage in pinning her abruptly vanished. She got an elbow in the ground and flipped us, pinning our arms with her legs.

"Dangerous," she finished.

«*That's my line,*» I said.

Spanov skinned her halter top over her head and leaned in to give us a deep kiss. The rest of our clothes were soon ejected, and we came together in a different kind of wrestling. Spanov, predictably, liked being on top.

In this new body, sex was a transcendent experience. Our skin was afire with scents, our nose was filled with colors, and our ears heard all the flavors of passion. The pleasure that had once been the province of a few square inches where we were joined now encompassed all the senses and our entire surface area. Add to that vision the sight of Spanov's athletic body arched in the throes of orgasm atop of us...

Color of Air had engulfed Spanov from toe to waist before I realized what was happening. She sank into our now-gelatinous body like a bather into a pool and with the same expression of bliss. Then, a squeeze, the crunching of bones, and the essence of Spanov was released to become part of Color of Air. It was an ecstasy beyond anything I had known before, any experience, any drug, any memory. I knew I would crave this moment for as long as I lived. The taste of cloves lingered on my palate, sweet and dark. Satisfaction curled inside me, thick as honey, so deep it felt essential, a need I hadn't known I had.

And then I felt the bones.

The wet snap, the crunching pressure—I had felt them break, inside me, inside us. And I had liked it. Finally, I came back to my senses. Those had been her thoughts, her urges. I hadn't understood how deep they ran. I hadn't understood what a drug they were.

«You killed her!"

«I needed sustenance, and she had useful skills to assimilate.»

Color of Air stood, a gross, misshapen lump of flesh, or plasm, or whatever we were. She walked to the toilets in the dressing room and sat on a zero-G waste disposal. She began to excrete the excess mass we had just absorbed. No, I couldn't let myself think of it that way. That was Grigoriva Spanov passing from this life. The waste disposal labored unhappily with the unfamiliar load.

We started to resume a human shape, first Color of Air's default shape, then shifting to my body. .

"Captain, what happened?" exclaimed Rapier as my form solidified. "I thought at first that Spanov had killed you, and I locked down the ship. But you killed her, didn't you?"

Color of Air replied in my voice. "She attacked me first, and I defended myself. Please delete all video and audio of this chamber since we entered."

"Let me hear that from the real Captain."

Good girl, Rapier. I knew you were sharp.

Color of Air gave me voice control. That was my chance to blow the whistle. Turn us over to Magid. Tell Rapier to self-destruct. Open the airlocks to vacuum. End this, somehow. But that wouldn't make amends. I had to play along for now and wait my time. "It's me, Rapier. Seal the records, my eyes only."

"Yes, Captain."

«How did she know it was you, but the first request wasn't?»

«We'll talk about that later. You just murdered a passenger on my ship, and we're going to have more trouble than we can handle if we don't think of a way out of it.»

«I couldn't help it! I was so hungry, and she was so willing.»

«We'll talk about morals later. For now, we need tactics. Grab our clothes and her clothes and get us back to our cabin.»

Color of Air did as I said. I was glad she was taking input and not shutting me out as she had done since the beginning. It was going to be ticklish with Magid still on board.

THE COLOR OF PAIN

WE HAD BARELY GOTTEN BACK to our cabin when Rapier paged me. "Captain, Magid is asking where Spanov is. What should I tell him?"

«You can impersonate Spanov, right?» I asked Color of Air.

«I can take her form and have her memories, but I don't pick up emotions or attitudes. I know the combination of her locker and where she stores her weapons, but I don't know if she likes Magid or hates him.»

«We'll have to wing it. Grab her clothes, and let me talk to Rapier.»

«Got it.»

"Rapier, tell Magid you are attempting to locate her. Wait

ninety seconds, and then tell him she has gone to medical with a sprained wrist."

"Aye, Captain."

We hurried to the medical facility, which wasn't more than a small room with first-aid supplies for little things and an autosurgeon for big things. We wasted another twenty seconds shifting form and changing clothes. I discovered that embarrassing and uncomfortable results occurred if those were done out of order.

«*Spanov is smaller than me. How do you do that?*» I asked as Color of Air pulled out a bandage and started wrapping our left wrist.

«*I can temporarily make my substance denser to become smaller. In the long term, it's less effort to discard some mass. Also, I would not fool a scale at the moment.*»

«*So that bowling ball in our stomach is your extra mass? I thought it was fear.*»

The shimmerdoor rippled as Magid entered.

"You're not answering your com, Spanov. Where've you been?"

"I left my com in my room. I was working out. Hurt my wrist when the gravity glitched at a bad time."

"Have you seen Captain Whitt?"

"No, he hasn't come out of his cabin since I came aboard."

Magid's eyes narrowed. "We still on course?"

"So far."

"Have you been monitoring the ship channels? I want to be sure he's not a sellout to someone on the far end."

"Nothing but standard navigation chatter."

"Keep your eyes open. And you had your night off last night. I want a bed warmer tonight. Be there." Magid left.

«Bedwarmer? I think I'm going to retch,» I said.

«That makes two of us.»

«I don't think it would be murder if you ate him. I'm reasonably sure he doesn't qualify as human.»

«I couldn't eat him. He would taste like (anthracite mixed with rancid limes).» The taste/smell that ended that sentence was graphic enough to make me glad that I didn't have a stomach.

«Enough of that. We have to keep Magid from becoming suspicious.»

«That means we'll have to keep on being Spanov today. Magid might call on her at any time. Can Rapier answer requests for you?»

«Even better, she can use a holo of me to make it seem like I'm really there. I mostly use it when I have tiresome guests. Or when the passengers are Offans. They eat carrion and smell like it.»

«Good, we'll go hole up in Spanov's cabin. Maybe I can contrive an injury or illness that will keep us from tasting him tonight.»

We gathered my clothes and Spanov's before going to her cabin. With the door locked, we could finally relax for a moment. As much as one could relax inside an unfamiliar body with a head shared with an eater of souls.

Color of Air surprised me by bringing it up first.

«Why do you object to me eating someone? You eat the flesh of other creatures, meaning you were once hunters, too.»

«First, there's the entirely practical consideration of not antagonizing the paying passengers. Second, we consider it immoral to kill other sentient beings.»

«Having eaten all sorts of creatures and absorbed their memories, I can tell you there is no clear distinction, only a matter of degree. Have you not killed? Your records indicate that you have.»

«In self-defense. Sometimes, when the job demands it, but I try not to take those jobs anymore.»

We sat silently for a while before I brought up the other part that was bothering me.

«Do you always have sex with people you eat?»

«It's the easiest way to get their clothes off. I hate eating clothes. It's not so bad if they're made of cotton, but these synthetic fibers just taste terrible.»

«Is that the only reason?»

«It makes the experience easier for them.»

I thought about that for a long time.

Much later, Rapier called. "Captain, Magid is looking for you. He knew he was talking to a hologram; apparently, there was something I didn't answer correctly. He's outside your cabin, demanding to see you."

«*Ah, shit. How are we going to get by him? Maybe I can get Rapier to draw him away for a minute...*»

«*Wait. Does this air vent connect all the cabins?*»

«*At least at the moment, it does, since we're all oxygen breathers.*»

Color of Air stripped off the clothes we were wearing on Spanov's body, then stood in front of the intake grate. She melted into a ball, then pressed herself into the grating. The feeling of the metal edges passing through our body was intensely strange.

«*Now, which way?*»

«*Left. Now up. Third right. Down. First panel is my cabin.*»

Another moment of being sliced up and reassembled followed, and then I stood in my own body in my cabin. Color of Air took some clothes from the hamper that looked appropriately rumpled, donned them, and then opened the door.

«*You're sick. I'm going to make you look flushed and bleary. You can do the talking.*»

"Magid? Sorry, something I ate didn't agree with me. Is there something the ship couldn't help you with?"

"Call me suspicious, but I don't like when the Captain stays in his cabin the entire trip. You're not usually this reclusive during a cruise. Come out and have a drink in the lounge like you usually do."

A rolling feeling swept through me, followed by the sick green stench of rotting algae. I took the cue as Color of Air clutched our midsection (which no longer contained a stomach, as far as I could tell). "Ungh, I couldn't handle that today. Sorry, I have to go lie down again. I'll take a rain check when my gut lets me."

Magid's eyes narrowed, but we must have turned a convincing shade of green because he let us go.

«He thinks something is amiss,» said Color of Air.

«It's hard to tell with Magid. He's always a suspicious bastard. It's a survival skill for him.»

"You might want to know that Magid is heading for Spanov's cabin," said Rapier. I was proud of how quickly my ship had adapted to the new situation.

"Delay him if you can. We'd better get back there."

"Yes, Captain."

Color of Air was already stripping off our clothes and diving through the vent. We rolled through the metal-acrid underworld again.

«Yech, dust and beetle droppings. You have a family of Grit living somewhere on board, too. You need to clean your air ducts more often.»

As we passed the lounge, I saw Rapier's hologram engaging Magid in a discussion about docking instructions for our destination. Good girl, Rapier.

We extruded out of the vent into Spanov's cabin. When Color of Air reached the transparent humanoid stage of her transformation, she stopped in front of a mirror. Flakes and bits of grit hung suspended within, drifting slowly as if stirred by internal currents.

«*Just look at all the dust I picked up in there. It's going to be hours before that settles out.*»

There came a pounding on the door.

"Just a minute, I'm in the shower," called Color of Air. She transformed our features into those of Spanov, then splashed water on our hair to make it look authentically wet. She went to the door.

«*Eh, clothes?*»

«*Grigoreva's memories say that this wouldn't be unusual for her. I can do the talking. I have assimilated her mannerisms now.*»

The door slid open. Magid immediately entered and looked about. His stance said he owned everything and everyone in the room. The glance he ran down our nude body emphasized *everyone*. I wasn't used to being on the receiving end of a look like that. Fortunately, Color of Air kept all of Spanov's assurance. Magid's gaze ran off like rainwater off a duck.

"Where've you been?"

"I walked about the ship, so I know the layout. You know, just in case. Like I always do."

"Hum. Well, stay away from the Captain. I know he's the type you like to jump, but he's acting kinda squirrelly."

"I saw a picture of a squirrel once. Why is that a bad thing?"

Magid fixed us with an ugly squint. "Can the sass. Just

listen for once."

«*Is it a good idea to tick him off like this?*» I asked.

«*He would be more suspicious if Grigoreva didn't give him some lip.*»

"I thought we took this ship because you trusted Whitt?"

"I don't trust anybody. Whitt's been steady in the past, but something doesn't smell right this time."

"So you're the expert on smell, now?"

Magid whirled, caught our Spanov-body by the upper arms, and pinned us against the wall. Our feet dangled six inches above the floor. Naked and not able to control my limbs, I hadn't ever felt this vulnerable. Not since ... focus! Color of Air could probably disable or kill him, but that would have undesirable consequences.

«*Don't tell him what you are, or it will be war!*» I warned her.

"I think our playtime tonight will be good for both of us," he said, low and close. I could feel the anthracite and rancid limes – more through his hands on our body than the breath on our face. That breath had a whole lot more going on, none of it good. "I need to break something, and you need some discipline. Again."

He dumped us on the floor and stalked out.

«*Do you think you overdid the sass?*» It was hard to convey enough sarcasm without a voice, but I managed.

«*This is how it usually goes,*» said Color of Air, sounding shaken. «*Now I see how those memories played out. He enjoys*» *breaking bones, and Grigoreva … actually likes it. They're really sick.»*

Color of Air crossed the room to lock the door. She shifted through several forms before settling into a clear, featureless, genderless humanoid. *«I had to get away from Grigoreva's form for a bit. The memories are a bit too much.»*

«Your memories are linked to form.»

«In a way. When I'm not wearing a form, I can pick up its memories and read a page like a book. When I'm wearing the form, it's more like I lived that life. Right now, I need to rest and reintegrate. Don't talk to me for a while.»

I sank into my thoughts and was surprised to see that hours had passed when Magid called on the intercom. "I'm ready for you," he growled.

We rose and took on the form of Spanov again. Before we left, Rapier said, "If you need an extraction, the safeword is 'tequila.' I'll be listening."

«You already knew the safeword, didn't you?»

«Yes, Rapier said it for your benefit.»

I felt a faint pulse of cinnamon warmth. I think she was pleased.

«What are we supposed to wear?» I asked.

«It seems that she would wear leathers if she were defiant, a robe if she was playful, and naked if she was contrite.»

«I suggest we go with playful, then.»

«Agreed.» Color of Air picked a sheer robe from Spanov's luggage. She picked up a small knife and held it against

her thigh. It sank into her flesh and vanished.

«You give new meaning to the term concealed weapon.»

We left the cabin and went down the corridor to Magid's quarters. The door opened as we approached.

The thrice-damned bracelet clamped on our wrist as we walked through the door. Magid was flattened against the wall to our left, ready to ambush us.

"Is this a new game, Magid?" Color of Air tried to maintain the charade.

"I've got you! I thought you were after the Captain, but it was my assistant this whole time. Ah, ah, don't try to shapeshift or stretch out of the cuff. It will detonate the instant you do."

"I don't know what you're talking about. Shapeshift? You've reached a whole new level of paranoid crazy, Magid."

"You sound just like her. She'd be defiant like that. But, see? Your sprained wrist healed much too quickly, and when I picked you up today, you were way heavier than my Grigoreva was the last time I threw her against a wall. I'm going to miss her. That was a heavier price than I was expecting to pay for you. But you'll make it up to me, won't you?"

«Stay in character,» I hissed. *«Try to sow some doubt.»*

"Magid, you're making a mistake. I don't know who you think I am, but I've been with you for six years since you picked me out of that labor camp ..."

Magid thumbed a button on his belt. Lightning shot through our body, tearing the world apart. Ozone, sulfur, brimstone, screeching orange, oily black, mercaptans, sandpaper on nerves, and lake-bottom ooze. Synesthesia made the torment ten times worse as it recycled it in so many ways. When Magid relented, we were in a heap on the floor, scrabbling and clawing. I thought our skin would be blackened and charred, but it was clear and unharmed.

"Just a microvolt trickle current at a Periphage's neural frequency. Disruptive, isn't it? A human wouldn't even notice it, so you can cut the protests. You're not Spanov. You're my property. Now, I will put you somewhere safe until we make port." Magid hauled us to our feet and marched us back to Spanov's cabin.

"Ship! I have apprehended a fugitive and am incarcerating it in this cabin. Lock this door to my ID only. This prisoner can appear to be anyone, including your Captain, so disregard all communications it might attempt with you. I have just sent you proof of my authority."

After a hesitation, Rapier said. "I understand and will comply." That meant she didn't like it and was looking for loopholes. It satisfied Magid, though.

Magid turned to us. "You can pay for what you did to Spanov while we complete our journey. It should also give you something other than your escape to think about." He triggered the bracelet, and the pain cracked through our body again. "It will stop for a few minutes every hour or so. You may think that's a mercy, but you'll find it's much worse for having a brief respite. Not knowing when or how long will be its own torment. I'll be back for you later."

It was days before the pain ceased, though the traitor clock said it was slightly more than an hour. It had all the horrible experiences of an eternal sojourn in the hell of a depraved cultist with the benefits of a full color/taste/smell sensorium. Let's not dwell on it. Rapier was calling my name.

"Captain! Captain, can you hear me?"

Color of Air gave me speech without a word. I responded, "Here, Rapier."

"Should I arrange an unfortunate accident for your passenger?"

"No, there's a good chance that will detonate the bracelet. If we survive, the entire Syndicate would be out for our blood. We would be exiled to the frontier worlds. We need another plan. How did you get past his order not to speak to us?"

"He said to disregard all communications with the being in this cabin. I connected the intercom in this cabin to the one in yours, so I can't say with any certainty that your voice isn't coming from your cabin."

"That's a loophole worthy of a lawyer."

"I've sworn to never use my powers for evil."

"That's comforting. Do you see any way to remove this

bracelet?"

"I have not found a way to remove, deactivate, or interfere with it. I am sorry."

«*Do you have any tricks up your sleeve?*» I asked Color of Air.

No answer.

«*Hey! Color of Air! Are you okay?*» I concentrated on her name's taste/scent/color as close as I could remember. Flavors of purple mint, with a tenor of red pepper and a downbeat of lilac at the end. «*Are you there?*»

«*Your accent is terrible,*» she said weakly.

«*What's the matter?*»

«*I don't know how much more I can take.*»

«*It hurts, but it's not actually —*»

The pain cut in again.

The intervals of agony were endless, but the respites between were anything but. Magid was right. Not knowing how long until the next onset was worse than enduring the pain. And the lack of pain just made the resumption all the worse. It seemed to affect Color of Air more than it did me. I didn't know if that was because she was insulating me from the full effect or if she was unused to handling pain. I had been tortured before. I knew how to take refuge in fantasy worlds and soothing memories. I tried to tell her how to do this during one break.

«*I don't know if I can do that.*»

«*Perhaps you can re-live the memories of some of the people you've ... absorbed?»*

«Yes, that ...»

The pain returned.

I tried for good memories again, but instead I landed on my encounter with the Medusa. Only one tendril had wrapped around my arm, but I'm convinced that pain far outdistanced this one. Oddly, that memory gave me the strength to endure. I'd been hurt worse before, and I was still here. If I gave up now, my business with the Medusa would be unfinished and my revenge on Color of Air would be forfeit. I would never find my sister. I reached a place where the pain and I coexisted, touching but untouchable.

At the next respite, she said, *«That helped. A little.»* Her voice still sounded weaker than before. I began to worry that this might damage her. Not that I had given up my desire for revenge. I hadn't forgiven her for eating me yet. But if she were injured, driven insane, or killed, the quality of my life might decline even further. I could wait for the right time.

«Magid is probably bluffing about the explosive,» Color of Air said.

«I've never known him to bluff. Why do you think that?»

«Would you want a bomb going off on a ship that you're on?»

«Umm, good point. It may be low-yield enough not to breach the hull and still smear us over the inside.»

«But he wouldn't risk it detonating while he's in the same

60

room, would he?»

«That's ...»

That had been a longer rest than average, so the torment's resumption was that much more devastating.

I lost track of the hours, even though they were marked by the cycle of Magid's torture device. It would be surrendering something to keep count, so I didn't. I just knew that one time, when it stopped, the door was open and Magid was standing there.

"Stand up! We've docked at Amyrium Station. We're disembarking. I need you to walk under your own power."

Color of Air moved feebly. She tried to push up to her knees but didn't quite make it.

«Let me drive!» I urged her. *«I'm in better shape. I can keep us going until you shake this off.»*

She tried one more time to reach her knees, then gave in. I felt our body respond to my thoughts. It had only been a few days since I could do that, and I missed it so much I could almost weep. I stood.

"Should I change? This robe might be conspicuous." We still wore the form of Spanov, of course.

Magid cocked a suspicious eye but couldn't deny it was reasonable and helpful. Probably, that made it suspicious in itself. "Go ahead. Put her leathers on."

I did that, fumbling with some unfamiliar pieces of female clothing that I had only taken off (someone else) and never put on. Magid watched, unselfconsciously.

"Now go ahead of me, down to the airlock." He stepped aside. As I walked past, I tried to plant a fast elbow in his kidneys, but he stepped back and pressed the stud on his belt. I was floored with the pain. Again.

It *was* worse when I was the one in control. I had some sympathy for Color of Air. This time, it was only a short pulse because he needed me to be functional.

"Try that again, and I'll cook you," he said in a conversational tone. He didn't sound menacing at all, which carried far more menace than any intonation could have.

As we walked, I tried to make some surreptitious hand signals to Rapier, but I couldn't tell if the message was received. She was smart enough to know she couldn't answer without tipping Magid off.

"Hey, ship! Where's your Captain?" Magid called.

"I regret that he's still unwell and has confined himself to his cabin in case it is contagious."

"Huh. Still acting squirrelly. He'd better get over it if he wants any more business."

"I shall tell him you said so, sir."

"Shut up."

I tensed as we approached the lock. This was a solid steel door, heavy and ponderous. No shimmerdoors for this function. Once we got past that, we were on the station, and it would be a lot harder to escape, unless I played a very long game waiting for him to drop his guard.

I hate long games.

As we reached the lock, I asked, "What about my luggage?" I started to turn to ask him the question. "I'm going to need …"

"Shut up and keep walking," he snarled, grabbing my shoulder to shove me forward.

I pivoted, fading away from his push and using that momentum to grab his wrist and throw him forward. He stumbled, and I tried to hook a foot around his ankle. This was not the body I was used to, however. It was Spanov's, shorter and wider, with a different balance over the hips. I missed.

Magid hammered down with both fists clenched together. It flattened me to the deck but failed to break my neck. Now that I was part of an amorphous blob, I don't think there were any bones to break. Probably no brains to slosh around inside and give me a concussion, either.

Magid reached for the stud on his belt. I knew that would incapacitate me. I lashed out with a foot. Again, my leg was too short. I was going to miss.

Dammit, I was a shape changer. I didn't have to put up with too short. I stretched my leg as I swung, adding a crucial couple of inches. My toe connected with Magid's hand before he could push the stud, knocking it away. He shook his hand and swore. I hoped for a broken bone.

Magid landed a solid kick in my side. It hurt, but it wasn't as disabling as it would have been if I still had ribs and lungs. I scrambled away and regained my feet.

I rushed forward to tackle Magid but fell flat on my face at his feet. One leg was longer than the other one. I scrambled away from a vicious kick at my face and regained my feet. I stumped backwards awkwardly on mismatched legs. Maybe I could disable Magid with laughter. If only he hadn't had his humor surgically removed.

I had to get a familiar body back to have a chance in this fight. I concentrated on my own form. I should be taller, with longer arms. No hips or bust to get in the way. How did I make myself change?

Magid was reaching for the stud on his belt again. I curled my shoulder and drove him into the wall. I felt a squishy sensation as I drove up into his chin with my fist. My arm looked longer, more like the one I remembered. I was changing. I remembered too late that my clothes wouldn't fit, as the buttons popped off my shirt.

Magid tried to grapple with me, but now with my longer reach, I broke his grip and rolled him over my hip, sending him flying into the airlock.

That was a tactical error. Now he was out of reach and had his finger on the pain button. I couldn't get to him before he pressed it. Now that I had attacked him, he wouldn't let up once he mashed it.

"Rapier, close airlock!" I called. Maybe I could cycle the lock and expel him onto the docks. Maybe I could put myself back together after a blast. Too many maybes. The door began to close like a doom.

«*Allow me,*» Color of Air said suddenly. She took control of our arm and shoved it through the gap in the closing door just as the pain hit. We collapsed, convulsing on the floor as the airlock sheared through our wrist, leaving the hand and bracelet on the far side. With Magid. The bracelet detonated. I could still feel the hand as the explosion consumed it.

Magid disembarked from the *Rapier Whitt* onto the docks, where he showed his papers to the bored officials. He made his way to the hotel, checked in personally, rather than using their automated system, and requested transport the next day at the concierge's desk. He even tipped a porter to take his bag to his room. The desk handed him a message with a communicator link.

Once in his room, he placed a call to the number in the message. Audio only.

"I just got in. No, I didn't get it. I don't think it exists. No one had ever heard of a Periphage there."

The voice on the other end, female, gravelly, blunt, said, "There is one. We tracked the cat down on Raxas. She said there had been one on her crew, and it got off on Damiron. I traced it through Elden, Kasra, and Cambrisa, then to Islae Station, where you just came from. Now I've lost track of it."

"No, I'm certain it didn't come with me. It was just me and the Captain on board. I don't care what the cat said. What's she doing on Raxas anyway?"

"That's not your concern anymore. Francis is disappointed. He took you off the assignment."

"I can't help that Francis is disappointed. If it's not there, it's not there."

He hung up.

Two hours later, a nondescript man emerged from a room in the next corridor. Probably not even building maintenance knew that a ventilation conduit connected the two rooms. He made his way to a bar; a little later he went home with a woman he had picked up there. The next morning, a conservatively dressed businessman left the woman's apartments, went to the dock, and presented papers for a departure on the *Rapier Whitt*.

When the airlock closed behind him, Rapier already had the mess cleaned up. "Welcome back, Captain. Is your trail clean?"

We changed into the form of Samuel Whitt. "Of course, Rapier. We're not amateurs. Neither one of us."

"I received word a few hours ago about an explosion in a hotel room. There's no doubt that Magid was in the room at the time. Even the bellhop remembered him checking in."

"Too bad. I wonder which of his enemies or employers finally got to him?"

"Suspicion is falling on someone named Francis, who was in contact with him shortly before that."

"Do we need to have Spanov disembark also?"

"The funny thing is, she didn't have any papers when she embarked, and there doesn't seem to be any record that she was on board."

"Well, that's that, then. File a plan to depart as soon as we get clearance. Destination: Abelard."

«We need to go to Raxas,» said Color of Air.

«Why is that important?»

«I'm not sure. We need to check it out.»

«It's my ship. Convince me.»

She had been letting me speak to the ship. She could just take back voice control and order Rapier to go wherever she wanted. (Whether Rapier would take that order was much more doubtful.) I wanted to see how she replied.

«Call it a partnership trial.»

«You want to see how we work together?»

«I think we worked very well together. Neither one of us alone would have overcome Magid. You did your best to get me through the torture, for which I'm grateful. You and I are more alike than different.»

«There are some differences that we need to discuss. I'm not ok with killing people. It's bad for business, especially when they're passengers.»

«But that's my nature — and yours now, too. I'm a predator. That's also how I acquire knowledge and skills. It's necessary for *me to consume new individuals from time to time.»*

«That's going to be a sticking point between us.»

«It may not be so much of a sticking point when the hunger sets in. You'll feel it, too.»

I didn't want to think about this right now. I wanted a shower and a good sleep. I wasn't going to get the sleep, but maybe the shower.

«Since you're driving now, could you steer us toward the shower?»

«Certainly. Who would you like to be in the shower?»

This was going to take some getting used to.

In truth, I wanted time to learn this body's abilities and discover my host's weaknesses. Could I bottle her up entirely, or cleave her off, or maybe even kill her and take over the body? I needed time. I told Rapier to amend our flight plan.

I thought about what she had said. We were a lot alike. It was very likely she was planning how to be rid of me as well.

THE COLOR OF IRON

THE PORT OF RAXAS would have been merely gloomy to the human senses that I once had. Those senses would have seen dimly lit corridors designed to build up a static charge of unease on the human particles navigating their crude waveguides. Now, Arilune senses could taste the blood tang of high-carbon steel and smell the skin particles of a hundred races exfoliated into dust and laminated onto bulkheads with layers of silicone lubricants. We could even hear the noxious stench of a grit, the reptilian rat-analog that had displaced the mammalian one from its niche across the galaxy.

Hearing a stench was something to which I was still not

accustomed. Synesthesia is a way of life for an Arilune (I had learned that Color of Air considered both Shapestealer and Periphage pejorative). Scents, sounds, and sights all tumble together and forget their proper place. Other things are fluid as well. Don't forget to use the right pronoun to go with the exterior shape. Make allowances for species that let you choose. There was a lot to keep track of.

The waveguide discharged us into a cavity. The anode at the far end collecting the charged passenger-particles was an array of immigration inspectors. Clutching the immigration forms that invited us to confess to several dozen infractions and felonies, we steered towards the nearest booth.

"Name?"

"Seamus Whitby."

"Purpose of your visit?"

"Pleasure."

The slab of vat-grown beef behind the counter raised an eyebrow. "Don't hear that too often here."

"All right. I'm a trader. I have nothing to trade this trip, but I'm looking for opportunities. That makes it a pleasure trip."

"Wise guy." He stamped our documents. I hadn't seen a stamp before. Elsewhere all documents are electronic and are signed cryptographically. The Raxians must be fond of the ominous finality of the *thud* of the heavy stamp.

At the next station, our luggage was facing down a

customs agent who came from the same vat as the immigration agent. The luggage was quivering with rage and flashing "Nothing to Declare" in green letters on its side. The customs agent was stolidly unmoving but didn't realize he was still standing only because we had commanded the luggage to keep the body count low.

Color of Air knew to hand over voice control to me whenever the luggage was involved. "Stand down," I told the valise. "He has permission to inspect." Hearing the code phrase, the luggage settled down with a sigh and reluctantly opened. Only we heard the puff of ten grams of recreational contraband vaporizing within.

The search was brief but disarranged every article within. The compulsive within me cringed as everything was crammed back in haphazardly. The customs agent looked disappointed that he couldn't charge us with something, though he clearly was trying to make the woman's clothing into a chargeable offense in his mind. «We should probably travel with only single-gender clothes,» I thought. «The variety could give us away if anyone is looking for an Arilune.»

«It's so hard to find the right size,» said Color of Air archly. She was getting the hang of sarcastic banter.

«I very much doubt you will get a chance to wear it on Raxas,» I replied.

In addition to the false name I had given the officials, we were wearing a good-looking but forgettable face from

Color of Air's repertoire. Call me paranoid, but after our run-in with Magid, I wanted to break our trail.

We exited through doors the color of finely ground despair and hailed a cab for the hotel. Horizons were close and cramped. Raxas was a small world, exceedingly dense with iron, which made up their principal export. We took a cab to the charmingly named Foundry Hotel and found refuge in our reserved room.

«*Now, are you going to tell me why we've come here? It's certainly not for the natural beauty of the scenery. If we're going to be partners, I need to know what you know. What are you holding back?*»

Cinnamon indecision. Chocolate basil — what did that mean? A hint of miso, which I was coming to recognize as her tell when she was thinking of lying to me. I headed her off.

«*Tell me if I'm wrong. You knew you were being followed. You know who this cat is. It was a surprise to you that the Syndicate had captured her. You're worried about what she could tell them – or has already told them. You want me to find her. And then what? You kill her?*»

«*No! Not kill her. She was kind to me.*» I noticed that she didn't deny the rest.

«*Did she know what you were? What form did you have?*»

«*I took one of her crewmates. That was my first form.*»

«*You ate her friend, and she was kind to you? Who was she?*»

«*It would be hard for a primate like you to understand. She's a*

72

Kaence, *not a cat. Her name is Nuritha. She is a predator, and she honors another predator. Being eaten is the fate of all life, whether by a hunter, by fire, or by worms. Better by a hunter than the other two — that's how her kind thinks.»*

I shuddered, but I had run into other species like that. Mantids were the sort of buddies you'd want at your back in a bar fight or a war zone — but if you see an egg case stuck to the wall, lock yourself in your cabin. And as for Medusas — no, there's no comparison.

«*So we're here to do what?*»

«*Liberate her, if possible. I have to believe that she is not cooperating willingly. Keep her knowledge out of the hands of people who would use it against my people.*»

«*How do you know she is not cooperating?*»

«*Because she told them I disembarked at Damiron. It was Aracelle. It was only my incredibly bad luck that Damiron was my second stop after Aracelle, and they picked up my trail there.*»

I whistled. Well, I thought about whistling. No lips. «*I don't believe in luck. There's your planning, and there's the adversary's planning. It was either a failure in your planning or the adversary has a plan we don't know about yet.*»

My features melted into hers so she could glare at me in the mirror. «*I was extremely careful at breaking my trail at every point!*»

«*But what if someone was watching for that pattern? Looking for what was missing instead of what was there?*»

She was silent.

«And there might be surveillance even in a private room, as illegal as that would be. We should keep to the face we registered with.»

She hastily switched back to the face that had cleared immigration.

«It seems that you have much to teach me about paranoia.»

We spent most of the day consulting databases and public records of comings and goings, taking care to look like we were doing no more than researching potential markets, in line with the interest that we had declared when running the iron gamut of the emigration hall. At last, we looked up and closed the connection.

«We've come up empty so far, said Color of Air. *We need to infiltrate the Palace. If she's not being held there, they would at least have more detailed records.»*

«I have another line of attack that I can use,» I replied. *«But we need to get some food first.»*

«But we don't need to eat, remember? At least not that way.»

«What if someone runs pattern matches for people who arrive on a planet but don't eat in public and don't order in? Not that ordering in is a possibility in this hotel, I checked.»

«You make me wonder how I made it this far.»

«Maybe at first they weren't looking for you. Now they are.»

«Fine. I can eat according to my shape. I can even enjoy it. Let's go.»

We took the elevator to the ground floor where there was

a … let's call it a food facility. It was more functional than a restaurant or even a mess hall. Since it catered to offworld clients, it was a cut above the normal Raxian eatery. It even had live servers. The elevator stopped halfway down, and a young blonde man stepped on. He smiled, which marked him as an offworlder as well. We both faced the elevator doors in the protocol that most sentient species (except the Blues) practiced in such spaces.

As Color of Air gazed at him out of the corner of her eye, I felt an attraction to his smoothly muscled body. His essence was grasses and pollens, open air, umami as of beef, salt, and esters. I felt overwhelmed by the sensations rolling through the body I inhabited. I wanted to invite him back to the room, wrap ourselves around him, feel his bones crunching within…

The deep revulsion that rolled through me sent Color of Air staggering back a pace. The man turned slightly towards us, raising his eyebrow. "Are you all right?"

"Yes, just … A touch of timeslip. My ship was a half-day out of sync with local time. I just need to eat, sleep, and reset my clock."

"I understand. If you want to get dinner sometime, I'd be glad of the company. I don't know anyone onworld yet."

"Not tonight, but another time, perhaps."

He nodded and exited the elevator. I would have slumped against the wall if I had control. That wasn't desire; that was hunger. «*Is that what you feel?*»

Color of Air conveyed a wry cinnamon … something. «*I told you that you would feel it soon enough.*»

Somehow we were in the restaurant, seated with a menu, before I was tracking external events again. There was a real downside to going everywhere together. Color of Air ordered an eclectic meal but turned down cocktails, wine, after-dinner drinks, and coffee. The server looked quizzically at us but shrugged it off as slightly unusual tastes. Her badge identified her as Rheem, though it didn't say whether that was first name, last name, or third name. (Raxian names can sound like a litany when you read them in full.)

When the food arrived, I understood. The crispy fried meat was a violet symphony in G Major, notes of pepper ringing out like bells among the starbursts. No human would have said the sweet pudding should have been on the same table, but it had the taste of wooden chimes in the wind that cooled the bombast of the meat dish. The bitter root vegetable was a favorite of an herbivorous species I hadn't heard of. It painted crimson sunset tones under the pepper and tannin of the other dishes.

«*Is that what food is like for you?*»

She was amused. «*It's what dining is like. A pleasant experience that is as nourishing as a concert would be for you. It's not the same as eating prey.*»

Rheem came by to ask if we wanted anything else. She had been attentive and chatty all evening. Color of Air turned my roguish charm on her and even dialed it up several notches. "What if I asked you to call on my room after you finish work? Would you like that?"

Rheem flushed down to her neckline and probably beyond, but her collar hid that. She looked at her feet. "Well, I don't really know you. It wouldn't be proper." She handed us the pad and stylus to sign for the meal charge. Our fingertips met as we handed it back. Met and lingered. She drew a sharp breath. "Come again for dinner while you're here. Ask me then."

She put her hand shyly on mine. Abruptly, Color of Air gave me full control, body and voice. I could feel the warm blood pulsing in her hand, taste the floral-orange-spice of her skin. I could see her as she would be in our bed, eyes closed in ecstasy as she sank within our embrace, releasing her flavors, her memories, her hopes and fears, as she joined with us forever. That was as it should be. That was our nature.

I leaped to my feet, stammering that I wouldn't have time to be back before I left, I was sorry for being so forward, please forgive me. None of these were things I had ever said to a young lady who indicated she was willing to be seduced. I rushed back to the elevator and back to the room without Color of Air revoking my driving privileges. She was silent until I reached the room, though I felt like she was laughing somewhere in the background.

«*Why are you doing this to me?*» I demanded.

«*You need to embrace your new nature. That hunger that you felt was all you. You're an apex predator now; enjoy it.*»

«*We can't afford to have people disappear near us. You might as well hang a sign on our hotel room door saying 'Periphage in residence.'*»

«*I suppose that's true,*» she said, sounding as if she was pouting. «*We'll have to hunt soon, though. The body demands it.*»

«*Isn't there a substitute? Meat? A wild animal? Raw fish?*» I knew even as I said that there was not.

She knew what I felt and didn't answer that question. Instead, «*You said you had something else to try to find Nuritha.*»

I extracted a small device from a hidden compartment in my luggage. It was a military-grade espionage tap from the sort of job I try not to take anymore. It clicked on the back of the computer terminal; within a second, it violated the computer's mind, drained all of its memory, and made it a slave to its will. The analogy wasn't lost on me.

«*This will start searching the dark network for mentions of Kaence, Nuritha, and Periphages. Now we wait. This could take a while.*»

I was particularly interested in turning up anything about Periphages. The evening reminded me that I was still an unwilling passenger in this body. Perhaps I would find a clue that would free me from my predatory host.

* * *

Two days later, we joined a tour of the Palace. The top honcho styled himself the First Citizen, wore military uniforms, and had "fair" elections every four years that he had every expectation of winning for the rest of his life. It was all straight from the playbook his kind has used since before the Caesars on Earth.

We still wore the form of Seamus Whitby to match the identity card we carried. The Raxians had a nasty habit of checking them frequently, making things difficult for an honest Shapestealer. We hung near the rear of the tour as we checked out the richly woven silk tapestries, the exquisite carvings, and the magnificent and elegantly crafted electronic surveillance systems.

«*Are we sure she's in here?*» asked Color of Air.

«*That's the last reference in the files that I was able to breach. After that, she was transferred into the Palace security system, which is air-gapped from the rest of the network. I can't find out anything more.*»

We were walking through the Great Hall of the Citizen now. Its most unusual feature was a ledge about ten feet above the hall floor, upon which a dozen black panthers sat with majestic boredom as the tour filed through. The guide was explaining, "Although the cats are restrained in no way, they are conditioned to never leave their perch above the hall. They have living quarters behind the gallery and are trained to come to the ledge and pose whenever people enter the hall." «*And so they symbolize the workers of this fine planet,*» I finished in my mind.

I spotted an alcove that shouldn't be covered by any security cameras I could see. We stepped within it while the tour trailed out of the far end of the hall. «*Quick, become a panther!*» I said. I could feel her startlement as she dropped our clothes to the floor. We started changing, but I could feel it was a strain for her. The form was blocky at first, the skin black but only suggesting fur, the posture stuck only halfway to quadrupedal. It took nearly a minute to settle into her usual flawless duplication of form.

«*Give a girl a little warning next time.*»

«*Now, up on the ledge. Look like one of the residents.*»

She lept to the ledge and took her place among the other bored panthers. As the last of the tour group straggled into the next room, the cats rose from their poses and padded back into their living quarters, taking us with them. I speculated to myself about what had caused her difficulty in changing forms. Was it lack of time to prepare, the fur, or something else?

The cat quarters were more luxurious than the hotel room we had booked, reputedly one of the better establishments in the city. Cats lounged on carpeted perches, dined from labeled bowls, and drank from a running waterfall along one wall. The walls were glass, not the bars I was hoping for. However, I spied a ventilation duct above one high perch. The grating would keep the cats out, but I'll wager that none of them could reshape a claw into a screwdriver blade. To tell the truth, it surprised me as well. In minutes, we were navigating the ductwork. Color Of Air adjusted our body to a more weasel-like proportion to fit the cross-section of the duct better, and when our belly dragged in the middle she added another set of legs.

A six-legged black weasel was an efficient duct-runner, but there were a lot of ducts. We looked into seemingly hundreds of rooms, many of which the Interstellar Trade Commission and the First Citizen's electorate would have found very interesting, though none held what we sought. Hours later, when we were beginning to feel our efforts were in vain, Color Of Air finally announced, «*She's here!*»

Another grating blocked our way down into the room. Instead of tediously unscrewing screws, we simply liquified and ran through, coalescing in a puddle on the floor that drew itself up into the form I recognized as the base to which Color of Air always returned. Naked, of course, since we hadn't carried our clothes with us.

A body hurtled across the room at us as we touched down. Reflexively, I took a low stance, ready to grapple an arm and pivot the attacker's momentum across my hip, following up with an attempt to break or dislocate an arm or two. It took a heartbeat for me to notice that our body had done none of these things. I wasn't in control right now. Fortunately, it wasn't an attack; we had our arms full of a furry form. Fur tastes like green pine sunlight set to a jazz beat. Just in case you wanted to know.

We held Nuritha off at arm's length. She had said nothing and only shook her head mutely. Despite Magid's people calling her a cat, she wasn't really feline in appearance. Her face was oval, and her ears would probably elicit the comment "elfin." Her race had never run on all fours as the panthers in the entryway had. But with the soft fur and the grace with which she moved, the comparison to a cat was inevitable.

Color of Air opened her mouth to speak, but Nuritha put a finger to her lips and pointed to her ears. Someone was listening. Color of Air nodded, gathered Nuritha in our arms, and began to elongate towards the vent in the ceiling. Nuritha struggled frantically as we rose; we returned her to the floor. She tapped on a collar around her throat.

«*That will incapacitate her or maybe even kill her if she leaves the room,*» I told Color of Air. «*She can't leave until we deactivate it.*» I felt a chlorine-sharp jolt of alarm as Color of Air remembered our experience with Magid's bracelet.

Nuritha laid her hand on our chest, over where the heart would be if we had one. She pointed to the air duct, then repeated the motion: heart, air duct, heart, air duct. She was clearly telling us to go and leave her.

Color of Air shook her head. We're not leaving. I wasn't getting much say in the matter, but I couldn't leave someone imprisoned like this either.

A door closed in the distance. Footsteps approached. Nuritha frantically pushed us toward the bed, then bent down to indicate we should squeeze under it. There was only a handbreadth of clearance, so we flowed into a jellylike puddle that oozed under the bed.

«*Yuck, don't they ever clean under here? I'm getting dust in my protoplasm.*» It tasted gritty and stale and ashen, with the ever-present tang of iron that this entire planet had.

«*Nuritha knows what you are, it seems. How did that happen? How did you not eat her?*»

«*I don't eat my friends,*» was her furious rejoinder.

I wished for an eyebrow I could raise. «*I suppose I didn't qualify? Just a one-night stand?*»

«*More or less.*»

Footsteps came to the door of the cell. Things clinked, clanked, and rattled for a few seconds. A radio squawked. A voice answered, "No, nothing's out of place. She's right there, on the cot. Crying again. Nothing has tripped the corridor sensors.

... I don't care if you saw a blip, there's nothing here.

... Oh, if you're so sure, you come down here and look.

... I thought so."

Footsteps, heavy, departing.

Nuritha remained face down on the cot. Color of Air extended a thin pseudopod along the wall, up on the bed, and nestled it into Nuritha's ear. "Thump once if you can hear me," she vibrated down the ear canal, a living audio earpiece. We felt a gentle thump against the mattress.

Nuritha continued weeping quietly into the pillow. She artfully wove a message of despair into her sobs. "How is anyone going to find me here?"

"Good girl, Nuritha. I had an adversary who let a clue slip out and a partner who found the location in their records."

"But anyone who comes for me would end up in a cage, too. Or dead. I don't want that either." She was doing a convincing job of talking to herself.

"We'll get you out of here," Color of Air whispered.

Two thumps vibrated the mattress springs. No.

"What? Why not?"

Silence. It wasn't a yes or no question. She must have been trying to find a way to work it into her monologue.

"Are there cameras here?"

Two thumps.

"Just microphones?"

One thump.

"I'll come up there with you."

We flowed between the wall and the bed and re-formed next to Nuritha. She pulled the covers up to hide us. It felt incongruously cozy and safe in the darkness, and the blanket concentrated the intense identity of Nuritha: raspberry, chocolate, cinnamon, musk, and lavender. Her fur felt wonderful. I felt the hunger rising again and fought to push back the raging beast. We don't eat friends.

In this cocoon, Nuritha risked whispering, no more than a breath of air against our skin. "I cannot leave. I have … a task." It was like a shout to our senses, but even a microphone directly above the bed would have detected nothing. Color of Air didn't hear through her ears; she heard through her entire skin.

"I can't leave you here."

Nuritha seemed to come to a decision. "Take me. Make me part of you. That's the only way I'm getting out of here. Then kill the First Citizen, steal his records, and escape. Expose him. Then I will have lived with purpose."

"Is that what you truly want?"

«No! We're not eating anyone today! What happened to not eating friends?» But our body said otherwise. Nuritha was sustenance, not friend. We needed to eat, and we already had her in our embrace. All we had to do was spread out, envelope her, pull her inside. The ultimate intimacy.

I don't know if Color of Air could sense my hunger or if I was sensing hers. But she responded to my statement. «A willing gift is sacred. It cannot be turned down lightly and must be consummated with all due reverence. I must give her a gift the equal of the one she gives us.»

«Is it truly the equal? We'll still be alive afterward.»

«And we'll be hungry again in a few days, a week at the most. Everything is fleeting.»

Color of Air made love to Nuritha reverently and passionately. By the end, I was nearly convinced it was the gift that Color of Air had claimed, and the moment we consumed her was transcendent. I could almost believe. But then I was left with the ashes of what we had done, wondering if Color of Air believed her own propaganda or if it was the rationalization of her species imperative.

Nuritha accepted her merging with wonder. <So this is what it feels like,> she thought, even as her mind dissolved within us. <To hear color, to taste light. Wait, is there someone here with you?»

«This is Samuel Whitt. He is my new … partner.»

«Whitt? … Captain …Whitt?» Her mind was gossamer blowing in the wind, torn and raveling. Thoughts were becoming disconnected. «Your sister … my ship …»

«What? What about my sister? Do you know what happened to her?» There was no answer.

It took some time to absorb Nuritha, letting her layers ablate away like an expanding nebula. At the end, her memories burst like a nova into our inner space. Streamers of remembrance were flung into the void: hunting with her siblings in a grassland park; training for trans-species medicine at an academy; a collage of planets and spaceports; memories of the crew of the vessel she served on. There, there was a glimpse of my sister still in first officer's uniform before she had made captain and gotten her own ship. What was their connection? The glimpses were all I had as the memory strands were swept up into Color of Air's … mind? Soul? Gestalt? Whatever barrier kept her from sweeping my memories up in that way also prevented me from seeing the memories she had acquired.

«*Tell me what you've learned,*» I pressed her. «*I can help.*»

«*I'm still sorting it out. Oh, this is not good. They know about me and know that Nuritha was my friend. They were using her to lure me here. There are traps at the doors; they expected me to take the form of someone in the Palace and come in from the outside. Nuritha gave us this knowledge the only way she knew how.*»

«*Then we should hustle back the way we came and resume our role as a trader. No, wait, if Nuritha disappears from her cell, they'll know we were here. They'll lock down the planet and set traps at the spaceport.*»

«*We'll stay right here,*» she said. Her thoughts had gone as grey and cold as the iron palace that held us. «*The First Citizen took Nuritha out from time to time to show off. When he does, I will tear the rotting heart from his corpulent body.*»

«*What? There's no profit in revenge. The profit is in getting as far from here as possible.*» Did I mention the downside of going everywhere together?

«*On your balance sheet, be sure to put down that someone knows who we are, wants to capture us, and is willing to bait traps with innocents.*»

«*Well, since you put it that way…*»

We arose, found the adjoining bathroom, and excreted the excess mass we had acquired. Standing before the mirror, we watched our form reflow into Nuritha's graceful lines. Color of Air had left the accursed collar in place when we absorbed Nuritha. (It had fortunately not been designed for Arilune as Magid's had.) I hoped we could get it off fast enough if needed, but it would raise an alarm if we took it off now. Then we waited, reviewing Nuritha's memories.

It was evening when a guard finally opened the door. He said only, "You're wanted for entertainment," and gestured for the door. He had a control box for the collar strapped and locked to his wrist. We wouldn't be able to simply grab it. We probably could slice his arm off if needed, though I would want to be certain there wasn't a deadman circuit built in.

As we left the prison cell, a red light suddenly scorched the anteroom. An archway had lit up as we passed beneath. Two other guards stationed outside were galvanized into action and pounced on the guard escorting us. "Shapestealer!"

Our escort blanched. "No! It's a false alarm! I'm not..." The other two jumped him and forced a vial of liquid past his lips. They held him and waited as he struggled. After several minutes, they looked at each other and said, "He's not melting."

"Of course I'm not, you idiots. If I were the Shapestealer, I would have set the alarm off going in. The bloody thing must be broken. Send for someone to fix it before I bring her back from the banquet. I'll be lucky if the captain doesn't write me up for drinking on the job."

I caught a whiff of alcohol in the air. Was there some elixir that could detect Shapestealers? What did it do to one? What were they scanning for that would detect us so easily? I was glad they were so fixated on their target using the frontal approach. It kept them from considering the other explanation for the alarm going off.

Our escort straightened himself up and motioned us ahead of him. We walked down endless corridors permeated with the tang of iron, punctuated with whiffs of machine oil, ozone, and solvents that signified we were on the level that had the support machinery for the Palace.

A service elevator was at the end of the corridor, small and cramped. We entered and stood as far from our escort as space allowed. «*Don't look demure,*» Color of Air thought. «*Nuritha would carry herself proudly, even when a prisoner.*»

I don't think that Color of Air considered how that would sound to me, prisoner in my own body. I spent the elevator ride turning that phrase over in my mind, like a lock for which I had no key.

THE COLOR OF STEEL

THE ELEVATOR let us into a serving alcove for a grand ballroom. That is, if grand were defined as spacious, imposing, and monumental but omitted terms such as lavish, splendid, or opulent. The overwhelming use of iron and steel in the columns, walls, and even tables was perhaps useful for impressing visitors with the nature of this planet's principal export, but as a design motif, it was on the oppressive side.

Our escort signaled to a majordomo standing near the head table, who bent and whispered to a steel grey man sitting at its head. He nodded, which was conveyed in reverse to the alcove. Our escort directed us to go to the table and await his pleasure and reminded us not to get more than thirty steps away from the control unit for the collar. Thank you for letting us know the range. We walked to the position indicated. Into every step, we put the dignity of royalty ascending to the throne. Every eye stopped and watched as we paced through the room until we halted and awaited the First Citizen's pleasure while conveying that we were granting him the audience with us.

In the hush that followed, the First Citizen suddenly burst into laughter and turned to the man on his right, who was sandy-haired and dressed to indicate that he was from offworld. "There, what did I tell you? Isn't she magnificent? She walks as if she owns the place, brazenly naked as if she were the lowliest whore, and stands before us without the least shame. Her kind must not be quite civilized yet, eh? Just barely beyond the jungle. Look at the pelt on her! Quite like the panthers we keep in the entry hall, isn't it? When she arrived on-planet, the police picked her up right away for public indecency. We took her in for her protection. All we ask for that protection is for her to perform some of her native dances for us. They're quite primal."

He turned to us. "Now, *mon petite bête*, do your dance for our distinguished visitor."

We gave him a withering look and turned our back to stalk away a few paces. Color Of Air was seething.

«Nuritha's people believe that clothing is an abomination. Their pelt is their ultimate pride; they shun any covering or ornamentation of it. To cover yourself in public is shame; to cover another is a deadly insult. She could bear captivity more easily than she could bear clothing.»

«Are you going to dance for him? Because I can't.»

«Tonight, we are Nuritha. She will dance for them.»

The First Citizen began a rebuke, but we — Nuritha — held up a peremptory hand and the room stilled. We were mere observers now, and Nuritha held us, and the room, in thrall. She held that pose as the silence stretched until everyone forgot their meals, their companions, their conversations.

She began the hunt. She was the mother of all her race, and she was born to hunt. Eschewing the stage, she made the tables her hunting ground, stalking softly, spear held high. The world was so young that it had no name; it was merely the world. A herd of antelope pawed nervously at the ground as she passed by. A family of monkeys chattered briefly but was cowed by a snarl. Storks near the verge of the meadow edged nervously towards flight. Nuritha paced past each of these as beneath her notice. Collective sighs of relief were breathed as each was confirmed as a lesser being, not worthy of challenge.

But then a great boar emerged from the rushes, tusked and bristling. Nuritha raised her spear, but the boar charged. She leaped, scoring a knife stroke on its hide as she vaulted over its back. Enraged, it whirled and charged again. Each attack was met with a feint, each pass with another slice, but the fearsome tusks gave no opening for the spear. Finally, bloody and weary, the boar turned too slowly, exposing a flank. The spear flashed home, and the great beast toppled at last. Nuritha stood triumphant before the head table, and the spell wavered a moment to reveal the First Citizen sweating and cowering in his chair.

Now Nuritha was dancing around the fire upon which the boar meat roasted. Many men were there who desired her, but none could match her in pursuit. Now came a new suitor, strong and tawny. She pretended indifference; he pursued. She sprinted away, vanishing in the forest. He hunted, he tracked her, he discovered her (perhaps she cooperated a small bit). The chase was on. Across the plains, over the mountains, across the oceans they ran. The world turned under them as they coursed and day and night took turns watching the race. Finally, he caught her (she may have let him) and he threw her down. Together they wrestled, joined by the flesh, tawny fur and black fur forming a single yin/yang union, and the world shook with their mating. And from their passion all the peoples of the land sprang forth.

The dance ended, and Nuritha's spirit passed from us, leaving us in control once more, swaying slightly but maintaining her final majestic pose. We did not bow because she would not have bowed. At the table of antelopes, one woman had fainted and the rest looked scandalized. At the table of the monkeys, they exchanged flushed looks and whispers of "Just wait until we get back to our room!" The storks resumed their duties of waiting on the tables. At the head table, the First Citizen had gone grey with shock, as if he had just received a death threat. (He had.) The sandy-haired offworlder had a dazed look as if he had just fathered all the people of the world (he had, but only in his mind).

The offworlder recovered and leaned in to whisper to the First Citizen. The latter looked shocked and replied in rather more than a whisper, "But she's barely more than a beast. We have laws against that here!" The offworlder was unmoved. He raised his eyebrow, and the effect was as if he had turned over his hole card. The First Citizen folded. He turned to the Majordomo and ordered, "Take her to the Ambassador's suite!" He emptied his glass and petulantly held it out, causing a stork to nearly trip in his haste to fill it.

Color Of Air was not pleased with the development. «That pig just wants to fulfill the fantasy we just painted him. We need to stay near the First Citizen and wait for a chance to put a knife in him.»

«It didn't look like he was going to let us get that close. At any rate, this solves the problem of going back to our room through that detector tonight.»

«Hmm, yes. If that alarm goes off again when we go through

it, even guards this dense will figure it out.»

Our escort conducted us through servant's corridors again, but upwards this time. We re-entered the land of the more equal on the ninth floor and were ushered to a door at the end of the hallway. The guard opened the door to let us in, then closed it behind us. I was briefly puzzled as to why he didn't check for escape routes before I remembered the collar and the transmitter that was strapped to his wrist.

Color Of Air reached for the collar but stopped halfway. »*It makes me itch to think that something that can kill us is around our throat.*» I remembered how Magid's torture device had nearly undone her.

«*Put your hands down. We don't want to make anyone suspicious. How long would it take you to get it off in an emergency?*»

«*About a tenth of a second if it doesn't disrupt muscle control too fast. What if it's rigged to explode like Magid's?*»

«*We'll have to take the risk that they're not crazy enough to use an explosive device in a crowded building. Plus, Magid intended to confine a shape changer who could slide out of it, but this is for a solid being.*»

We didn't have much longer to wait. The Ambassador walked in, loosening the black tie that went with his dinner jacket. Color of Air stood proudly in the center of the outer sitting room of the suite.

"Your Excellency asked for me to be sent to his

chambers. I can only assume you wish a personal re-enactment of my performance this evening."

"Stars, no! I don't employ abused and unwilling prisoners as entertainment. Your rights as a sentient being ..."

Color of Air crossed the room in a bound and slapped her hand over his mouth. "If you value your life or mine, don't finish that sentence," she breathed in his ear. "They're listening."

"They wouldn't dare. I have diplomatic immunity." I noticed that he whispered no louder than she had. Good. He might stand on principles, but he knew that others might not.

Color of Air spoke in a normal voice. "I assure you that I'm not a prisoner, and I'm not unwilling, especially for you. I had my eye on you at the banquet. I'm glad you picked up the signal."

The Ambassador broke into a sweat, probably overloaded by the overt and hidden messages in that sentence. "Well, I ..."

"Come to your chamber. That dance is so much better with a partner."

«You're not going to eat him, are you? That would blow our cover.»

«This isn't my first dance,» she replied coldly.

She plucked at his jacket fastenings as she led him to the bedchamber. "So what do I call you?" she murmured in his ear.

"Oh, Stars, where are my manners? I am Alexander. And what is your name, my dear?"

"You can call me Nuritha."

"What a lovely name. It sounds like a purr. It seems fitting for one…"

She used her teeth. "You weren't going to say feline, were you?"

"Er, no, of course not."

"Good. We are not descended from cats, though we have fur and we hunt. We *don't* purr."

"Of course. I've visited your world, and it's as beautiful as you conveyed in your dance. Your people are proud and are accomplished in the arts, and I know of your cultural avoidance of clothing. I wasn't as shocked as the Raxians pretended to be."

She pushed him back on the bed. "Then tell me why I'm still the only one not wearing filthy garments?" Once that was rectified and we were snug among the (iron gray) blankets, we could whisper.

"Why are you really here?" Color of Air breathed. Alexander shivered; she has that effect on people.

"To dig up enough dirt on the First Citizen that the Concordium can't continue to ignore his sentient-rights record. Sentient trafficking and slavery would be a major card for us to play."

«*Let me speak,*» I petitioned. Color of Air yielded.

"Raxian steel is too valuable to the interstellar trade for them to let you rock the boat. Both the Syndicate and the Concordium cooperate to keep a strongman in power here, to keep the flow of ingots coming." Alexander went up on one elbow to look at us in surprise. He wasn't expecting a political analysis, and I reprimanded myself for not staying in character. He took it at face value, though.

"The First Citizen has gotten greedy. He's squeezing the Syndicate's margins on high-quality steel. They want someone more … pliable … in that position. The Concordium wants free elections and democratically elected leaders. And, of course, an end to his barbaric practices. We find our interests aligned with the Syndicate, as embarrassing as that may be."

"What do you want from me, then?"

"I want to smuggle you onto my shuttle when I leave tomorrow so you can testify about your experience here."

"Have you forgotten this collar I'm wearing?"

"I'm sure I can remove it…"

"Before it kills me?"

"Before it what?"

«*This guy is terminally naive,*» I thought.

«*Yes, I thought he was playing dumb, but he's not playing.*»

«*Can you knock him out without hurting him?*»

Color of Air snuggled closer to him."Leave that for morning. I have a better way to fill the empty hours." His protestations that he wouldn't take advantage of a prisoner soon grew weaker. His scents, which I had been striving to ignore, rose about me: grasses and pollens, open air, umami, salt, and esters. The hunger grabbed me by the throat. This was prey, bones to break and memories to sop up like gravy. Wouldn't it be better to eat him, take his ticket offworld, and dispose of the evidence? I didn't do any of these things. I've survived this long by recognizing rationalizations when I heard them,

His scent, though, was familiar. Where had I encountered it before? I worried about it through several minutes of increasingly distracting activity until I had it. He had been in the elevator at the hotel, and we had spoken briefly. What had a diplomat been doing in a hotel like that one? But the face wasn't right. Could more than one person have the same scent?

I didn't have many minutes to ponder it. He didn't last long and fell asleep immediately. If this had been a real date, I would have been disappointed. As it was, it solved our problem.

He held us closely, which presented a slight difficulty. We softened into a puddle and streamed from under his arm onto the floor. We reformed again, but this time into a faithful replica of Alexander. Dressing in his clothes took only a few minutes. We pocketed the collar on the way out.

Outside the door to his suite, the startled guard barred our way. "Please return to your quarters. It is after curfew."

We put on a bemused air. "What is the reason for this?

It's not lawful to detain an ambassador from the Concordium."

The guard smirked. "Conspiracy to overthrow the duly elected government of this planet isn't lawful either. Nor is consorting with lower forms of life." The smirk broadened into a leer. "Was the little mink good, Ambassador? Does she bite? Uhhh…"

I suppose that, technically, he got the last word in. The next-to-last word was our fist in his solar plexus, driven by Color of Air's rage. He fell like a tree, heart ruptured by the force of the blow.

«Alexander wasn't very discrete; they're on to him. He's in danger now as well.»

The guard was still wearing the controller for the collar locked to his wrist. We grasped his hand and let our flesh flow around his. (Look away if you're squeamish.) Moments later, we had absorbed his hand, leaving only a smooth stump, and the controller dropped off. We stopped there. We didn't want to absorb this guy's memories; they looked unpleasant.

Pocketing the controller, we headed for the lift. The controls were a schematic of the Palace, with the top floor conveniently labeled [Private]. Seemed like the place to start. Tapping the floor, however, only produced a red [Unauthorized] icon under our finger.

«It must be fingerprint keyed.»

«Let's hope the guards are authorized.»

Our hand morphed into a replica of the guard's missing hand, and we tapped again. This time, the destination illuminated, and the lift began to move.

«*Neat trick, that.*»

«*All it takes are a few cells.*»

We examined the controller that we had lifted from the guard. There was a big button marked [Activate] and a smaller one marked [Unlock]. We pressed the second one and the collar snapped open. «*I feel better now that it's not armed,*» commented Color of Air.

The lift opened directly into a sumptuous apartment. Draperies billowed languidly from an open balcony. The living area appeared deserted, but faint sounds came from the bedroom. She started towards the bedroom, but I called «*Wait!*»

«*What is it?*»

«*Do we want to implicate Alexander? He's innocent.*»

«*You're right.*» She slipped off Alexander's clothes and took Nuritha's form. «*Nuritha would want her name on this revenge.*»

I had something more anonymous in mind, but she was striding towards the bedroom again. I was about to say something when I saw sparkles in the air. There was a slight puff of vapor from our skin, and I yelled, «*Get down!*» Red alarm lights thundered pungently through the dim room, followed seconds later by a dozen guards.

* * *

I awoke, restrained and alone. Color of Air's by-now-familiar presence was absent. I couldn't feel much of anything, though I could smell various scents. Salt. Grass. Yellow. Tweed cinnamon and paisley pomegranate. The ever-present bite of iron. Yep, synesthesia was still in full force. I could perceive my surroundings but not make sense of them without my host. I had harbored a desire to be rid of her, but if her absence meant an eternal psilocybin trip, I could put up with the snarky comments.

After a long time in the darkness of colors and smells, I felt something stir.

«Samuel?»

I was unreasonably happy to hear her voice again.

«You're not dead?»

«No, there was blackness. Time seems to have passed without notice. I have a gap in my memories.»

«You were unconscious.»

«I've never known that state before. I don't want to repeat it.»

«Can you make any sense of where we are? I can't tell what these scents mean.»

«They are just static, filling in the blanks where there is no input.»

«Are we blind?»

«No, enclosed. We are in a human-shaped iron caisson, completely sealed. I can find no flaw in it to escape.»

«It sounds like the perfect way to confine a shape changer. They had detectors, but we should have expected they had *weapons and cages as well.»*

«It seems that we have to wait for them to open it. They didn't kill us, so they must have wanted us for something.»

«Waiting is a very bad idea. We have to break out. How much can you expand in volume? »

«Maybe double? But the caisson will not allow it. »

«Have you ever seen ice shatter a pipe? An expanding liquid can exert a surprising force. Try it.»

There was a pause. *«Have you started?»* I asked.

«I'm trying to think of a large enough life form I've been before. It's easier if I have a target since I don't have any external feedback.»

«Is that why you had trouble shifting into the panther earlier?»

«Exactly. Maybe a Deepwater Lamplighter will do.»

Those weighed about a tonne and had lights on the ends of their fingers to attract fish two miles beneath the surface — their native habitat. *«That sounds big enough. When were you a Lamplighter?»*

«Hush. I must concentrate.»

Nothing happened for long moments, then the static became tinged with purple. I didn't hear her groan or grit her teeth, but there was a sense of great strain. The purple brightened to a violet, then to something I had no name for other than angry. The caisson cracked down the middle. Color of Air threw the metal shards across the room with a great heave, fortuitously smearing two of the four guards across the wall. The Lamplighter's fists were even more effective than the metal plates in liquifying the other two. She grabbed the remaining figure by the back of its lab coat and dangled it in front of our face. From what I remembered of the being we were currently mimicking, abject terror was an entirely appropriate response to even a friendly specimen, and we were anything but friendly.

"Why are you trying to trap me, and what did you use upstairs?" Color of Air roared. Really, in this form she couldn't help but roar.

«*Let me talk to him,*» I said, «*I have a better way.*» She yielded control.

I tried to modulate the voice to a merely thunderous level (less than volcanic, at any rate). "I want your credentials and clearance. Open all your files on Periphages, or you'll end up like the rest." He nodded assent. I let him fumble through the login, then broke his neck. I hadn't promised *not* to kill him, after all, just not as messily.

«*I'm sending these to the ship so we have them somewhere safe. Adding a backdoor for later. Destroying these records. Done. Let's get out of here.*»

«*Not yet. I promised Nuritha that I would complete her mission.*»

That struck me as suicidal. It was also honorable. I wasn't one to put honor before survival, but I could respect those who did. It wasn't often that those two principles were in such direct conflict.

«I don't know where to find the First Citizen. His bedroom was a trap. He's probably staying in some hidden safe room. In the meantime, reinforcements will be here sooner rather than later. Let's find a quiet place to lay low while we locate him.»

Color of Air agreed, so I turned the skulking over to her. She took the technician's form and then his clothes. His body went into a closet, where we hoped it wouldn't be discovered for a while. Then, we openly walked out of the room we had been held in.

This area was a prison crossed with a laboratory, which was just as unpleasant as it sounds. Many different species of sentients were locked in rooms here, some with the scars of torture or experimentation. Alexander would find plenty of evidence against the current regime if he didn't end up here himself. It was still the middle of the night, so there was little activity. We found an unoccupied office where we would have a few hours to plan.

There was a terminal here. Color of Air turned it over to me to dig through the network for more information. I could get into the lab systems with the back door I had installed but didn't have access to security information, such as the location of our quarry. But kick over a log, and a lot of unpleasant things can crawl out.

«They're looking for ways to give Arilune abilities to other species. This report alleges that a lab secretly run by the Starlane Corporation on Pinwheel has made breakthroughs and may have

captured some Arilune for experimentation. Starlane is a huge conglomerate that does military and intelligence technology for the Concordium. They use it for black ops that they want to keep off the books. There are three documented cases of individuals appearing with different faces and body morphologies. Since all three were revealed through freak accidents, it's assumed there are many more undetected agents. Wait ... I think we've discovered a fourth one.»

«Who's that?»

«Alexander. He's the same guy we encountered in the hotel elevator but with a different face. They both have the same scent.»

«You're right! I'm glad I didn't reveal myself to him as a shape changer. He thinks he slept with a Kaence. I can't help thinking he's too naive to be an agent.»

«Unless ... that's got to be it. He's Partitioned.»

«What's that?»

«The side of his mind with the mission objectives and the skills to accomplish them is sealed behind a barrier. Lie detectors and mind probes can't penetrate to scan that side. It's an unbreakable cover story.»

«So, is he a good guy or a bad guy?»

«It's complicated, like most people. He's almost definitely working for the Concordium, both as his cover story and his deep mission. It's almost morning. We must get out of this complex before someone finds we busted out of that diver's suit.»

«How about if we hide among the panthers again?»

«That's a terrible ... actually, that's not *a terrible idea. We'll head there once this search completes.»*

The last of the report flashed up on the holodisplay and Color of Air switched it off. Not before I saw the appendix listing the expeditions that had searched for the Arilune home planet. There in the list was the *Dry Whitt* commanded by Samara Whitt. My sister. Nuritha had known my sister and Color of Air had known Nuritha. It was all connected in some way I couldn't see yet. It underscored that I had more reasons not to trust Color of Air than I had known. It roiled like a cloud of oily smoke in what would have been my stomach if I still had one.

We found our way to the entrance hall by following the orange and purple musk of the big cats that hung visibly in the air (to us). We stashed the technician's clothes and ID next to the ones we had left earlier as Seamus Whitby. Either might be handy later, and I was glad they had gone undiscovered. My name was still clean on Raxas.

We vaulted to the perch we had used before and entered the panthers' backstage lounge. The big cats didn't notice us, seeming preoccupied with their empty food dishes. It was their feeding time, and I've noticed cats are quite good at telling time if it involves their meal schedules. I've had ship cats that knew their feeding time down to the second because I had delegated that task to the ship AI.

«We can hide out here during the day and find a way to locate the First Citizen when it's quiet. We can try the info systems

again or maybe capture and impersonate one of his lieutenants who has access to him.»

«We have to remember that they have Periphage detectors. I saw faint lasers in the First Citizen's bedroom before we got zapped. They probably vaporized a few skin cells and analyzed their spectra to match your signature. Do you know what they would look for?»

«Cyanide, graphene, long-chain carbon compounds, and a fair bit of silicate.»

«No wonder you're tough.»

«Not to change the subject, but the cats are getting restless.»

They were, indeed. They were milling about, rumbling with anticipation, having little flare-ups of temper with each other. But they weren't facing the food dishes; they were eyeing a door in one wall that I hadn't seen open yet.

«Something's happening...»

«Maybe this wasn't the quiet hiding place we were looking for.»

The door rose into the ceiling. The panthers crowded eagerly through the opening and into the featureless room beyond. They knew what was going to happen and looked forward to it.

«I think we had better go with the pack if we don't want to stand out,» I said.

«It's called a pride, not pack,» she replied archly. We followed the pride, staying in character.

It was a smooth-walled room, easily washed down. It

was all of iron, of course. A walkway was halfway up one wall, on which stood the First Citizen and Alexander. A couple of the cats jumped at them, clawing at the wall. The rest waited patiently below.

«*This does not look good. I think Alexander is getting the blame for letting us loose.*»

I felt Color of Air bunch up her (graphene, silicate, cyanide) muscles, ready to spring. *Do we save him?*

I did some risk-benefit analysis. «*He's the ambassador from the Concordium and sounded like he wanted to do the right thing. But if he's got a face made by Starlane — he might be working for the Syndicate, and we'd be jumping from the frying pan to the fire.*» But if he was Partitioned, he might be something else entirely. I didn't think that out loud. Color of Air might not understand.

The First Citizen was holding Alexander by the upper arm. He started to push. Alexander teetered on the edge, fighting for his balance, turning his foot inward to shift his weight backward. The panthers snarled and fought for position underneath. We remained poised, coiled and indecisive.

Alexander staggered, but I saw how it put his foot behind the First Citizen's ankle. I knew that move. I knew who had taught it to me. «*Go!*» I shouted inwardly.

The walkway was higher than the cats should be able to jump. Just barely higher, to instill an appropriate feeling of fear as they leaped and fell back, ever so close to making it up onto the platform. We leaped with stronger muscles, a body that could stretch imperceptibly longer, and a paw that elongated and clung in a way the others couldn't match.

Alexander kicked the First Citizen's feet out from under him just as we hooked the other ankle and dragged him down. I couldn't tell which one of us brought him down as we all fell together, but his death was a group effort among our black-furred and ravenous cellmates.

We stood over Alexander and roared, defending him from the real panthers. They turned aside, ready for the easier red meat that still drummed a tattoo on the floor. We grabbed Alexander in our jaws and dragged him back through the door, down the hallway to the perch where the cats would later sit to clean the bits of Citizen from their whiskers. We dropped him to the floor and leaped down after him. By the time he picked himself up and whirled to defend himself, we had resumed Nuritha's form.

I nudged for vocal access. "Quick, go down that way and out of the Palace. Make your way to the port. You should be able to get there before they order all traffic halted and searched."

"Come with me, or they'll recapture you and kill you."

"No, I have more to do. I can take care of myself."

Alexander looked at us with narrowed eyes. "Who are you really?"

"The enemy of your enemy. Now go."

He had a good self-preservation instinct. He left at a run.

«*Now we should get out of here ourselves. Seamus Whitby should go to his ship as quickly as possible. Is your debt to Nuritha discharged?*»

«*Yes, it was a fitting end for that beast. Let's go.*»

There was a moment of melting, rearranging features, and then I looked down on my familiar body. Familiar, yet it felt a little strange after having so many shapes since I last occupied it. I stood for a moment, waiting, but nothing happened. I thought about donning my clothes, and my body moved to obey. Huh. She had given me control.

I dressed, a familiar action with novel implications. Did my body balance the same as before? Did the fabric feel the same? Yes to the first, no to the second. The fabric felt smokey green with lime. Still the synesthesia. No time for details now. I hurried out of the Palace.

We didn't have any trouble getting to the port. No one was looking for Captain Whitby. En route, I used my communicator to tell *Rapier* to prep for departure and to tell my luggage to check out of the hotel and meet me at the ship. Stars help anyone who stood in its way.

In the departure concourse, I saw a face I had seen once before. I sidled near. I sensed grasses and pollens, open air, umami, salt, and esters, but the face was the one I had seen in the hotel elevator. On impulse, I said, "Did you find someone to have dinner with after that first night?"

His head jerked around and he gave me two smiles. The

first was a polite acknowledgment as he tried to place me, then an easier one as he mentally pictured me in the elevator. He didn't know that he had seen me an hour earlier wearing a coat of black fur.

"Yes, I did, thanks, but they were rather tedious. I'm sure you would have been a much better conversationalist."

That was an even clearer pickup line than the one at the hotel. He may not have been my type, but I certainly seemed to be his.

"But you're leaving now."

"Yes, I'm off to meet with my next set of clients. Raxis has too much iron and Caelum doesn't have enough. I think there's profit to be made."

"Good luck."

"Thanks, Captain ...?"

"Whitby, Seamus Whitby."

He offered his own name as John Drake, though I was sure it was as phony as mine.

«I have a strange feeling we're going to see him again,» I said.

«So do I. One other thing, Samuel...»

«Yes?»

«I have an admission to make. When we were breaking out of the lab, I was looking through all their research on Periphages for methods I could use to, um, excise you from myself.»

I had had the same goal, I thought guiltily. Had she found something? Was she going to hold it over my head, or was this predator's honor to tell me before using it?

I can't stop you.

No, I didn't find it. But you got us out of a tight spot … again. You acted with honor to Nuritha and Alexander. Our partnership is working better than I expected. And … I thought I might be lonely if you weren't there anymore.

Huh. I hadn't expected that. I had to admit I was coming to like our banter. I still had a problem with her diet of sentient beings, though. What would I do if I found a way to separate us? I didn't know.

I would miss you, too. There were many ways to interpret that. Surely one of them was true.

THE COLOR OF SEA

"WELCOME, CAPTAIN WHITT. Our most private seaside room, as you requested." The hostess unlocked the door to the bungalow and bowed, low and graceful. I entered and pretended to admire the appointments while looking for bugs, traps, and sabotage. Color of Air and I had worked out an arrangement where I got control of body and voice for part of the time, and part of my specialty was threat assessment. We still didn't trust each other completely, but our working relationship had improved.

My luggage was still standing in the doorway. "Sit!" I commanded it. It walked over to the foot of the bed and sighed open as it settled into position. I relaxed. It would have stayed tightly closed if it had detected electronic surveillance in the room.

"A most exotic piece of luggage," commented our hostess. She had no idea how exotic. "May I hang up your clothes?"

"I picked it up at the Titanium Bazaar on Three Axis Station. One of its quirks is that it's quite particular about who takes items out of it. Please let Housekeeping know to leave it strictly alone. A few ports ago, I had to buy a replacement hand for someone who had tried to tidy up a little too much."

"A dangerous portmanteau for a dangerous man. I'll also instruct them to be careful of the needle gun when pressing your jacket and the knife when polishing your shoes. Are there any other services you desire?"

I raised my eyebrow slightly at this simultaneous warning and innuendo. I declined, even though we were becoming hungry again. Especially because we were becoming hungry again. This hunger was not something felt in the stomach; it was a whole-body ache that became increasingly difficult to ignore.

After the hostess left, Color of Air took control once again, morphing into what seemed to be her base form. She had let slip that its name was Tammartin. It seemed to be the first sentient that the Periphage had ingested to become sentient itself. I itched to research that name, to gain more clues about her past. It was hard to get the privacy to do so.

«*Why would Erissa tell us that she knew how well we are armed?*» asked Color of Air.

«*Erissa?*»

«*It was on her name tag. Your attention was probably several inches lower, as usual.*»

I ignored that. «*What do you think? Work out the scenarios if she's enemy, ally, or neutral.*»

«*Ok. If she's neutral, she's well-trained in security and is putting us on notice that she's flagged us as someone to keep an eye on. If she's a potential ally, she's letting us know some of her abilities and is making an overture to get closer. If she's an enemy, she's given away some advantage by putting us on guard, though her purpose may be to make us curious enough to engage with her.*»

«*Good. I'm glad you said* potential *ally. We don't have enough information, so we should do nothing and let her make the next move. By the way, she's at least as well-armed as we are. I counted five concealed weapons.*»

«*Six.*»

I spent the next half hour wondering which one I had missed.

We walked by the sea while Pinwheel was still high in the sky. Pinwheel was known throughout the Galactic Arm as one of the most spectacular suns visible from a settled planet. Pinwheel was actually two stars of nearly equal mass in a close orbit. Only twelve times their diameter separated them, so they spun around their center of gravity in just over six hours. Tidal forces peeled a bridge of sun-stuff from their surfaces, which formed a glowing spiral of plasma around each disk. The pair was distant though bright. The planet orbited a third star, Cinder, which provided warmth and stability. A brown dwarf, Cinder smoldered darkly in the sky, upstaged for the moment by its actinic sisters.

The beach also had attractions: golden sand, warm blue water, and a lack of people. We had paid well for a secluded spot and a private beach. Still wearing Tammartin's form, we walked down to the water's edge and watched dolphins play in the waves offshore.

«*Are dolphins native?*» asked Color of Air.

«*No, they were imported, along with most organisms. Pinwheel sterilizes the surface with X-rays every time Cinder crosses the plane of their rotation. Terraformers built up an ionospheric shield before seeding the planet. Now, they simply get spectacular auroral displays every 45 years.*»

«*We'll have to come back for the next one.*»

«*I'll put it on our calendar in 23 years.*»

«*Immortality has its benefits.*»

We watched the waves for a while, the picture of a vacationing traveler, though neither of us had personalities suited to idleness.

«*Are you sure about those coordinates?*» asked Color of Air after a while.

«*That's what was in the files. About two kilometers that way.*»

«*There's nothing but ocean there. It could be a misdirection. We're supposed to know to add ten degrees to the longitude, or take the opposite sign.*»

«*There's only one way to find out. I wonder if we can rent scuba gear without being too obvious.*»

«*We won't need to. Let's go for a swim.*»

She stood and dropped her light sundress on the beach. The needle gun in the pocket weighted it down.

«*I feel naked,*» I complained.

«*I am naked.*»

«*I mean, without a gun. And it's not waterproof.*»

«*We'll just take it with us.*» She formed a pouch in our thigh and slid the needle gun into it. She threw a towel over the sundress to keep it from blowing away. I felt better dressed now.

We walked down to the water, feeling the air play across our skin. The air carried salts from the sea — we tasted violet sodium and umber potassium, but bromine was a song in A-minor wafting in the air. It conveyed a harmony of kelp, krill, barnacle, and mussel on its back, each in its distinct shade of rainbow flavor. After the sterile air of the ship and the iron dust of Raxas, the assault was dizzying.

We waded into the gentle waves. When it was up to our waist, we dove forward into the water, propelled by powerful strokes. We were streamlined and graceful in our element. Color of Air looked back for my benefit, and I saw a fluked tail like a dolphin's, merging at the waist into a more human back. Long hair flowed around our shoulders.

«*A mermaid!*»

«*A Cyraenan, one of the inhabitants of Cetus 127.*»

Our eyes adapted to the water, giving us the clarity of diving goggles. The tastes of the sea assaulted our skin, with an almost overwhelming roar of salts leading the way. After that was quickly filtered out, we could taste the shrimp hiding in the rocks, the anemones swaying in the currents. A school of darters flashed yellow citrus that twinkled as they changed directions. A small predator fish exuded a whiff of meat from its previous meal.

«*I don't see anything out here.*»

«*It would be farther out if it's here.*» We struck out to the west, away from the shore.

«*How long can we stay under?*»

«*I don't need to breathe, so pretty much indefinitely. The Cyraena can go without air for about fifteen minutes.*»

I lost myself in the exhilaration of gliding through the watery world. I wanted to flex and soar, not be a passive passenger in someone else's body. But the vistas of peaceful green light filtering from the surface onto shoals of rainbow fish were entrancing enough to keep me from complaining about my lot. For the moment.

A little over a kilometer from shore, the sea floor dropped away into the abyss. Dolphins congregated here, diving down the cliff face and returning with octopus-like creatures in their jaws.

«*Unlikely that there's anything farther out unless it's a deepwater research station. The cost of supplying a habitat goes up astronomically with depth. We should sweep north and south.*»

We picked north at random. I never bet on even odds so I expected it to come up empty. Which meant that we soon struck pay dirt. (The law of low expectations can trump the laws of chance and perversity.) A seabed habitation appeared in the distance, unlike the hidden stronghold I had expected. (If this were fiction, I would have used the word "lair.") This was open and brightly colored, lit by the dappled sunlight from the surface above. Applying the term "airy" to an underwater structure seemed a stretch, but this came close. The seafloor had risen as we swam northward, putting the highest towers of the building only five meters below the waves. It felt like a resort or a summer palace. Color of Air swam down to peer at it from the shelter of an outcropping of barnacle-covered rock.

We were interrupted in our reconnaissance by a taste like fresh sashimi with a burr of black pepper. We rolled over to find that a dolphin was checking us over. It was a full-sized male, the normal gray-and-white of the species, with the exception of a single fin that was black. It didn't look friendly. Color of Air tentatively stretched a hand out toward us. "Nice dolphin. See, we're not a threat."

«*Watch out for those teeth. They'd make a sushi chef die of envy.*»

«*We're a lot tougher than maguro. You should worry more about him hurting himself on us.*»

The dolphin lunged, narrowly missing us but dealing us a blow with its tail. We went tumbling through the water, head over fluke. Color of Air righted us with a few strokes, only to be rammed in the midsection by our attacker. Yeah, it didn't drive our breath from the lungs we didn't have, but it hurt. A mature dolphin at full speed packs a wallop.

«*I've ceased worrying about hurting him, despite your advice. How do we get out of this?*»

«*I'm about ready to have dolphin for my next meal,*» Color of Air grated.

I'd lost track of our nemesis while recovering. A blow in the back told me he had circled and taken another pass at us. I was glad we didn't have a kidney in the normal location. I also saw another figure in the distance.

«*A Cyraenan is coming. No eating anyone or changing shape. We don't want to blow our cover. Especially if this is really where they are researching Arilune technology.*»

The dolphin was lining up for another charge. The approaching Cyraenan whistled and clicked some commands. The dolphin reared back momentarily, but then he charged anyway. The Cyraenan darted in front of us, repeating the command. He gestured with a silver rod, clearly telling the dolphin to leave off. It retreated but was still fixated on us. It came back for another sally. The Cyraenan touched it with the tip of the silver rod, and we tasted electric current in the water.

The dolphin squeaked in frustration and turned to dart away, unharmed but cowed. The Cyraenan took us by the elbow, gestured to the surface, and gently but firmly escorted us towards the light.

Surfacing, we got a good look at his face. It was born of the granite cliffs at the edge of the sea, with eyes of black pearls from the dark canyons. Enduring, rather than aged. His chest was broad and smooth, bronze shading to dolphin mottling on sides and back. Midnight hair was swept back in a circlet and tumbled to his shoulders behind. He steadied us in the water and looked us over for damage.

"My deepest apologies for Blackfin. He has been trained better than that and should never behave so towards one of the Folk. I am Remus, brother to the Hierarch, and would make amends to uphold the honor of our family."

«Well, well, it appears we've been assaulted by the favored pet of the Prince of Cyraena.»

"I am Amaya, my Prince. I would have swum elsewhere if I had known these were your waters."

"Just Remus, Amaya. Here, I am another tourist, and these waters are free to anyone. How did you come here? Ours is the only ship on the planet fitted for aquanauts."

"I am traveling in a human ship. I have a cabin fitted for

my comfort."

«*Every word true, and a complete misdirection. Beautiful.*»

«*Thank you. Now shush.*»

"It must be an interesting arrangement to work with Drylanders. You must tell me how that works."

Color of Air affected a self-deprecating air. "I'm their intermediary for trade with fully aquatic species. The Drylanders find it useful, and most aquatics tend to trust one of us more, even though we breathe air."

"You must come to take some refreshments with me at our offshore resort. I would like to know more of how one such as yourself works with humans."

«*Put him off for a bit.*» I prompted her.

«*But I want to see what they're hiding out here.*»

«*We'll be back, but we'll choose the time.*»

"I regret I have duties this evening that would keep me from accepting your hospitality at this moment."

His face darkened. "Few of my brother's subjects would dream of turning down such a request."

"May I accept your invitation after I discharge my obligations? I am only concerned with upholding the honor of our Folk among the humans we deal with."

<*Good one,*> I said.

«*Hush. You'd better be right.*»

His smile quirked through the clouds on his face. "I cannot reasonably insist when you put it that way, can I? You make me even more desirous of learning more about you. We could use someone with your skills and diplomacy at the court."

"You flatter me; I am a simple trader. But I must go now."

"Come soon to attend me."

"I will." We turned, executed a flip in the water, and struck out strongly for shore.

«*Why did you put him off?*» asked Color of Air petulantly.

«*Now that we know who is out there, we can do some background checks before going in. But most of all, we don't want to appear too eager. He becomes the pursuer if we play hard to get, making him less cautious.*»

»*He didn't strike me as the cautious type to begin with.*»

We changed back into Tammartin just before we surfaced. Erissa was sitting beside our clothes, waiting. Color of Air ducked her head momentarily as she melted into the form that Erissa would expect.

«*Did she see us?*»

«*Don't know. Only our head at most. Just have to bluff it out.*»

Nothing for it but to walk ashore. We stood up and walked towards her. Not showing off, but nothing to hide either. I reminded myself that we might be nude but we weren't naked. I was glad that the needle gun was concealed in our thigh and not in our clothes. She could well have gone through our clothes while we were hobnobbing with the Prince.

As we reached the shore, she stood smoothly and held

out a robe. That was a nice solution to the "only one of us is dressed" problem. Given enough time and a willing co-investigator, I considered exploring other solutions to the problem. Then I realized that it was hunger, not lust. It had been too long since our last meal.

"Did you have a refreshing swim?" Erissa inquired.

"Yes, the water is lovely. Warm and quite clear. There's an abundance of interesting marine life to study just offshore." I gave Color of Air the mental equivalent of an elbow in the ribs on that one.

"You must be very good at holding your breath."

"I got a biomod for water breathing some years ago when I worked for an underwater mining company. It comes in handy at times."

"I can see that. I must try it sometime. I love diving, and to go completely free, in nothing but my skin, sounds like a dream."

Erissa motioned to a beach blanket that she had spread. "Pinwheel is going to set soon. Shall we watch it go down?"

We settled down on the sand. She made sure to settle close, almost touching. I could feel the warmth from her tanned skin, taste the lavender and lemongrass that was her essence, glimpse the soft curves within the flowing cotton dress.

"Was there someone else swimming with you?" Erissa asked casually.

"No, just me."

"Ah. It must have been a trick of the light, then."

Pinwheel was nearly touching the horizon. They were stacked vertically at the moment, with Pinwheel Alpha kissing the ocean and Pinwheel Beta a degree above it and to the right. The combined rotations of the suns and the planet made a unique dance. Alpha slid sideways along the horizon while Beta plunged into the sea beside it. Then Alpha was tossed back into the sky like an acrobat briefly before following its sister down into the benthic chroma.

Only Cinder remained in the sky, freed from the competition of Pinwheel's show. It hung bloated and hungry in the darkening sky, glowing a mottled and baleful red just above the visible threshold but providing most of the planet's heat. Bright storms smeared through the equatorial zones, streaked with cooler regions among the upwellings. It was a brown dwarf, a jovian planet that had drunk Dr. Jekyll's potion of hydrogen to grow into Mr. Hyde — a near-star that achieved a fitful ignition and muttered madly to itself in the darkness.

"I've never seen anything like that on the fifty-seven worlds I've visited. It outdid even the marketing brochure."

"Every Pinwheel-set is different. That was called the Juggler. Other conjunctions are called by various names, such as the Dolphin's Eyes, Hidden Palace, the Virgin's Breasts, and Pearl of the Sea."

«*Is she baiting us?*»

«*I can't tell yet. Don't volunteer information. And eating her won't solve anything.*» Although I had to admit she looked delicious.

"Shall we go inside? I can have a light meal delivered to your bungalow." She was definitely being forward. I murmured an assent. Or Color of Air did. It was getting hard to tell.

Erissa bent to pick up our towel and hand me the clothes underneath. She froze for an entire second as she compared the wispy sundress to my two-meter frame. My assumptions about her training told me we must have caught her completely off guard. The next instant, she drove her elbow into our solar plexus, rolled away, came up with a needle gun in her hand, and pulled the trigger.

A desolate click was the only response.

We held the needle gun's clip in our hand. "Sorry for the precaution. We didn't want ..."

She didn't wait for any explanations. She whipped a strand out of her hair and leaped on us. I identified it as a molecular monofilament just before it cleanly separated our head from our neck.

«*I didn't see that one coming.*»

«*That was number six.*»

«*You could have warned me.*»

From our position on the sand a few feet away, we could see our headless body holding Erissa down, still struggling. An Arilune is much stronger than even a boosted body, so after the advantage of surprise was lost, it was no contest. We rolled across the sand to them. One arm reached down, picked up the head, and plopped it back in approximately the right place. A moment of queasy adjustment later, we were whole again.

"Someone who is frightened might draw a gun as a threat. You pulled the trigger immediately. Then you sliced off my head, something that's fatal to most lifeforms. What's the deal? I thought we were having a nice time out here until then."

Her face was stony. "I didn't want to get eaten."

"What makes you think I would do that?" It wasn't a denial, though of course it could be taken that way.

"You're a Shapestealer. At least ten people on this planet have disappeared in evident Shapestealer attacks. I was sent here to track it down. I know it wasn't you—you just arrived—but that doesn't mean you're not just as dangerous."

Color of Air didn't have to feign her surprise. "There's something very wrong. None of us would so wantonly kill so many people. I'll track them down myself and end them."

"But you do kill people, don't you?"

We were still on top of Erissa, holding her arms down in the sand. "Can we have a truce for a moment? If I was going to kill you, I could have already done so. Can I let you up?"

Erissa didn't have many options, but she nodded anyway. Color of Air arose and helped Erissa to her feet. Then she sat cross-legged on the sand a pace away and waited. Erissa hesitated, then took one more pace away before sitting down.

Color of Air continued with Erissa's last question. "I have to eat. But I don't destroy. The last person I consumed … well, let me have her tell you.

Color of Air stood and melted into the form of Nuritha. She sat gracefully once more but about a half pace closer.

"I'm Nuritha. I've known Color of Air since the beginning. I was recently in a prison on Raxas, with no hope of escape. Color of Air found me and tried to free me, but there was no way. I asked her to absorb me, to end my captivity, and to complete my mission on Raxas. She did all of that. I couldn't have asked more of a friend."

"But you're not really Nuritha, are you?"

"I'm her memories and her essence. I'm not sure what I am right now, but I am content. You can trust her."

"I'm not sure how reassuring that is."

We stood once more. We melted into the form of Tammartin. When we sat again, we had moved another pace closer.

"This is my base form. My original host. I'm afraid she had no choice, but I wasn't sentient before we joined. I don't show this face to many people."

"So, you won't eat me without my consent? Just so we're clear, I'm not going to consent. Ever."

"You have my word. We have a common enemy. You help me, and I'll help you." Color of Air put her hand on Erissa's thigh.

Erissa looked up into our eyes, searching. "Who is this form you're wearing? What is your real name?"

Color of Air smiled. "Let me tell you my name." She leaned in. Our lips met. After a few moments, the conversation deepened. It lasted most of the night.

It was near Pinwheel-dawn when we returned to the bungalow.

«*That was almost as satisfying as a full meal,*» Color of Air thought dreamily.

«*The advantage is that you can go back for seconds. The other is so ... final.*»

«*The information she gave us on Prince Remus will come in handy.*»

We opened the door. There was a faint scent in the air inside.

«*Someone has been here.*»

«*The luggage is undisturbed. It's not holding any detached body parts.*»

«*There's something on the table.*»

«*A bottle. And a card. "We wish the honor of your attendance at a private party offshore tomorrow evening. Regards, Remus."*»

«*It's some kind of liqueur.*»

«*There's something not right about this.*»

«*Seems authentic. It smells like a fresh sea breeze.*»

«*Samuel! Don't drink it!*»

«*Too late. I thought you told me nothing could poison us.*»

«*Quickly, into the bathroom. Lock the door.*»

"Luggage! Guard this door." The squat shape walked over to block the door.

«*I'm feeling woozy.*»

«*You're feeling very drunk.*»

«*On one sip?*»

«*Don't argue. Close the tub drain.*»

«*Fingers won't close. They're dripping.*»

«*Lean on the lever!*»

«*It's like putty.*»

«*No, we're putty. Push!*»

«*Got it!*»

«*Get in the tub! Now!*»

«*What's the puddle in the bottom?*»

«*That's us.*»

«*Oh...*»

Pinwheel was low in the sky. It cast long double shadows across the room, slowly merging and separating again, with a six-hour half-life.

A hand emerged from the bathtub.

It had two fingers. After a struggle, a third emerged,

destabilizing the other two. The hand subsided back into the tub.

Once more the shadows did their dance before the hand tried again. This time, it levered something resembling a body into a sitting position. An amateur clay face failed to cohere and slid like a mudslide in a downpour. The figure leaned forward to grope for the lost face. The entire head dropped into the tub. The torso belched an exhalation that might have said, "Shit!"

A half-hour later, a vaguely human golem successfully arose from the tub, staggered to a chair, and sat with its head in its hands. The playback ended. The holo monitor above the luggage switched off.

«And I still have the worst hangover of my life.»

«Just remember, no alcohol. It messes up the neural impulses that keep our shape.»

«I got that already. At least we know no one came in while we were incapacitated.»

«It wasn't for that reason, then. But something's still wobbly about this. If Remus sent Amaya a message and a present, why did the resort staff deliver it to our room? They had no way to connect Amaya with Samuel Whitt.»

«That is pretty dodgy. Who could connect us?»

«Erissa. Maybe. With a lot of guesswork.»

«We kept her occupied all night. She didn't have time.»

«I don't know, then. Should we attend the party?»

«I think we should. We need to learn if our cover is blown.»

«Right. That gives us an hour or two to find a Shapestealer hangover cure.»

By the time we finished firming up, Pinwheel was touching the horizon. It had taken most of the day to recover from one sip of liqueur. We would be fashionably late and reasonably sober. We took the liqueur bottle with the vague notion of discovering how it had come to us.

Tonight, the twin suns were bisected precisely by the horizon at the same instant as they set. *«That must be the Virgin's Breasts Erissa mentioned.»*

«I don't know. It's been too long since I've seen any.»

«Breasts?»

«Virgins.»

«You're terrible, Captain.»

We waded into the Cinder-lit sea. As the warm water lapped our flanks, we flowed beneath the waves. Male melted into female, legs into flukes, Samuel Whitt into Amaya. We began to swim and found the bottle troublesome.

«How about another pouch, like the gun?» I said

She obliged, ostentatiously tightening the cap before storing it. *«Don't let it leak out,»* she added.

«That lesson is still fresh. Why didn't you warn me about alcohol?»

«I did decline every time it was offered.»

«That's not an answer.»

«I was afraid ... afraid that you would use it against me. Even

if it harmed you.»

That gave me something to chew on as we swam.

This sea was alive with noctilucent life. The firefly fish we had seen the previous night broke sparkly through the surface on reentry from their flights. Glowworms swayed as backup dancers to showy fish. Much of the sea life on this planet sported light-emitting organs, whether through natural selection or the design of the terraformers, we didn't know. Even the octopus whirled galaxies of blue and green lights as it jetted toward us in the shadowed sea. We slowed to watch it come close and undulate in the water before us.

«That octopus looks mighty curious.»

«I've heard they're highly intelligent creatures. Probably just checking over someone unfamiliar.»

This one floated just out of reach and followed as we resumed swimming toward the undersea resort.

I had expected something on the theme of Atlantis. Ancient Greek architecture, perhaps. Kelp-encrusted stone blocks, covered with barnacles and anemones. Instead, we found a crystal palace, open to the flow of the tides. Luminescent sea life was cultivated at the base of the walls to imbue the interiors of the walls with enchanting and shifting pastels.

We undulated through the front gates and surfaced in a spacious reception area. There was nothing as ordinary as a front desk or a concierge, but within seconds, a scrupulously precise functionary was facing us, his nose held at exactly the angle that would allow him to look down at us if he deemed it necessary.

Color of Air took the offensive. "My name is Amaya. Prince Remus requested that I attend him this evening."

The functionary raised the pad in his hand, prepared to sneer that many young women imagined they could bluff their way in on the strength of such a claim. His expression as he found our name on his list was worth the price of admission.

With a suddenly obsequious expression, still tinged by the suspicion that someone was pulling a fast one on him, he conducted us to a private room where we found the Prince holding forth with his cronies. The room was designed for mixed gatherings. The Prince lounged on a submerged couch, his humanoid upper torso at ease in the air, his dolphinesque tail immersed in saltwater.

"Amaya!" he boomed. "How good of you to grace us with your presence his evening. Come and take your ease with us." His eyes flickered to his left; the Cyraenan on the adjacent couch excused herself gracefully, gesturing that we should take her place. As she dove beneath the surface, she ensured we saw the poisonous glare and the Prince did not. It didn't matter. We wouldn't be wearing flukes for long enough to threaten her position. I just made a note not to accept a drink from her this evening.

The Prince leaned close. "I'm bringing together scientists and industrialists to invest in Cyraena. You've probably been trading in our bioscience products since that's where we're the most advanced. But I'm tired of hiring rides in the starships of other races, as you have on the *Rapier Whitt*. It may have been good enough for my father, but it's time to modernize. We need to catch up in the physical sciences. That's why I'm interested in your contacts among the humans."

One small mystery solved. The Prince had linked Amaya to my ship, perhaps by comparing arrival times. Amaya hadn't been on the passenger manifest or registered in any hotel, so he had sent the invitation (and the bottle) to the Captain. I still had lingering doubts, though.

Color of Air nudged me to speak. Trade was my specialty. "I'm sure that we ... I ... can arrange some meetings with some interests that would complement yours nicely. I have contacts with many races beyond the humans." I almost lost it when I said "we" instead of "I." Was my existence as an unwilling passenger starting to affect my thinking? "Who are your current partners?"

"None officially, yet. We located here because there is a major Starlane research complex here, on the land side. We're trying to interest them in investing in us. At the very least we're hoping to attract some of their talent to join us. Officially, there's no partnership. But people move between our two organizations more often than you'd think."

Another Cyraenan had drifted over (I would never think of that term in the same way in non-aquatic parties again). Remus introduced him as an aide to the finance minister. Others started to come over as well, to make my acquaintance, impress their Prince with their wit, and probe whether Remus was up to something (and whether they wanted a piece of it). Most were minor nobility or lower-level functionaries, both corporate and govern–mental. It didn't seem like this enterprise had the backing of the Cyraenan establishment.

There were a few other species as well. There was an entirely aquatic fellow who resembled a Terran sea horse, but one as tall as I am, er, was. In my own form. Never mind. He (She? It?) had a companion (pet?) like a meter-long paramecium. Neither said very much.

On the other side of the room, where the drylanders congregated, I spotted a Blue. Think two-meter-tall hairless blue llama with arms. I was glad they didn't come over. They communicate via messenger chemicals on their extremely long tongues. Conversations with them are either erotic or embarrassing, and I wasn't in the mood.

Then, a human surfaced. As an air-breather, he wore a thin mask that conformed to his face and chin, leaving his long black hair to trail in dramatic melancholy in the faint currents. He was a sallow-faced and taciturn man who seemed to enjoy the gathering considerably less than the rest of the entourage. The Prince introduced him as

Rayche, an exotic chemist, and added a stage whisper that he was on loan from Starlane. I felt Color of Air's interest perk up.

"A what now?"

"I find compounds in exotic biologies with medicinal or recreational uses in other species. Or tactical," he added. He had languid eyes that expressed great ennui with a world that was just molecular chains to his mind. Or he was completely stoned on one of his recreational compounds. It took me a moment to parse his last utterance.

"Tactical? As in chemical weapons?'

"Nothing so crude. I don't deal in blunt instruments."

"I trade in light, high-value cargo with flexible schedules and clients. Perhaps you might need a service such as mine?"

"So you're a smuggler?"

"Insufficiently imaginative bureaucrats might term it that, but I'm sure none of those words would be used in your presence."

Rayche turned to the Prince. "Hoy, Remus, since this party's pretty dead so far, how about I take your guest on a tour of the labs? We can see if we have any mutual interests, and I can have her back in time for the afterparty. You weren't planning on making a move on her until then anyway, am I right?"

Remus let a flicker of annoyance show before clamping

down on it. "If that is what Amaya wishes, then certainly. I invited her this evening because of her unique position on a human ship. We need more ambassadors between us Cyraena and you Drylanders. Go along and tour the labs, and see if you can find some mutually beneficial venture."

«The Prince is taking this graciously.»

«Oh, he's steaming, but he can't afford to show it.»

We followed Rayche away from the resort's upper levels. We found a small city beneath it, with shops, residences, offices, and industry. Everything was enclosed despite the mild ocean at this latitude and the gorgeous reef. Once people accumulated possessions, stores had inventory, and offices had records, they ceased to find it amusing when the contents were rearranged by stray currents or carried off by curious wildlife. Such is civilization.

We traveled by corridors and through open spaces and concourses. Doors were as likely to open through the ceiling or floor as the walls. We swam up through a final door into a recognizable research area. Much of it was dry. Rayche pulled himself onto the floor, shedding the flippers he wore on his feet as he did. For me, channels were strategically placed where a Cyraenan could remain half-submerged and swim alongside their host. So I did that. No need to reveal that we could be as bipedal as he.

"Cyraenan biosciences are highly advanced. Since water-dwelling species are disadvantaged in the physical sciences due to the challenges of maintaining high-temperature processes in water, they tend not to develop metallurgy, smelting, or nuclear chemistry. Instead they concentrate on biochemistry, which the diversity of marine life supports admirably. All of this," he waved expansively, encompassing the building and all of the equipment within it, "is grown organically rather than manufactured."

I was impressed. Other than a preference for rounded edges over right angles, the equipment was finely made, with thin, even cases, digital displays, and regular sizes. Now that I looked more closely, it did seem that no two pieces were identical. Each item was bespoke, made specifically for its place and function. A design aesthetic of balance and harmony made the variety appear planned rather than haphazard. I started to salivate (meta-phorically) about the trade possibilities.

After talking with Rayche about high-value goods and potential markets for about an hour, Color of Air came to alert. «*I smell Periphage,*» she said. She seized control of the vocal cords.

"I have a buyer interested in bodyguards/assassins with natural camouflage or even armor. Have you done anything with skin layers to enhance people in this way?"

Rayche gave us a hard look. I began to worry that she had blown our cover. Then he gestured for us to follow him. We submerged and swam through the corridors to steadily more unfriendly territory. By the time we passed through a heavily armored door, I was beyond worried and into making contingency plans around the topic of survival.

"These are our Starlane labs, where we do our work on technologies like the one you're asking about. We have a program to develop an entire entity along those lines— and I'm guessing that you already know that, or at least your 'buyer' does." Rache conducted us to a cell, where he slid open a panel in the wall. We looked into a spare but comfortable room. A single man sat, reading in a chair. He was naked, well-muscled, seemingly cut from the cloth of a thousand faceless agents who guard the important and the well-to-do.

Rayche rapped for attention on the glass, then spoke into the panel. "Q3, please assume form undercover number five." The man stood, impassive, and let his features flow into those of a featureless, sexless manikin, then into a slender female form with hair the hue of ripened wheat. Her features were suddenly animated with a saucy expression as she turned to look over the point of one shoulder at us as she assumed a sexy hipshot stance.

"Very good. Now armored form two." The subject gave us a final pout, then flowed into a stocky gorilla-like being with a skin like rhinoceros hide. The hipshot position looked ridiculous until he shifted to a more belligerent stance. He needed more practice.

"I'd heard some rumors that some Concordium agents could change their faces, but this is an entirely different level."

Rache sniffed. "They grow clone bodies for the agents and use epigenetic therapies to change their size, facial features, or gender. Primitive stuff. Though their consciousness-transfer mechanism is something I'd like to get my hands on. They can move from one clone to another in seconds."

"This is much more than cloning; this is true shape-changing. How is it accomplished?"

"We discovered a slime on a faraway world that ingests and mimics whatever it touches. The fascinating thing is that it also absorbs skills, abilities, and some degree of personality, though not specific memories. We have tried to duplicate some of the mechanisms in isolation for purposes such as limb and organ replacement or fully organic body modification, but sadly, we have failed so far. Only full ingestion by the slime yields results."

Rayche turned to us. "But you already knew that, didn't you? You arrived on the *Rapier Whitt*. According to the little we know, Captain Whitt is the only person, or I should say the only person still living, to visit the homeworld of the slime. A planet whose very existence is now classified and whose location is wiped from the network. Where is the Captain now? Whitt's the person we want to do business with."

«What? I never visited your world. Did Samara? Are they confusing me with her?»

«Hold that thought.»

"I didn't travel on that ship, and I don't know your Captain Whitt. Check the passenger manifests. I wasn't on the *Rapier Whitt*."

"No, you're not on any manifests. And Captain Whitt has a certain reputation for leaving small details off the official manifest. The coincidence that you show up the day after the *Rapier Whitt* lands is too much. So where is the Captain?"

"I couldn't say."

"It doesn't seem that you're of any further use to us. At least you alerted us to look at the recent arrivals. We might not have noticed he was here otherwise. You're free to go." He indicated an exterior door, not the one that returned to the complex. He probably didn't intend for us to hear his final comment. "Q1 needs some practice."

As we swam outside, we saw we had emerged much deeper down the coastal shelf. Less light filtered from the surface. Tall strands of kelp reached upwards towards their photosynthetic rewards. Anything could have been lurking in the shadows.

«We're in trouble, aren't we?» asked Color of Air.

«Undoubtedly. He wouldn't have revealed all that detail about the Periphages if he intended to let us go. He also wouldn't risk us warning "Captain Whitt" too soon. At least he didn't realize Captain Whitt was in the room with him.»

«Or an Arilune. He would have loved another test subject. But

about that whole Captain Whitt business...»

«Hide! Something is cruising above us.»

A shadow passed through the dim light above. My first thought was a drone, but this was a race of biologists. It was a dolphin, moving purposefully as though on patrol. It rolled as it made a turn, revealing a telltale black fin.

«That's the Prince's pet!»

«Something tells me that's no dolphin.»

«What's a dolphin afraid of?»

«Not much, except maybe an orca. There's no way I could manage to become something that big.»

«How about a rock?»

We were meshing so well that I couldn't tell which of us had each of those thoughts. Was that what fully merging would be like?

We drifted down to the seafloor and formed a rock. I hoped it was sufficiently rock-like to pass inspection. A rock doesn't have good senses for regarding its own rockness.

The shadow returned. It almost passed us by but then stopped to nose around our edges.

«Does it know that this rock wasn't here a few minutes ago?»

«It may be that it can tell that it doesn't smell like a rock.»

«I thought you could give off whatever scent you wanted.»

«It's partly the form. Rocks don't have many options for producing or receiving scents. I can't sense anything from our opponent.»

The shadow over us changed. It was less of a compact, torpedo-shaped darkness and more of an irregular, undulating darkness. Strong arms began to pluck at us and rock us in our depression on the sea floor.

«*Did Blackfin bring reinforcements?*»

«*No, it's the octopus from before - and he has one black arm!*»

«*He's an Arilune?*»

«*Also known as Specimen Q1, I imagine.*»

«*What does it mean that he always has a black appendage?*»

«*It's probably an old injury — like a scar.*»

I filed away the information that Arilune could be injured. I had thought they were close to invulnerable. Today I had learned about alcohol and scars.

Blackfin — hmm, no fins, maybe Blackarm — managed to pry us out of the seabed. After all, we didn't mass more than we had as a humanoid. It smashed us against another rock, which was more injurious to the dignity than the body. That gave it ideas, however. It picked up another rock and raised it over its head to smash us.

Color of Air assumed Cyraenan form in the fastest transformation I had witnessed, flukes in motion even while the rest of our body was still amorphous. We were out of range before Blackarm had time to react. It jetted futilely after us before giving up. A jetting octopus is fast, but only for a short sprint. It began to transform back into Blackfin as we rounded a boulder and looked for a hiding place. We squeezed into a crevice just as Blackfin flashed by overhead.

«We can wait for him to think we escaped, then sneak away when he's looking elsewhere.»

«So tell me what you know of my sister while we're waiting.»

She gave me the mental equivalent of a flat stare. It tasted of slate and calcium with a hint of lime. You need the right senses to get the idea of that.

«Yes, she was the Captain of the expedition that found my planet. Tammartin was her exobiologist.»

I let it go. Something still didn't add up.

After a time, we cautiously left the crevice. Blackfin/Blackarm was nowhere in sight. We swam up the coastal shelf towards the shore. As we crested a rise, a patch of sand reached up a tentacle and snagged our tail. Of course it did. Even a normal octopus can change color and disappear before your eyes.

We thrashed, but it had an iron grip. I felt bones grating, nearly as painful as walking into a stupid and obvious ambush. Color of Air reached for the needle gun concealed in the pouch on our side, but Blackarm got another tentacle around that wrist. We struggled mightily to keep the other one free and searching for a weapon. Another tentacle coiled around our waist.

«Why isn't he trying to absorb us yet?» I asked.

«Natural defense. The skin of one Arilune will repel another. Until one is crushed and broken enough to allow the other one entry.» The despair in her thoughts tasted like charcoal.

«We have no weapon to use against it.»

«In a fight, everything is a weapon. The needle gun is trapped against his body. Can you trigger it?»

«No. Even if I could press the trigger, I wouldn't have the dexterity to move the safety slider. You take control. You have combat experience.»

Did I? I didn't remember being in combat, but somehow I did know how to fight. I sent my senses down our torso, looking for anything to use. A buckle, a bit of metal, a belt for strangling. Unfortunately, we weren't wearing anything. The octopus threw another tentacle around our torso and began to squeeze. I felt a rib crack.

Anything can be a weapon.

I flexed and pulled that rib until it broke off, jagged and sharp. It took no dexterity to shove a rib out through our skin and into the body of our attacker. Dark fluid stained the water bitter iron (yes, it's a color). Blackarm thrashed and keened a graphite note of pain that no real cephalopod could ever utter. Its grip faltered momentarily, giving me hope that we could break free, but then it surged forward, getting all eight arms around us and capturing the one arm that we still had free. He started bending us backwards, threatening to snap our spine.

«Can you change into something else? An eel? A jellyfish? I'd like to sting him until his eyes water.»

«Not unless we can get away for a moment. A Periphage is the most vulnerable to absorption while changing until the new skin

forms.»

I made another try for the needle gun, but there was something in the way. I felt around it for a moment until I remembered the bottle of liquor we had stored in a pouch.

Everything is a weapon.

«Can we crush this bottle? I can use the shards as weapons...»

«I don't want to get the contents on us.»

Everything is a weapon.

«That's it! Move the bottle close to the surface. Push the needle gun up against it.»

«I will try. It's hard enough to make a pouch, let alone move it around. I can't make very many modifications while in solid form.»

Slowly, the bottle and gun migrated to the surface. Eons later, it was in place.

«Now, bear down on the neck. When it cracks, shove.»

Color of Air struggled. She tried to create additional leverage between the butt of the needle gun and some ill-used ribs. It *hurt*, almost as bad as the real ribs I've broken on several occasions. The octopus was still straining to crush us by main force but was also drifting towards the sea floor, shifting its grip to free up one tentacle. It meant to pick up a rock to bash us.

«Push!» I urged. The bottle grated against ribs as we bore down. The octopus squeezed, threatening to pop it out like a seed from an orange. We would lose our only weapon if that happened. I felt one trapped arm give way as the bone

shattered. The octopus's free tentacle curled around a boulder the size of my head. I hadn't thought a cephalopod's eyes could show triumph. I was wrong. It raised the stone to strike.

«*Roll!*»

We twisted just as he flung the rock at us, pushing the neck of the bottle out. The rock slammed into the bottle, knocking the neck off. Blackarm recoiled reflexively from the jagged glass, allowing me to get one arm free. I grabbed the bottle and shoved it deep into his baggy head, releasing nearly a half-liter of alcohol.

The triumph in its eyes dissolved into dismay, dismay into fear, and fear into horror, which slowly washed away on the gentle currents. Bits of protoplasm glinted in the Cinder light until overrun by a squadron of firefly fish. The last was a tang of charcoal and iron filing, washed clean by the living sea.

We came ashore in exhaustion, made it to the bungalow, and tumbled damp and naked into the bed.

A few hours later, the door opened. A figure entered, stood by the bed, and let the robe slip from its shoulders. It lifted the sheet. We felt a warm fragrance of lemongrass and lavender in the darkness.

"Luggage, light," I ordered.

The light came up to reveal Erissa. Black tresses, as artful as always, tumbled concealingly about her. Our needle gun was held to her throat.

"You are predictable," she said with amusement.

"So are you." Her needle gun was pressed into our side.

"What can I say?"

"Thank you would be one thing. I took care of one of your problems."

"The Shapestealer?"

"There are at least two. One is dead now. The other seems to be confined to a cell. I think they are still training it."

"Training? Dead? Pick one and start explaining."

We stared levelly at her in the dim light. I'm unsure which of us had control since we both had the same reaction.

"Please," she added.

"I found a secret lab where they create and train Shapestealers as guards and assassins. They sent one of them after me with orders to kill. I prevailed."

"How did you kill it?"

"Trade secret. I want you to call in a strike force to eradicate that lab."

"Consider it done."

"From what I learned, I think they captured these two Shapestealers and have been brainwashing them to do their bidding. One of their people knew of Concordium efforts to find the Shapestealer homeworld, which tells me there's a leak somewhere."

"That's useful to know. I'll put someone on that. What do you want in return?"

"Forget that you met me."

"That would be very difficult," she smiled. "I can neglect to put it in my report, though."

"That's all I ask."

"I do have one other reward for you."

"What is that?"

She leaned close and whispered. A name. A place. It punched me in the gut. Metaphorically. I don't have a gut anymore.

«Damn it, now I want to eat her,» I grated.

«Not now, I have other plans.» Color of Air sounded amused.

"I'm … not sure that was a reward," I said. "But thank you."

"Shall we pick up where we left off?" She bent down for a long kiss. "What other shapes can you show me?"

"I think you'll like this one…"

THE COLOR OF SMOKE

THE WORLD'S NAME WAS CAELUM, an obscure planet in an unremarkable system in a metal-poor sector of space. No one knew what had swept the heavier elements from a 15-light-year sphere of the galactic arm. Scientists worried about what caused it, while normal people went elsewhere. The residents called themselves Caelamities.

That's a slight exaggeration since Caelum was a pleasant enough world. Low gravity (no metals), good agricultural ecosystem. The locals learned to make miniaturized technology without the profligate waste of metals that others could afford. For building materials, stone was just fine. They were renowned for the beauty of their stone architecture.

And here we were.

This was the place that Erissa had whispered. The name she had said was one I knew well. It was also the destination that Alexander had mentioned when we parted. Coincidence? In a galaxy this large? Not likely.

«How do you plan to find Acanthemblemaria when we have an entire planet to search?» asked Color of Air. *«We're not likely to find her in the merchant's quarter, I take it.»*

«Decidedly not. We are *likely to find black market contacts who can get us closer, though. This is the place to start making contacts.»*

We were on a cobblestone street running between modest but handsome buildings that housed businesses of the mercantile sort. The *Rapier Whitt* occupied a berth in the port under a false flag, call sign, transponder code, registry, captain's name, and an inconspicuous new shade of shimmerpaint. *Rapier* had forged papers to match the short, stocky, blond female captain named Salton Jonas who emerged. I felt a glimmer of appreciation for the usefulness of this ability in my trade, unwillingly acquired though it was. Still quite handsome, too, I thought as a passing window reflected my new form back at me.

A few discreetly folded bills passed to a spaceport official had gotten me an address. That address was across the street and a few doors down as I scoped out the storefront and the possible places that could be employed for its surveillance. Its carefully curated ordinariness nearly warned me off with its perfection. A red tile over the doorway decided me. It would attract traffic that a decoy wouldn't want.

The store bought and sold curios. Near the door, it displayed actual mechanical watches, while the back had a collection of oil lamps. I imagined the lamps could change hands with substances more valuable than oil hidden inside them.

The proprietor was a tall and distinguished man. Salt and pepper hair (rather light on the pepper by now) and thoughtful lines around the eyes and mouth conveyed the image of someone you could trust. His hands were those of a much younger man, contradicting that message for anyone who took the time to notice. To Color of Air's senses, he was slate and heather, with something not quite old leather that I struggled to put a name to. A small placard on the counter mentioned that his name was Smanester.

"What may I help you find today?" he asked.

"Oh, I'm not sure. Something local, something handmade. Something that I can only find here. I'll know it when I see it."

"A souvenir? Or a collectible item?"

"More the latter. Not necessarily for me. I have clients who pay for the unusual. I'm always looking for items that check the right boxes for one of them."

"You're a trader then?"

"I would call myself a procurer. Tell me what you want, and I'll find it for you."

The proprietor was unmoved. "Feel free to look around. I have many fine items that would interest off-world buyers." He didn't comment on my offer.

We feigned some interest in an intricate mechanical timepiece that showed every bit of the ordered chaos within. It claimed to be adjustable to any rotational period. «*I don't think we'll get any information out of him,*» said Color of Air.

«*Probably related to the speed at which he pegged us as offworlders,*» I agreed.

After picking up and examining several other objects, I turned back to him. "I think that clock would interest one of my clients," I said. "How much is it?"

Smanester named a price ten times what I was expecting. I offered a much more reasonable figure. He said, through a tight smile, "You seem to be mistaking this for a flea market. That was a price, not an opening bid."

I put the clock down. "That wouldn't be a price I could pass on to a client. Perhaps you could suggest other establishments that might be a better fit?"

"Now you're mistaking this for a chamber of commerce."

"Then could you direct me to the…"

"No."

"I see. Thank you for your time."

Back on the street, Color of Air commented, «*That didn't go well.*»

«*Maybe he doesn't like offworlders. He would only be satisfied selling to one if he could shaft us.*»

«*I wonder how he stays in business?*

«*Good question. I suspect that his main business is money laundering. He breaks financial trails by buying and selling outrageously priced "collectibles."*»

«*So he might be the contact we need, but he won't do business with us?*»

«*Exactly.*»

«*Let's watch the shop for a while. Maybe we can impersonate one of his usual customers.*»

We ducked around a corner long enough to melt into another form. After making a few wardrobe adjustments (we had worn a reversible jacket and adaptable clothes to accommodate a variety of standard personas), we returned to the street as someone the shop proprietor wouldn't recognize. Nothing remarkable happened until closing time when a young man put a closed sign in the window and locked the door.

«*I never saw him go inside,*» I remarked.

«*He was already inside. Check his scent.*»

It was faint at this distance, and I wasn't very good at the nuances yet. I concentrated. Heather. Slate. Hmm. That third component, not leather… ambergris? I had sensed that combination recently.

«Is that Smanester?»

«It is. He wore makeup to make himself seem older and more dignified. It probably gives him an edge in negotiating — or insisting he doesn't negotiate.»

I had noticed the hands that seemed too young and kicked myself for not making the connection.

We followed Smanester down the street. The ambergris component of his scent nagged at me. It was like the scent of soft, aged leather but with overtones of smoke. I had encountered it before.

The neighborhood changed from tasteful retail into a district of drinking and dining establishments. However, he didn't stop here but continued into somewhat seedier neighborhoods. He turned a corner to the left. When we arrived at the intersection, he was nowhere in sight.

It was little more than a dimly lit alley with doors that you had to know about to find. Its only virtue was that it wasn't as dark and foreboding as the smaller alleys that branched off it.

«I've lost him,» Color of Air grumbled in frustration. *«Everything stinks here.»*

«Move along the alleyway slowly. Check the scent near each door.»

«I won't be able to pick out just one scent from this foul stew.»

«We're not looking for his *scent.»*

We moved along the left side of the alley. I was glad to hit paydirt a few doors down without venturing into the smaller, less inviting passages. We weren't carrying enough firepower to feel comfortable in their stygian gloom.

«He's here. It's a Bluedrift den. That's why Smanester smelled like ambergris.»

We pushed through the door into a dim room. There were a few clients here and there, bent over small stone bowls from which curled tendrils of smoke. A stratum of blue smoke hung at eye level. Whorls like turbulence in a stream traced a path to a table where Smanester sat with his back to the door, watching intently as the Keeper heated a small stone bowl for him. A handful of other patrons huddled over their own stone bowls, in which glowing squares of resin fed the atmosphere of the room. None of them paid us any mind. We slipped into the restroom unnoticed.

Color of Air had packed the filmy little dress she had worn when I first met her. As I wondered how she had slipped it into the small shoulder bag without my notice, she transformed into the cinnamon-skinned seductress with wheaten hair and eyes that I remembered so well. I hadn't seen this aspect since that evening.

And then it occurred to me what her intentions were.

«No! We're not eating him.»

«Dear Samuel. First, it is my nature. Second, we will get the *information we need, which he was unwilling to share. Third, he wasn't very nice to us. Finally, while I've come to respect your opinion, it's my body, and I need to feed it. I'm sorry you need to watch.»*

I gritted my teeth because she was right on all points. Especially the one about watching. There was nothing I could do to stop her. I just wanted to switch off until it was over.

The seduction went much as mine had, but faster. The mild euphoria induced by inhaling Bluedrift made him more receptive, less questioning. We ended up in a rooms-by-the-hour place across the street. I say we, but I was a passenger, helpless to stop the murder that was about to take place, unable to even cry out a warning.

Smanester wasn't much for stamina or experience. It was probably the best night of his life, short as it was. Would he have willingly traded the rest of his life for it? It was too late to ask him now.

Color of Air reveled in it. The tumescent joy of wrapping herself around him, giving him pleasure that would be amplified back to her, the orange snaps of the bones as she broke each one, culminating in the final pure white orgasmic bliss of absorbing his memories.

I felt it all. It was a drug.

The worst part of that moment was that it felt so good that it would be hard to deny her again.

* * *

We walked back to the shop in the body of Smanester. I didn't participate. I was furious at Color of Air for her unilateral action. I was furious at myself for feeling pleasure in cold-blooded murder. I told myself it was second-hand pleasure, which led to the even worse knowledge that I wanted to feel it again. I *needed* it again. My rage escalated from volcanic to stellar.

My feelings either leaked through to Color of Air, or she accurately guessed the meaning of my silence. «*You're pretty hung up on this for someone who pulled a needle gun on me within ten minutes of meeting me. What gives?*»

«*I may threaten force easily, but I only kill when necessary, like Magid or the guards on Raxas.*»

«*I have to eat, and I'm an obligate carnivore. More, I'm an obligate sophovore. It's my nature. If I don't consume intelligent beings — sophonts — I, and you, will cease to thrive and will eventually perish. That doesn't make me evil. I've been considerate of your sensibilities. I've made do with less since you've been with me. Alexander and Erissa are still alive because of you. Probably that cute waitress back on Raxas, too,*» she said with asperity. Asperity was umber, felt like fine sand, and smelled like pocket lint.

I had no answer for her.

We unlocked the door with the key in Smanester's jacket pocket. I was stubbornly silent while she fumbled with the door, but my self-preservation instinct kicked in. I don't know if 10,000 volts would injure us, but it wasn't a thing I wanted to learn experimentally.

«*Stop! You have to disable the security system before entering!*»

«*Where?*»

«*Look in the door frame. Those little bumps disguised as screws will electrocute anyone who doesn't know how to disarm them. Didn't you get that from Smanester?*»

«*Oh, yes.*» She held her thumb against one corner of the pane of glass in the door. There was a faint click.

«*Why didn't you know to do that?*

His memories are available to me, but I must look for them. I didn't think of booby traps until you shouted at me. Then I could look for the memory of how to disable them.»

I filed that away for later. The night had passed and it was almost time for the shop to open.

«*Do you know how to do Smanester's job here? Do you have the memories of his inventories, contacts, and clients?*»

«*Yes, I've been reviewing them. I checked first if he knew contacts who know Acanthemblemaria, but no. We'll have to inquire.*»

»*You can call her Maria. She goes by that name unless she's being cruel, which isn't infrequent. We can't ask directly, or we'll be shut down just as quickly as Smanester shut us down. We'll have to look for an opening.*»

«*We'd better open the store then.*»

«*Forgetting your makeup?*»

«*Oh stars, he made himself look older. I did forget that.*»

She walked us into the living quarters, where we found a mirrored vanity with all the necessary makeup. She regarded the paints, putties, and hairpieces with distaste. «*I never learned how to apply makeup, let alone a disguise.*»

«*I could try my hand at it,*» I said dubiously.

«*No, I'll do it my way.*» She sat at the mirror and stared at it.

«*What are you doing?*»

«*Shush. I'm replaying Smanester's memory of his face in the mirror as he finished the job. Trouble is, he did it so automatically that he hadn't really looked at himself in a long time. Don't say anything. I'm almost there.*»

After another minute of intense concentration, young Smanester's face suddenly aged twenty years. Skin sagged and lost some rose from the cheeks. Lines appeared around the eyes and mouth. Hair grayed and thinned, eyebrows grayed and grew bushier.

«*Not bad,*» I judged. «*Should fool most people.*»

«*I want you to know what a virtuoso performance that was. It's incredibly difficult to make a face that isn't one I've ingested. At least I had the genetic code and could run the clock forward a few decades. I wasn't even sure I could do it.*»

«*You mean every form I've seen is someone you've eaten?*»

«*Pretty much, except the big cat on Raxas, and that was wrong in so many details because I didn't have a model. Good thing no one looked too closely.*»

I added this to the list of disturbing revelations about my partner.

We opened the store and waited. Business was slow. The first customer came in about an hour after the local lunch hour, which we had observed by hanging a sign in the window for that time, even though we needed no lunch.

This was not a customer at all, but a courier to pick up a package. "You have a piece that Councilor Vidon ordered." It wasn't a question; his intonation was completely flat.

"I believe so, just a moment."

We went into the back and found a small sculpture of questionable taste. The tag had that name and a breathtaking price. We brought it back out to the front. "Here it is. Would you like me to pack it in a box?"

"Naw." The man looked at me strangely. We were probably supposed to recognize him.

"I see. The price is …"

The courier placed a somewhat bulging envelope on the counter and pushed it towards us.

"Thank you for your business," we managed to say.

"Yeah. You been clubbin' all night again? Not too sharp today."

"That must be it. Thank you and come again."

The courier snorted and left. Color of Air slumped mentally inside. «*That was harder than I expected. I don't usually try to replace someone in their daily life.*»

«*You can let me drive when the next customer comes in and*

feed me memories in the background.»

«That might work.»

Nothing much happened for the rest of the day. After closing, we followed Smanester's usual practice. We walked to a nearby bank and made a payment on a line of credit using the cash we had received, then sold the land that had been used as collateral for the loan and deposited that in an account that had a fictional name on it (and we had ID to match). Back at the office, we electronically transferred the now-clean money to the agent of the "artist" who had made the sculpture. A normal day in the shop for Mister Smanester.

The next morning, one of his artists walked in with another piece for sale. This was a retro calculator/phone with all of the circuitry on the outside as some kind of statement. It seemed familiar.

She glanced at the clock we had attempted to buy on our first visit and made a face. "Still haven't sold that yet?" Ah, that was her art piece as well.

"Haven't found the right buyer," I said noncommittally.

"What are you asking for it? Have you priced it to sell?"

I was going to answer with what Smanester had told us, then reconsidered. I knocked eighty percent off his figure.

"Wow, really? That would be great, but honestly, who's going to pay that much? I'd rather get the sale than have it sit on the shelf with a price tag I can be proud of. Pride doesn't pay the rent."

After she left, Color of Air commented, «*So he's shafting the artists on their commissions?*»

«*Yep.*»

I felt better about having eaten him.

Near closing, a woman came into the shop. She didn't look at the merchandise.

"I saw the red tile over your door. Do you have connections with the Daughters of the Road?"

I kept my voice noncommittal. "I've heard of them." I wanted to give Color of Air time to sort through Smanester's memories.

"It's my cousin. I've brought her all the way from the southern continent to find help for her. She was in ..."

"A bad situation," I interposed. "It's best if I don't know the details."

"I've heard the Daughters can give her a new identity, teach her new skills, let her have a chance at life."

Color of Air picked it up, using Smanester's memories, I presume. "They can do that. One of the finest lawyers I know was a waif that the Daughters took in."

"So they teach more than just sewing or music or ..."

"I know they're still very ... traditional down south, but yes, the horizons are broader here."

"How do I find them?"

"Don't write this down. Memorize this address." Color of Air named a place on the outskirts of the city. "Go there, look for the red tile, and tell them Smanester sent you. No, I'd prefer if you didn't take my card; we stick to word of mouth alone."

"I don't know how to thank you!"

Color of Air smiled Smanester's smile, a fair bit warmer than the one he had given us. "Prosper. Stay safe and prosper. That will be enough."

After the woman had left, I asked Color of Air. «*Is that really what Smanester would have done?*»

«*Yes, his memories of working with this group go way back. Who are these Daughters?*»

«*They're a loose network of women helping women. They pop up everywhere. I've run into them on many worlds I've visited. Sometimes, I think they're inter-dimensional.*»

That left me thinking about how the same man had been rude to us, spent the day laundering stolen money, shafted artists on their commission, and then did an act of kindness like this. People are complicated.

I felt bad about eating him once again.

THE COLOR OF STONE

«**WHY DON'T WE TRY** *some of Smanester's underworld contacts?*» asked Color of Air the next morning.

«*We've been through his memories and his rolodex and we don't have anyone we can just approach out of the blue. We'd set off alarms if we did.*»

«*Rolodex?*»

«*It's an old word for a contact list. No one knows what it originally referred to. Maybe the name of some old programmer.*»

Our opening came through the door mid-morning on the third day.

It came in the shape of a middle-aged woman in conservative clothes who spoke with a sophisticated mid-

169

Aquila accent, all rounded vowels and fashionably clipped endings. My first thought was "tourist," and I was ready to give her Smanester's snooty reception to get her to move on. But her accent was nice to listen to, so I let her go on for a bit.

"You have some lovely things in your shop, but I shouldn't mislead you about why I'm here. I've been to every shop and supply house in the capital and can't find some components I desperately need. They won't talk to me in the front rooms at all, even though the items aren't technically illegal. Well, maybe somewhat. But in the back rooms, a few have whispered to me that Mister Smanester can find anything. I hope that's true."

What the heck was this? A rich family's nanny fronting for a drug lab? "I'm flattered, I think. What did you hope to obtain?"

"I'm trying to find some selenium neural transistors and a small quantity of positronic matrix substrate." She said this as if she were looking for some baking supplies.

I blinked. "I beg your pardon. This is an art and souvenir gallery. Why would you come here looking for those?"

"I was told that you had connections who could supply such things. I wouldn't trouble you if I could get them through normal channels and if it wasn't so urgent for me to find them."

«He does have contacts who can get those things,» Color of Air supplied, reading from the Smanester memory banks.

"I can ... make inquiries. It may be delicate. Those are not items I usually trade in, which might raise questions."

"I can tell it troubles you, so let me be forthright about my need. My name is Emmalyn Renshawe. I'm a doctor, and I have a patient in very unusual circumstances. I need to create an exoskeleton for her, a sort of full-body mobile life support system. These are components I need to fuse the exoskeleton into her nervous system so she can move around unassisted. You can see that this is not a business venture, so there's no profit I can offer to split with you. However, I am prepared to pay reasonable rates for the components and a good commission for you as well."

«*I vote for helping her,*» I thought. «*It does us no harm and it seems to be the compassionate thing to do.*»

«*Smanester wouldn't have put himself out for her.*»

«*She doesn't know that.*»

«*All right, I'll go along with you.*»

«*It will also be the perfect opening to get into Maria's network. This is the type of thing she deals in.*»

«*Why didn't you lead with that?*»

I didn't say that I wanted to see if she was capable of altruistic motives. I think she suspected anyway.

"Black market and reasonable rates is rather an oxymoron," I pointed out to Doctor Renshawe.

"I am aware of that. I'm also aware of the cost and availability of these materials on worlds where they are legal. I have no time to travel offworld to get them, and I doubt my ability to smuggle them in." She handed me a credit chip. I popped it in a reader on my wrist and raised an eyebrow. "You should be able to obtain them for enough less than that amount to make a tidy profit on the deal. I would like you to deliver them via courier to the address on the chip."

After Doctor Renshawe left, we got to work on Smanester's network. Mostly, I got to work since black market trading was part of my hustle. As expected, we were greeted with some suspicion since these were not items that Smanester usually traded in. Since we had a good story about a doctor and a patient (though I toned it down from full-body life support to a mere prosthesis), and the quantities were much less than were needed for something really illegal (like building an unlicensed AI without Three Laws safeguards), we found a supplier by the end of the day and arranged for a courier to pick it up the next day.

«*I don't think we should go as Smanester,*» I said. «*Do you have another persona that would be a good fit?*»

In reply, I got that odd feeling that the walls of the world were melting that accompanied one of her shape shifts. I walked to a mirror and saw a solid, unimaginative-looking guy with a bodyguard face. You know the one. The face that seems to be incapable of showing fear, compassion, interest, or the slightest hint of humor. The only expression it can handle is threat assessment.

«I guess that looks like a courier. But I'm going to be looking over my shoulder to see if I'm following us.»

The pickups went smoothly. I had hoped to make some contacts among Maria's networks, but we only met low-level operatives who had been instructed to transfer certain packages to someone bearing the right encryption token. Then we went to the address Renshawe gave us.

As we stepped into an elevator, I said, *«I think a more sympathetic face is for this meeting. It's just a hunch, but I want to cultivate the contact with this doctor. It's one more angle to play.»*

«You're getting more creative with your euphemisms.»

«You know what I mean.»

«Yes, but do you?»

I felt the shift, so I checked my reflection in the elevator's mirrored wall (why that is a thing on so many worlds, I'll never understand). My original face looked back at me. At least it had the advantage that I didn't have to change clothes. *«I guess that will work. Is that the best you could do?»*

«Just be yourself.»

Ouch.

I spoke the address to the elevator. I was startled when it went down, not up. It went quite a long way down, then opened on a small lobby. Lobby? It was more like an airlock, with another door facing the elevator and blank walls on either side. I pressed the annunciator by the door.

"Yes, who is it?" came the doctor's voice.

"I have a delivery for Doctor Renshawe from someone named Smanester."

The door slid open. The Doctor stood behind it. Behind her was not a living area, as I had expected, but an extensive workroom with lab stations, information consoles, micromanipulators, fabricators, and printers. She had an eager expression and far too little suspicion for her own good. She was clearly as inexperienced with the underworld as she had said in Smanester's shop. I decided to improvise.

"Here are the neural transistors," I said, handing her one of my packages. "But I'm required to install and activate the positronic matrix myself. If you could show me where it goes, I can take care of it right now."

"That wasn't part of the deal."

"That's the deal between my boss and Smanester. If it's going in a prosthetic, that's only moderately illegal. If you're making an autonomous sentience — a robot — that's very illegal, and the price is something you don't want to know about."

"I swear that it's going in a prosthetic. That's not enough for a robot brain." She had lost the posh accent she had employed in the shop.

"See, the thing is, it isn't by itself. But put together a few purchases from different sellers, and, well ..."

"It's not ready for installation yet. If you can just leave it, I'll take care of it."

"That's fine. I'll come back later when you're ready. There's only a small extra charge for an extra visit."

"No, wait." She chewed her lip. Career advice for her: stay away from poker games.

"Who is this, Emmalyn?"

Another voice grabbed our attention. The speaker had skin as dark as a quiet moonless night, high cheekbones, and a direct and penetrating gaze. She was also in a wheelchair. There was a translucence to her as if from a long illness.

"The courier with the components, Zuri. He says he has to install the positronic matrix himself."

"Let him do it. We have nothing to hide. I'm sure he'll let you check his work before he leaves." As wheelchair-bound as she was, Zuri was a force to be reckoned with. Renshawe led the way to a worktable covered with bits of carapace and wires. It looked like a humanoid insect had molted and left its abandoned skin behind. I suppose that wasn't far from the truth, though the process was going in the other direction. This was meant to be worn by Zuri.

Renshawe pulled a helmet towards her, a thin shell, barely more than a skullcap. She peeled back the top to reveal the receptacle for the positronic matrix, a circular plate ten centimeters in diameter. She stepped back and gestured to me. She didn't need to say "I'm watching you" out loud. Her entire posture said it.

I placed the sealed case on the tabletop and pressed my

thumb against the lock. A layer of protection to guard against the package being stolen from the courier. I gathered that there had been a rogue AI about fifty years ago. Someone had omitted the definitions of financial harm from "A robot may not injure a human being or, through inaction, allow a human being to come to harm." It had laid waste to the banking system. Someone had gotten enormously wealthy and had left the AI to take the blame. Even fifty years later, they're still twitchy about AIs here.

I lifted the fragile, shimmering mesh from its bedding and placed it in the skull's receptacle. It fit perfectly, as it should, having been grown to the specs that Renshawe had given me, er, Smanester.

Using a microprobe, I touched the connection points around the perimeter of the mesh. Each touch caused the mesh to send tendrils into the surrounding network, more like repotting a plant's root system than connecting wires. Renshawe watched with a gimlet eye.

"Please do the key exchange now," I told her, watching as she entered the symmetrical encryption keys that made the system nearly impossible to hack.

I looked up to find Zuri watching me. She had large, liquid eyes. "Well done. Where did you learn your craft?"

Where had I learned it? I had known that I could do this when I made my plans. The procedure seemed familiar to me. But when she asked that question, I couldn't remember learning this skill and couldn't remember any times that I had used it. Was it something that Color of Air had supplied to me?

I covered up my confusion with another question. "Offworld, obviously. Not many schools here. So, you're going to wear this?"

Renshawe looked up sharply at the personal question, but Zuri took it in stride. "Yes, my body doesn't do what I want it to anymore. My muscles have grown stiff, and I have almost no bones left."

My eyes widened. (Putting my own poker prospects at risk.) "And ... you lived?"

"I see you know what that means. Yes, I escaped before I was too far gone. More accurately, I was rescued."

I looked back over the exoskeleton on the table. Some features now made sense. "And you're going back?"

"You're connecting dots that you shouldn't be able to. Who are you, exactly?"

"Carl Whitby."

«Original.» Color of Air blew a raspberry. Which didn't smell or taste even vaguely raspberry-like.

«Quiet.»

Zuri waved her hand. It was a faint gesture; she could hardly move. "Names don't mean anything. Have we met? You look familiar."

"I'm sure I would remember if we had."

She wasn't having any of the gallant misdirection. "Hmm. I think it was a photograph. An image in a file. In a dossier. Ah, in Acanthemblemaria's files. Labeled dangerous."

"Probably in good company. I'm guessing your dossier is in there, too."

"It is now. I've lost the element of surprise, but I'm preparing some new surprises."

"Perhaps we can join forces."

"Who do you work for?"

"I'm a freelancer with a grudge. How about you?"

"I was with the Concordium. Now they consider me compromised and disabled. I could let them recall me, shake their heads over me, and retire me and my wheelchair to a low-G habitat. Freelancer with a grudge? Maybe that's me, too."

Zuri considered, but made a quick decision. That seemed a trademark of hers.

"You can help with the suit, but the mission is still mine. Clear?"

"As long as I can try to convince you otherwise as we work."

Zuri turned to Renshawe. "I want to try the suit on now."

"We need to do some more tests."

"*I* need to try the suit. *I* need to relearn how to walk. *I* need to know my abilities – and limits." The last was said with a catch that said she wasn't used to limits.

Renshawe prepared the back half of the suit, ready to

receive Zuri like a form-fitting coffin. I told myself that was not an example of positive thinking, but knowing what she was about to face made it a hard simile to shake. I lifted Zuri from her wheelchair and laid her on the table next to the suit. We had to remove her clothes, which would interfere with the suit's function and cause bruising when squeezed between skin and suit. Renshawe shot me a glance. "Those hands had better not go anywhere out of bounds. Eyes either."

I gave her my best indignant stare. "I'm all for undressing a beautiful woman, but only with her consent and cooperation. I would not take advantage of someone in Zuri's position."

Renshawe nodded shortly. I lifted Zuri's shoulders to let Renshawe pull her jacket off. As I bent over, Zuri whispered, "Do you really think I am beautiful?"

"Believe it," I whispered back.

She smiled and relaxed, which made our task a bit easier.

Color of Air had a different comment. «*That idea — consent — is important to you, isn't it?*»

I had the same response. «*Believe it.*»

We removed Zuri's clothes, her muscles strangely stiff and unresponsive and her bones frighteningly light and fragile. This could have been me, or worse.

The exoskeleton closed around Zuri like a clamshell, molding to her contours like skin. It was so form-fitting that she would have to wear clothes to not shock the rather conservative local culture. We watched as her chest rose and fell as the suit began helping her breathe. It covered her completely except her face.

"I can't move yet," she said.

"Be patient. The positronic matrix is still integrating. Concentrate on moving your right index finger. Just that."

Long minutes passed before we saw the first twitch. Her finger tapped on the table, three times. Then her hand clenched and unclenched, and she raised it in front of her eyes to look at it in wonder. "I can move again."

"Take it slow, dear one."

"Slow is for people with time to spare. I have things to do." She sat up on the table, much as a robot would, bending straight from the waist without assistance from the arms. One would expect to see abdominal muscles ridge and flex as she did, but her tummy remained smooth. It looked enough like a marionette that I almost checked for strings. She swung her legs over the side of the table and paused there for a systems check. She raised each arm and put it through its range of motion, the same with each leg. She rotated her head on her neck and flexed her back. I know what I told Renshawe, but I couldn't take my eyes off her.

"I'm going to stand up now," she announced.

"If you go too fast and injure yourself, it could set you back weeks," warned Renshawe.

"You know I like to push it."

Renshawe colored slightly. I do believe there was a double meaning in those words.

She stood. Wobbly and uncertain, but she stood. It was a triumph for someone with more than halfway petrified muscles. Then she fell.

We helped her back up, but she was waving us away the whole time. This time, she walked a dozen steps and back, but she was too weak to lift her feet entirely off the floor. It was more of a shuffle than a walk.

"Zuri, the artificial muscles aren't delivering their design force, which was already marginal. We'll have to add more layers of contractive fiber to them."

"You know that we're already at the point of diminishing returns with them. More fibers will add more weight than strength, and then heat dissipation will become an issue. At least I'm mobile. I can get there and do what I need to."

"You'll either kill yourself trying or Maria will flick you with her little finger and knock you over, and that will kill you. You can't go like this."

«*I'm taking over. I can fix this,*» said Color of Air.

We walked to a nearby lab bench. I watched to see what she was going to do—not that I could stop it if I wanted to. She picked up a very large and sharp surgical tool. Both Zuri and Renshawe turned their eyes on us.

Color of Air brought the knife edge down on our hand and sliced off two fingers.

Stars, that hurt! No blood spurted; there were no

protruding bones or trailing tendons. Just two fingers lying on the table. Color of Air picked them up and turned to Renshawe. "Do you have some alcohol?"

Some pure ethanol was produced and diluted to fifteen percent. Color of Air placed the two fingers into the beaker and swirled it around. The fingers slumped and liquified, dissolving in the solution. I could see that the two fingers had already grown back on our hand. "I'll need a large syringe and access to the nutrient port on the suit," she said.

Renshawe was backing up, her eyes wide. "Periphage," she whispered.

"Most of what you've heard isn't true," said Color of Air. "But this will help Zuri."

"Do it, Emmalyn. I'm willing to take any risk to see this out."

Renshawe shook her head in denial but retrieved the requested syringe at a glare from Zuri. Color of Air connected it to an input port in the back of the suit and slowly emptied the contents into its fluid circulation system.

Zuri tried to make light of it. "Trying to get me drunk, sailor? I can drink you under the table."

"I'm sure you could," said Color of Air soberly. "It wouldn't take much. Now, this shouldn't take long."

Zuri's hand twitched. Then a tremor started in her leg, almost dumping her on the floor. We picked her up and laid her gently on the table, which only underscored to Renshawe how strong an Arilune was. It didn't help.

Zuri's heel beat a tattoo on the table, then she was flailing around with no control over the suit's muscles and none of her own. I hoped this wouldn't injure her internally with the brittleness of her bones. For a long moment, she went completely rigid and finally collapsed like a rag doll.

Renshawe started clawing at the suit, trying to get it off Zuri. When we restrained her hands, she wrenched free and stabbed us with the knife we had used to cut off our fingers. Color of Air calmly removed it from the bloodless cut. (Our jacket wasn't so lucky.)

"You've killed her! I'll … I'll …" She realized she had few recourses against a stronger opponent. Calling the authorities in the middle of an illegal operation wasn't attractive either.

"No, Emmalyn. I'm fine."

Zuri swung her legs off the table and stood, this time with confidence. She twisted experimentally from side to side, then walked across the room and back. Then she sprinted around the outer walls of the lab and back to the table. She leaped six feet in the air and landed on the table.

"I'm more than fine! I'm ready to take on Maria on my terms this time!"

Renshawe backed away, even more horrified by this transformation than the seizure of a moment ago. "You put that stuff into the exoskeleton. What if it eats through to your skin? Are you going to become like *that*?" She waved in our direction. Since we were wearing my face at the moment, I felt offended. It's a good-looking face.

"If that's what it takes to get my mobility back. If that's what it takes to get in there and finish the job. I'll pay any cost to take Maria down."

"Even if the cost is me? I can't support you if you take this path. This …" Again the gesture. "… is a phage. A carnivore. You're going to lose yourself, and more. Are you willing to pay that cost?"

Zuri tried to meet Renshawe's gaze but dropped her eyes to the floor after a few seconds. Renshawe knew that was her answer. She turned and left.

We gave Zuri some space, but she was still pumped from the new strength the exoskeleton gave her. She threw one last look at the mute seal of the elevator door that had just partitioned her life into before and after. She turned to us and asked, "Is that a possibility? These muscle fibers in the suit are now made of your substance, aren't they? Can they consume me?"

Color of Air shook our head. "No."

Inside our head, I heard her think, «*I don't think so. I've never tried this before.*»

"Your demeanor changed when you cut off your fingers. Your speech patterns are different. Are you multiple people or just a chameleon?"

«*She seems to be accepting what you are pretty readily,*» I commented.

"Yes. Both." Color of Air flowed into Tammartin form. My smartly tailored jacket hung limply on her smaller frame.

"My name is Color of Air, and I can take many forms and personalities. But Samuel is a passenger and has his own personality. It was his face I was just wearing."

"What sort of a name is Color of Air?"

We took a step closer and tilted her face up to ours. Our lips introduced her to the name for which Color of Air was just a translation: flavors of purple mint with a tenor of red pepper and a downbeat of lilac at the end.

«*Moving kind of fast, aren't you?*» I commented.

«*I have to get her to trust us.*»

«*Her colleague, probably her lover, just walked out the door.*»

«*Sigh. I don't get relationships.*»

She shifted back into my form, signaling that I should carry on for now.

"What's your game, then?" asked Zuri. "You're not just a courier. You didn't just happen to be the one picked to deliver this and just happen to have a face that's known to Maria. You didn't just happen to have the key to making this exoskeleton work."

"That last one. Honestly, that was a complete coincidence."

"Meaning you don't deny the first two."

"Maria has something that was stolen from my sister. I'm looking for a way in. When I heard about the components that Doctor Renshawe was looking for, I figured I would find a way into Maria's underground network on one end or the other of the transaction."

"I wasn't planning on taking anyone with me."

"Plans can change when you see an opportunity. I have skills you can use. I've been in one of her compounds before. I've gotten out. Different planet, but I know how she works. I know the formula for an antitoxin."

"Stop right there. There's an antitoxin?"

"Yep. Now let's negotiate how many are in the party."

Zuri sighed. "All right, you can come along. But my objectives come first, recovering your property comes second. Deal?"

"Deal."

"Now, what's this about an antitoxin?"

"It's not complete protection, but it slows down the effects enough. Load up on enough stimulants that she doesn't lull you to sleep, play dead if she catches you, and give her the slip when she's not watching. Worked for me."

"Might not work a second time, but I'm planning not to run into her."

"Better prepare for every eventuality."

"You have a point. You can make this antitoxin?"

"I'll bet all the materials are right here. I'll get started. By the way, you should crank up the cooling on your exoskeleton; the new muscle fiber gives off more heat than the old one."

Zuri's eyes narrowed. "How did you know I'm getting hot?"

I worked very hard not to let my eyes go round. Let's keep those poker creds up. I did some handwaving and some it-stands-to-reason explanations. But how *did* I know she was getting hot?

I could feel her.

Just like when I felt our severed hand as it burned in the airlock along with Magid, I could feel the fibers in the suit even though they weren't connected to us. Now, if *that* wasn't distracting.

«*I hadn't expected that, either,*» said Color of Air.

«*Can she feel us?*»

«*I wouldn't think so. The tissue is in the suit, not in her.*»

Soon, we had an antitoxin prepared. One dose was in Zuri's exoskeleton, ready to inject her if necessary, and I carried a hypospray with the other. I had no idea if we were susceptible to Acanthemblemaria's toxin or if the formula I had prepared would help us. I was going to try very hard not to find out the answer to either question.

"Ok, how will we get in, following your plan?" I asked.

"I have bribed one of her staff members to report a clogged drain and call a plumber. We're the plumbers."

"If that isn't a cliché. Does anyone still fall for that?"

"It's a regular occurrence at Maria's compound. You

should see what she tries to flush down the toilets."

I had seen it. I shuddered.

Zuri sent a signal to her contact and waited for the fake service order to come in. She put on a plumber's coveralls over her exoskeleton and pulled a knit hat over the suit's skullcap. The suit only showed at neck and hands, and the hands just looked like she was wearing gloves. She would pass a quick inspection. She found a second coverall for me but gave me a critical look after I had donned it. "Maria knows your face. That's a problem."

Color of Air said, "Not really." She shifted to the bodyguard face we had used earlier for the component pickup.

Zuri took a half-step back. "Whoa, that's awesome. I may try to recruit you as a Concordium agent after this is over. We could use you."

"Eh, I like freelancing." She must have been a low-level operative who didn't know about the Concordium dark ops.

Before long, we were driving a van towards Maria's compound. It was an authentic plumbing van from the company that Maria's staff usually called out. They hadn't yet noticed they were missing one of their older vans that was due to be traded in. She thinks ahead, this Zuri.

A gorilloid met us at the back gate. (I'm not making cheap shots about his physique or his intelligence. He really was an uplifted great ape.) "You're not the usual crew," he said. If his brows lowered any further, they'd have to send out storm warnings.

"We're new. Marg and Peter are on another job right now," Zuri replied.

"What you see here, stays here. Got that?"

"We know the rules. We signed the contracts. We saw the death penalty clause."

The gorilloid touched his communication wristband with a finger nearly as wide as my palm. "Plumbers are here," he snorted into the speaker. He retreated into a small kiosk next to the gate and lurked there.

A staff member came from the main building across a courtyard. Human, male, slightly pudgy. He didn't make any small talk, just beckoned for us to follow.

"My name is…" I started to say.

"Not something I need to know," he replied curtly.

I guessed this was Zuri's contact and he wanted as much deniability as possible. He led us into the main building and into the servant's wing. We had to cross the opulent main hall to get there. I checked the painting-laden walls as I passed, looking for one in particular that depicted a planet sitting amid a sea of stars. It was a blue world, with many seas and lacy chains of islands connecting a few larger land masses, and the stars had been rendered with exquisite brightness. It wasn't there.

Damn, I was going to have to find it.

Our guide led us to a room of porcelain and steel, only

partly in character with the elegance of the rest of the dwelling. This was a combination of toilette and abattoir, a place where Acanthemblemaria disposed of her victims after digesting them. The clog was not a fiction. It was absolutely horrific and the stench was indescribable. This stench could stain the light purple, strip skin like acid, or fill the air with the sound of a stopped heartbeat. With Shapestealer synesthesia, it did all of those things.

Our guide gagged despite his familiarity with this place. "We had a banquet this week. I hope you'll be able to clear this quickly. Maria will be entertaining again soon."

He turned to leave, hastily. Zuri pulled a metal rod from her belt and struck a blow to the back of his head, laying him out unconscious on the floor.

"Hey, was that necessary?" I protested.

"It was part of the deal. He may be dismissed for this, but if Maria thought he was an accomplice, he'd be just as dead as the guests from the last banquet. It would just take longer and involve a lot more pain."

It was a better deal than Smanester had gotten.

"Let's split up," said Zuri. "You can look for your stolen property, and I'll look for the object I need."

"Works for me."

We went in opposite directions. It was a big place and I wasn't sure how to search it all. I hoped the painting had been hung in one of the many rooms. If it had been put in storage, I might never find it. If it had been sold …

I realized we could still feel Zuri through our connection to the tissue in her exoskeleton. We kept a general awareness of her direction and distance and her level of physical exertion. Useful, perhaps, but also disturbing.

Off the main hallway was a gallery I hadn't seen before. At first, I thought it looked promising, having the appearance of an art gallery. There were rows of stone statues down both walls. All were nudes. It slowly sunk in that Maria had boldly put her victims on display where any visitor could see them. It was a sign of how powerful she had grown that she could do that with impunity.

Acanthemblemaria was a Medusa.

All of these people had died in her embrace, turned to stone, silicate hearts no longer able to pump blood of sand through their arteries. Many had expressions of rapture or ecstasy. Death by Medusa was reputed to be the best way to go. A few had expressions of horror. These were most likely thrill-seekers who had gambled on having a night of pleasure and escaping the consequences. I had, and Zuri had, though at terrible cost.

I checked several more rooms, finding no paintings but finding an appalling number of statues. The death toll of this creature was enormous.

Color of Air had been pensive. «*You have encountered her before?*»

«*Yes, several years ago.*»

«*Do you see me as you see this Medusa?*»

«She's in a different league entirely.»

«That wasn't entirely a denial. We both need to eat other beings to survive. Is it just a matter of degree?»

«Maria also kills just for pleasure and delights in torture. You don't have either of those faults.» Was I condoning Color of Air's diet?

«So intent matters? Perhaps Maria just needs a conscience.»

Did she mean she had a conscience, or was that supposed to be my role?

I heard footsteps in time to hide in a doorway. Several servants were hurrying to the front entrance, adjusting dark glasses as they went.

«Shit, Maria's home.»

The servants opened the door and bowed, knowing better than to look upon the Medusa who swept through the opening.

Acanthemblemaria was an orb floating in midair, surrounded by a waving mass of hair-fine tendrils. If a Medusa had visited ancient Greece to spawn the stories of the terrible monster, scholars hadn't translated the word for her hair correctly, or the ancients didn't have the right word, just as they didn't have a word for the color blue. It didn't resemble a nest of snakes, other than it was in continual, seething, hypnotic motion. On the other hand, a Medusa can make you see whatever you most desire, so perhaps whoever saw one and lived to tell the tale had a snake fetish. Perseus would have needed more than a mirror to escape her psychic field.

At the moment, she wasn't exerting herself to project any imagery. She didn't know I was watching, and mesmerizing the servants was probably counter-productive if she wanted any work out of them. She sailed through the entrance hall and moved towards the living quarters.

Which is exactly where Zuri had headed.

«*We need to help her out,*» said Color of Air. She took control, and we started moving swiftly in pursuit.

«*Careful! This is one of the most deadly creatures known. If Maria already has Zuri, we can't help her.*»

«*Zuri is still at large and unharmed. I can sense her.*»

We took a wrong turn, ending up in another trophy room. And then in a library. Who knew that a Medusa read? And then a workspace with information screens and some very strange keyboards for Medusa tendrils to operate. If we survived, I wanted to return here to track down the painting in her records.

About to double back, a sudden pain across the back of the neck laid us out on the floor. I tried to move, but Color of Air was still in control. She was slightly slower to react but rolled over as another line of pain wrapped around one wrist. I had thought at first that Maria had ambushed us from behind, but there was no one there. Maria could make you see things, but as far as I knew, she couldn't make you see nothing. I was confused. What had hit us?

«It's the exoskeleton. Maria has got Zuri, and we're feeling it.»

«We have to get out of here.»

«No, we have to rescue Zuri.»

«It's too late for her».

«Do you want to experience her death firsthand? It might kill us, too.»

I was ashamed that it took that argument to keep moving towards Zuri and Maria. Maria terrified me.

We left the workspace and cast about for the way forward.

«This place is a maze.»

«I feel Zuri off that way. But there's no door.»

«Go back one doorway and go right.»

«That's going away from Zuri.»

«Trust me. That's the way Maria thinks.»

I could feel Color of Air wondering if I was stalling. I was ashamed to admit I had thought about it. But a Medusa loves a maze in a certain pattern. No one knew why. Maybe they evolved in aircoral habitats that were useful for trapping prey. Her lair would be at the center of a clockwise spiral.

We had just made the turn when another stripe of pain went down our back.

«Zuri's exoskeleton has been compromised.» I think we both said that simultaneously.

We staggered back into motion. I navigated through another few turns before we were suddenly on fire from the waist up.

Color of Air gasped, «*Take over, Samuel. You have a greater pain tolerance than I do.*»

Our feet responded to me once again. I thought about turning around and running like hell. But by now I had worked up enough rage to keep moving. I got the hypospray out of my belt. I stepped through the next door and into Maria's lair.

Maria was standing in the center of the space, holding Zuri in her tendrils. She had manifested as a beautiful hermaphrodite, which must have been an image taken from Zuri's subconscious. She was peeling the armor from Zuri's left arm and side as one might peel a shrimp, leaving husks on the floor. Zuri was already wrapped in tendrils from the waist up.

«*The suit has been shredded. Why are we still feeling what she's feeling?*» I demanded of Color of Air.

«*My substance must have gotten into the neural interface in the brain. We're wired directly in.*»

That was bad news. A Medusa infiltrates the victim's body with those tendrils, replacing carbon compounds with silicon compounds through molecular exchange. The reaction also siphons all the calcium from the bones, leaving them little more than jelly. If this sounds incredibly painful, it is. But the Medusa tricks the victim's brain into interpreting pain as pleasure to keep the victim docile while being consumed. At the end, all that's left is a stone statue.

Zuri's face wore a combination of ecstasy and horror. It felt like the best high in the universe, and she knew it was killing her.

We didn't have the benefit of rewiring the pain center. To us, it was unabated agony.

«*Shift back to my face,*» I snapped to Color of Air.

I advanced as I felt my features re-form. "Maria! Let her go! I'm the one you want!"

The beautiful face turned towards me. First in puzzlement, then anger, then gloating. "You again. I hate that name. You'll die this time, but I'm going to make you say Acanthemblemaria ten thousand times before you do, each time you beg for your life. I might let you go if you can say it exactly right."

Maria lunged for me but didn't release Zuri as I had hoped. I thrust forward with the hypospray, trying to inject the contents into the Medusa. A tendril snapped around my wrist, freezing me in place.

"What is it about this painting that is so interesting, eh? You tried to steal it once before, then this little one tried, and now you're both back looking for it. I'm starting to think it's more than just artwork."

I looked to the side and saw that a tube lay on the ground near Zuri, and the painting that had been stolen from my sister lay on the floor, slightly ragged-edged from being cut away from the frame. We had had the same objective without even realizing it. What could Zuri want with that painting? As far as I knew, it *was* only artwork.

"It belonged to my sister, that's all. I want it back because that's all I have of her since she went missing." I struggled to turn the hypospray towards Maria.

Zuri moaned and opened her eyes. I must have diverted enough of Maria's attention to break the spell. She took in the tableau, eyes flicking to the hypospray we were struggling with. I saw her hand strain towards her own hypospray in her belt.

«*Can you still shapeshift?*»

«*Yes. We'll take some damage from the tendrils, but survivable. What's your plan?*»

«*What's the scariest form you have?*»

I gave a superhuman yank to overbalance and distract Maria. The serene golden face that was only a projection of her thoughts wrinkled with the first hints of concern. "What are you? Not much food in you. Just a silicon soup with a nervous system. I can still torment you, but you're not worth eating." More tendrils coiled around me, some releasing their hold on Zuri. Enough?

"Then how about you just let us go? Release both of us and the painting and we'll let you live."

In a holodrama, a grandiose and empty threat would cause the villain to laugh, just as the hero manages to pull it off, following the principle that irony tends towards a maximum as dramatic necessity increases. I gave Maria one beat to conclude it was just a ruse, then a half beat to begin thinking I might have something.

«*Now!*»

We erupted into the form of a Deepwater Lamplighter, every bit as large and scary as the last time. In the moment of change, when we were most vulnerable, the tendrils sliced deep. The shell of the Lamplighter cut them off in the next instant, but they had done their damage, disrupting tissue and slicing nerves. Pain seared through arms and back, where they had gripped the hardest. Worst of all, our claw couldn't hold the hypospray, which went clattering to the ground. Well, damn. I needed that for my plan.

The sudden change shocked Maria into recoiling for an instant. Both Zuri and I found ourselves free. Zuri used the still-functioning right arm of her exoskeleton to whip out her hypospray, press it to Maria's head, and trigger it.

A typhoon of flailing tendrils ripped through the room, smashing everything that got in the way. Our carapace fended off most of it, and Zuri hunkered down on the floor. «*I need a human form. A sturdy one,*» I called to Color of Air. I was a little surprised that she chose Spanov, but Magid's assistant had been compact, strong, and fast. I pounced on my hypospray on the floor then went after Maria. I almost lost the device twice as she battered everything in sight, but I finally got hold of a handful of her tendrils to hold her still and rammed my own spray home. She went limp, hanging from my hand.

"Good work, Perseus. You slew the Medusa and cut off her head."

Zuri's voice was weak and shallow. I dropped Maria's head and hurried over to her.

"You've studied your classics," I said as I checked her vitals. Eyes cloudy, skin cold and hard. If there was a pulse, it couldn't be felt through dense silicate layers. Her rib cage could barely expand to draw breath. It didn't look good.

"That wasn't an antitoxin, was it?"

"No. It was Medusa nerve agent. I never had a way to save you other than keep you away from Maria, but I could take her down if she consumed you. Or me, I had the same safeguard."

"I would have done the same."

I held her for a while, listening to her breathing become more labored.

"If you consume me, I become part of you, or so I've heard."

"Something like that. We keep your memories, or most of them anyway. Much of your personality. We can take your form as needed."

"Like the one you're wearing now?"

I looked down. Still Spanov. "Yes, she was quite a person."

"Will I still be aware of myself?"

"Only for a short time, until you're fully assimilated." Unless you were the one odd case like me.

"Please let me join with you. You'll get some Concordium intelligence that you probably should have. In return, please do one thing for me."

"What's that?"

"Go see Emmalyn before I fade. I have to apologize to her."

"I don't think that's such a great idea ..."

"Promise me."

"All right."

I shucked off my clothes and started more gently divesting Zuri of her exoskeleton. "Hurry, please. I don't have much time."

I did that and held her while Color of Air enveloped her and let her spirit and soul suffuse us. All the extra silicon was only a minor inconvenience. We sloughed it off as so much waste material. We gathered up the painting and left. I sorted Zuri's memories to find why she was sent to retrieve it, but her higher-ups in the Concordium hadn't told her what made it valuable. To her, it was just an object to find and extract. Very little of her intel was of material interest to me. Oh well, at least I got the painting. Now to find out why it was a big deal.

We went to Zuri's apartment to change into her form and dress in her clothes. Then we went to Renshawe's apartment and knocked on the door. I thought she was about to fall over when she came to the door. She scooped us up in an embrace, then realized that we weren't wearing the exoskeleton.

"What's happened? You survived, but you're back to normal. That's not possible." We could see the thoughts run across her face as she added up the conflicting information. "You're not Zuri, are you? You're that *thing*."

Color of Air channeled the fading remnants of Zuri. "I'm in here, Emmalyn. I had to merge with Color of Air to keep some part of me alive. I accomplished my mission but Maria jumped me before I could get away. We killed her. Together, we killed her. But I was mostly stone by the time we were finished. I didn't want to die like that. I wanted to see you again and say I was sorry for being so bull-headed. This was the only way to do that."

Renshawe's face was as stony as the statues in Maria's trophy rooms. She shook her head. "No, you're not real. You're just a Periphage. That's what you do, you trick people." She closed the door.

I could feel Zuri's heart breaking. It may have been a virtual heart, but that feeling lives in the mind, anyway.

«Let me go,» she said to us. «I had to do that. I knew I had to say goodbye. I wish she had listened.»

Color of Air had been holding Zuri's memories together with an effort of will. Now she changed from Zuri into Tammartin and let the memories and personality fade away.

«There's one more thing to do. What happens to Smanester's shop?»

«I presume he'll be declared missing, and it will default to his creditors or the tax collectors.»

«I have a better idea.»

A half-dozen women were in the shop, ranging from three girls in their teens to a silver-haired matron who stood to speak for them.

"I want to thank you so much, Mister Smanester, for donating your shop to the Daughters upon your retirement. It will be a place for our girls to learn about business and a much-needed source of income for our chapter. After all your years of generosity, this came as a tremendous surprise. We had no idea that you were planning to retire so soon."

"Something came up, and I have an opportunity to travel offworld. I'll be gone by this evening. I couldn't think of anyone more deserving to take my place."

«And we've told all his former contacts that this shop's new management will no longer do money laundering for them.»

«No, it didn't seem to be the sort of life skill we should teach these girls.»

After a little more speech-making, we grabbed the tube containing the painting we had come for, turned the keys over to the Daughters of the Road, and headed for the *Rapier Whitt*. I wanted to start deciphering the puzzle behind the painting as soon as possible.

THE COLOR OF SWORDS

THE RAPIER WHITT stood where we had left her. The shimmerpaint I had applied gave her an air of genteel decay, a dusty silver as if weathered but not quite neglected. Shadows suggested that old insignia had been removed when the ship had been repurposed. Possibly two or three times. Non-functional storage pods had been strapped on to change her profile. Anyone keeping an eye out for *Rapier Whitt* would pass this ship by without blinking.

Someone was waiting by the entry hatch.

"Good day, Captain Jonas," he said. "The name's Batson. I had an alert set for the next private ship to file a flight plan for Auphari. When I saw where you were going, I hustled right over to see if I could land a berth with you."

"I wasn't planning on taking passengers," I said, "and I'm not planning to call at Auphari on this trip."

"It's directly on your route. I can make it worth your while." He stepped closer, holding out a data pad.

Beneath a sum of trade credits that would make it worth our while to detour many parsecs from our filed plan, the pad said ::I can help you.::

As I stared at the message, Color of Air commented, *That's enough for first-class passage on a luxury liner. Why is he so eager to get on a tramp freighter?*

She couldn't see the message. I had to look a second and third time before I could see what was actually there: a set of mundane coordinates that you would just skip past and enter into the nav system — unless you knew the code. I apparently knew the code and Color of Air did not. I changed my mind about taking this passenger. I wanted to learn more.

«We can use the cash,» I argued. «We didn't make anything on the last three trips, our supplies are low, and our credit balance is on the ropes.»

«But we don't want to go to Auphari. You just said so.»

«It won't take long and then we'll be set for several months.»

At that moment, we both got a whiff of grasses and pollens, open air, umami, salt, and esters. «It's Ambassador Alexander aka John Drake from Raxis,» hissed Color of Air.

«He gets around more than a bad check, doesn't he? We still don't know who he works for.» But he had just used a Concordium cogni-cipher. Double take. How did I know that? And why did he want to help me?

«What's he doing here? And why would he choose this ship out of all the ships in port? This sounds like a trap.»

«He did say that he was heading to Caelum for a trade deal. But if it is a trap, better to walk into one we can see than wait for one we don't.»

"All right, Mister Batson, we'll take you to Auphari."

«Now just wait a minute. I didn't agree to take him. We've been working well together, so I've granted you some autonomy. But if you're going to ignore my misgivings and make dangerous decisions, I can revoke that autonomy just as quickly.»

«If we back out now, we'll just confirm any suspicions he might have.»

Color of Air seethed a crimson organic smell that I couldn't place, but which was thoroughly unpleasant.

I placed our palm on the lock plate next to the hatch. The door sighed open. We motioned for Batson to precede us so that Rapier could get a good look at him for threat assessment.

"Rapier," I called. "We have a passenger."

Rapier appeared in her kimono-clad avatar on my signal to welcome our guest.

"This is Batson. He'll be traveling with us to Auphari."

"Welcome, Mister Batson. Should I send for your

luggage?"

"I travel light." He hefted the small valise slung over his shoulder. "Though if you have a replicom, I wouldn't mind a few changes of clothes. I recycled all my spares before leaving. Caelum outfits would be out of place on Auphari. They'd be out of place nearly anywhere, truth be told."

"Certainly, sir. I've taken your measurements, so you only need to select your fabrics and styles. If you follow me, I'll show you to your cabin." Nice way to put Batson on notice that he'd been scanned. She'd have a report of weapons and contraband waiting for me. We headed for my cabin.

We had a dilemma to work out. I said, «*For now, we have to decide whether to stay in this form or revert to being Captain Whitt. Auphari is known for its zealous and well-equipped Customs agents. The ship's disguise won't hold up there, and it will raise red flags if I'm not at the helm.*» Color of Air didn't reply. She was still smoldering over my decision to take Batson on board.

The cabin door shut behind us. Color of Air subsided into her base form with a palpable feeling of relief mixed with annoyance. The clothes we had been wearing hung loosely on Tammartin's more compact body. Color of Air took them off and tossed them aside but didn't immediately move to put anything new on. I itched for a shower, but Color of Air didn't move in that direction. She didn't need showers. Her surface was self-cleaning, absorbing dirt and blotting out odors all on its own. I wanted control for a while so I could indulge some of my desires. I really needed to scratch an itch that didn't exist.

Rapier cleared her throat discreetly. "Batson has submitted his specifications for clothing and accessories. I have checked them over for possible hidden weapon components and removed three, but you may want to look at them before I make them. There's a specification I don't understand."

I commented, «*I'll bet he put those three pieces in there for us to find. He wanted us to think we found everything.*» Color of Air reluctantly yielded control to me again.

"Let me look," I said out loud. Rapier put the specs for the clothing on the screen. They were terse notations in the maker language, closer to a computer program than human language. I scanned through the instructions, finding most of them straightforward. The belt buckle was intricate, but I satisfied myself that it wasn't a weapon. Then I came to the part that had stymied Rapier.

The pattern was convoluted and probably impossible to build. I scanned it and found it had a cancel command at the end, rendering the entire block a null operation. So why leave it in? Was this a standard order for him where he had commented out an unneeded option? But what did it do? The prospect of a black ops virus subverting Rapier via the replicom was not one I wanted to overlook. Then I saw the cogni-cipher hidden in the code.

::I can help you. I know how to free you.::

I stared at it for a moment, dumbfounded, then swiftly moved the block to quarantine.

«*What was it?*» asked Color of Air. She had noted my pause and was suspicious that I was hiding something from her.

«*Probably junk, but I'm not taking a chance that it's a virus. He could be testing us to see how we react.*»

The next morning, we ventured out in Captain Whitt's form to have breakfast in the common room. Batson joined us a short while later. He did a convincing double-take as he entered.

"Good morning, the name's Batson. I didn't know there were other passengers on board."

"Samuel Whitt," I said, extending my hand. He made no sign he recognized the name. Well, it hadn't been the one we were using on Raxas anyway. "I'm the ship's owner."

"I see. And Jonas?"

"She acts on my behalf when I need a different face." I was really sticking our neck out to get a rise out of him. "Depending on the locale and my, ah, history there."

He finally reached out and took our hand. His grip was as precise and hearty as that of a sales droid, and consequently, just as false. The salt and pollen in his aura spiked, suggesting a nervousness beneath his calm surface —or perhaps walled off behind a Partition in his mind.

"Are there any other passengers aboard?" he enquired.

"Perhaps enough for a good game of poker?"

"I couldn't say."

"You … don't know if you have other passengers?"

I smiled a small smile. "No, that's how discreet I am." Let that keep him off balance. We could produce more passengers if needed. Just not all at the same time.

"Maybe a game of chess, then."

"Rapier plays a mean game of Go, though I can still beat her on a good day."

"I would be happy to have a new partner," said Rapier from the air above us. "Captain Whitt has been growing predictable lately." Most people hated an AI who could lie, but to me it was one of Rapier's best traits. She *was* lying, wasn't she?

"Ok, I'll take you up on that. Right after I hypnoskim a book on Go strategy. I was also wondering if I might use your replicom a bit more. I've a few more things I'd like to get ready before we reach Auphari."

"Shouldn't be a problem. Let me see the materials manifest so I can ensure we have sufficient stocks." I knew that Rapier would comb all of the designs for booby traps and weapons. I suspected that I would receive more surreptitious messages that way.

Batson departed. I intended to stand also, but nothing happened. Color of Air had taken back control. «*He's up to something,*» she said.

«*No doubt. No point in calling him on it just yet. He'll just try a different angle, one we may not anticipate. We'll monitor his replicom logs. He'll slip up.»*

«I can't believe I'm accusing you of being insufficiently paranoid, but really?»

«You have yet to plumb the depths of my paranoia. Batson thinks he's the cat and we're the mouse, but he's mistaken. Now, let's get that painting hung in its proper place.»

«It really is meant to be hung for viewing?»

«It is.»

«And it was worth braving the Medusa to recover it?»

«Most definitely. It belonged to my sister. No one else deserves to have it.»

Rapier produced a custom frame in the replicom. However, the canvas was jagged at the edges, and the portion that had been folded over the former frame was lost. I placed it in the replicom and set up a repair program. When finished, it was framed again and the missing sections extrapolated to the edges. You couldn't tell that it had been damaged.

I held the finished piece against the wall of the lounge. "How's that look?"

"I'll hold it; you step back and look," said Rapier. Contact points on the frame clicked to magnetized spots on the wall. I took four steps backward.

"Just a little higher." The painting glided up the wall. "I think the left side is low."

"You should report to the medical bay for an eye examination. It's level to more zeros than you can count. At least three."

"I know, I'm just pulling your leg."

"Alas, I have no legs."

"You have very nice legs. I specifically requested them."

"Don't make me report you to the Cybernetics Bureau for AI sexism. Again."

We were still laughing when Batson came in. He tried to hide his reactions, but his eyes snapped immediately to the painting on the wall. His pupils widened. Other than that small giveaway, he made no outward sign of interest.

"Oh, there you are," he said. "I brought you the manifests you requested." He handed us a data chip. I reached to take it with my right hand. It didn't move. Instead, Color of Air coolly reached out with her left hand and accepted the chip.

"I'll make sure we have the materials on board for these."

"There's nothing exotic on the list; I don't foresee any problems in that regard."

He turned to look at the painting we had just hung.

"That's very nice. Did you paint it?"

I tried to answer, but Color of Air had taken control. "My sister did. She's missing, but I heard a collector on Caelum had it, so I went there to acquire it."

"Missing, you say? Did the collector have any leads on

where your sister might be?"

So he had an interest in locating my sister? Interesting.

"Unfortunately, no, that was a dead end."

"Well, you must feel good to at least have it back in the family." He cast an appraising eye on the painting. "It's quite good. You could almost navigate by it." He nodded and departed in the direction of his cabin.

By now, I was fuming.

«Why did you cut me out of the conversation?»

«I could handle it. It's my body, you know.»

I wanted teeth again just so I could grind them.

Color of Air walked back to our cabin and sealed the shimmerdoor. She placed Batson's chip into a reader and said, "Rapier, please verify that we have all these materials on hand and that they're safe to let Batson play with."

She dropped my clothes in front of the mirror as she turned back into the form of Tammartin, and then she cycled through Spanov, Nuritha, Zuri, and a few others. I hadn't met some of them yet. Shapestealer calisthenics?

«I'd like to know what Batson is up to,» she said. «He might spill something to a different passenger.»

Not a bad idea. «He might know Zuri. They might even work...»

«I know,» she snapped. She settled on Spanov, who had fortuitously left her valise on board, so we had clothes that fit. Color of Air pulled the kit out of a storage compartment and pulled on Spanov's leathers.

Behind us, Rapier said, "Here's the manifest that Batson gave you. We have sufficient stocks to cover everything."

"Give him the green light, then. But verify the patterns he uploads before feeding them to the replicom."

"Of course."

Color of Air left the room without glancing at the manifest on the screen. There went my chance to check it for encoded messages.

"Rapier, where is Batson?"

"Is this the Captain speaking?"

"Yes, it is."

That was the wrong answer. Rapier would be on her guard now. But there was no reason not to give us the requested information.

"Batson has just left his cabin and is walking towards the workshop with his plans."

"Perfect, thank you, Rapier."

I could sense Batson coming long before he was in sight, via Color of Air's olfactory senses. She used that to time her arrival at the central lounge just before Batson's. He looked up as we entered from the door opposite and made a small sound of surprise. "Well, hello. I didn't know anyone else was on board. My name's Batson."

"I am Grigoreva Spanov," Color of Air said in Spanov's husky voice.

"Captain Whitt implied there weren't any other passengers. Are you crew?"

"Let us say that I am a guest."

"Nice to meet you. At the moment, I have some work to do, but I'm sure we'll see each other again?" He didn't exactly exude friendliness.

"That would be a pleasant diversion. I myself am on my way to do a workout for a few hours. I wish every ship I took passage on was as well-equipped as this one."

Batson eyed the leathers we were wearing. "Uh, what sort of workout are you planning?"

In an echo of Grigoreva's come-on to us, Color of Air said, "Martial arts."

"Ah. Maybe another time. Enjoy your workout." Batson continued towards the workshop with the air of someone who'd been interrupted in an important task.

«*Huh. Unless I miss my guess, he's well-trained in hand-to-hand combat,*» I said.

Color of Air offered no comment as she continued towards the exercise room.

«*You don't need to work out, do you? Your muscle tone is whatever you want it to be.*»

«*Practice helps keep skill sharp and reactions automatic, just as it does for you solids. It helps pass the time. And sometimes, you just have to punch something.*»

On that, we could agree.

She selected a *bokken*, a type of wooden sword used in Kendo. After warming up for a while doing forms, Rapier addressed us. "Would you like a sparring partner?"

I kept quiet. This could be entertaining.

"Batson didn't seem interested."

"I would be happy to provide you with a suitable opponent."

The image of Rapier materialized in the air, dressed for Kendo with breastplate and hakkama. She took a stance opposed to us.

"Am I supposed to dance with shadows? You're just a hologram."

Rapier brought her *bokken* down sharply on our shoulder. Cinnamon-lemon pain shot from the impact. I knew that this body could take a lot of hits without damage but it was still uncomfortable.

Color of Air raised her *bokken* to block. "How did you do that? You're not real."

"I use shimmer technology to make the form solid. I keep the intensity and reaction times to human norms to simulate a typical opponent." She feinted, then landed a tap on the forehead.

"You've been able to do this all the time I've known you?"

"Only in the exercise room, the medical bay, and the galley. I don't have shimmer projectors anywhere else. It's illegal for any other use." She tapped our upper arm again.

"Is that so? You're on."

Several hours later, hot and sweaty, we returned to our

cabin. I'm pretty sure the sweat was just Shapestealer mimicry since there's no reason for a formless being to have sweat glands. The hot part was understandable since muscle contractions involve chemical reactions that are endothermic, no matter whether the tissues are carbon or silicon-based. Rapier had matched Color of Air blow for blow, parry for parry. I was impressed since I had left the sparring program set on level eight, which usually gives me a thrashing. I kept to myself the news that there were four more levels above that.

As luck would have it, Batson turned the corner just as we were entering the Captain's cabin, wearing the wrong face.

"Oh, hey, Spanov. Is the Captain in? I've been looking for him."

"He is not. I have not seen him in a while. The ship can locate him for you if you ask nicely."

"I guess I haven't been asking nicely enough. The ship refuses to tell me. Can you tell him I uploaded a new set of pattern files? I need his sign-off to finish my work." Batson stopped by the door and tried to peer past us into the cabin. This guy needed to learn about boundaries.

"I will tell him when I see him," Color of Air said, stepping through the shimmerdoor and opaquing it behind us.

We could still hear Batson in the corridor, smirking, "Guest, eh? Well, I guess rank has its privileges."

«I liked his John Drake persona better,» I commented.

«You shouldn't have brought him on board. He's trouble. Who knows what he's making in the replicom?»

«Better to keep him where we can watch him. Rapier will keep him from making anything that can be used as a weapon.»

«Better hope so.»

Color of Air stripped and reverted to her base form, which I took to mean she wasn't giving up control anytime soon. She never gave me control of this form.

The sweat vanished, reabsorbed into her omnivorous protoplasm. She never needed a shower, and I missed them.

Rapier said, "I have the patterns from Batson for approval. I don't see anything concerning, but they have the unreadable comment blocks the first one had."

"Delete the comments and let Batson use the plans. It'll keep him from stalking me for a while," said Color of Air. She didn't look at the display.

There went my second chance to read the messages Batson had embedded in the design files. Could I ask Rapier to restore them later so I could read them? Not, I decided, without alerting Color of Air of my interest. It was like living in a glass room with microphones, without any place to escape the surveillance. I was watched twenty-five hours per day, ten days per week. Heck, I couldn't even scratch my nose most of the time. It was wearing. I missed my freedom.

Color of Air settled down cross-legged on the bed. She seemed ready to go into one of her trances. She didn't sleep, so I still wasn't sure of the function of these spells of inactivity. Maybe it was just a way to pass the time. For me, it was insanely boring.

«Hey, can I read or watch a vid while you're napping?»

«No.»

I could feel her shutting down. I no longer had any input; no sounds, smells, or sights. I was alone with my thoughts and they were poor company.

Sight/sound/smell crashed into my prison. Burnt chocolate taste of air scrubbers, saffron-scented light from the overhead panels, oboe notes of the texture of bedsheets against skin. I was back in my cabin.

«What's our position? What year is it?» I asked.

«No need to be dramatic. I simply needed to meditate, and it's only been fourteen hours.»

I pushed my complaint. *«I had no idea what was going on. I had no sense of time or space. Total sensory deprivation.»*

«I was fatigued by the workout yesterday and felt I might have some residual Medusa toxin in my system. I needed the time to flush it out.»

That was a plausible explanation for needing a deeper and longer rest period than usual. I wasn't in the mood to trust plausible explanations.

«I need a cup of coffee,» I grumbled.

Color of Air was amused. «*That's just a habit. Caffeine doesn't do anything for us. But I do enjoy the aroma. We can go have a cup if it makes you feel better.*»

She stood, putting on first my body then my clothes. She let me drive. As we made our way to the galley, I couldn't help but feel she was being falsely conciliatory.

Batson was sitting at a table in the common area, working on his own cup of coffee. He went down a notch in my estimation when I noted that he was having granola for breakfast. I would have gone for a bearclaw previously, though the thought triggered revulsion from Color of Air. She had a diet of sentient beings; who was she to be a judge of pastries?

I got my coffee and sat down, cradling the hot mug. I took a sip, for form, but the aroma was the best part. Had I always thought that, or was it a fabricated memory?

"Good morning, Captain. I was just contemplating your painting over there." Batson gestured towards the newly-framed canvas.

I nodded. "I'm glad to have recovered it."

"It's quite a piece. I'm sure it has a deeper significance. I'd like to speak to the artist about its inspiration." He emphasized the last sentence in a peculiar tone of voice. Almost a command.

"I would, too. I haven't seen her in years."

Batson shook his head. "That's too bad. How was your workout yesterday?"

I was still thinking about the painting. "Oh, it was fine. A good way to unwind, you know?"

It took me a moment to remember I had been wearing a different body.

I looked up in time to see Batson drawing back an elastic band on ... a slingshot? The band snapped, a disk flew across the table. Color of Air seized control, reached for a weapon.

I hate gambling when I don't know the odds. Or the stakes. Batson said he knew how to free me. That made him an ally — right? I made my choice. I resisted giving up control to Color of Air. I could only slow her for an instant, but that was enough.

A disk slammed us in the sternum, driving us back in our seat. It buzzed like an angry Raxian hornet. I tried to rise from my seat, but I couldn't move. We were paralyzed and cut off from each other. The inner voice was gone.

"Sonic resonance," said Batson conversationally. "Useful for imparting order to amorphous liquids. A standing wave holds the blob immobile. But I need to talk to you separately." He turned a dial on his slingshot device.

The angry hornet rose in pitch. A rending pain tore through my chest. The vibration shredded our shirt and raised a bullseye on our chest. It looked like the strobe-frozen splash of a rock in a pond. Then the central peak split in two. Ribs shattered, organs sundered, a rift grew from sternum to crown. I held onto my sanity and told myself I'd been through worse. I was good at lying.

We liquified into two amorphous blobs. Clothes fell in shreds on the floor. Each blob stretched upwards, forming into transparent mannequins tinged with light blue. The color of air, I thought to myself.

The other mannequin assumed the features of Tammartin, low-res and undetailed. I presume mine looked more like me.

Batson pointed his device away from me, holding it on Color of Air. My paralysis eased. I could turn my head and see she was still frozen. I looked back at Batson.

"So what do you want?" I snarled.

"I want to talk to Samara Whitt."

That floored me. I thought it was about the Periphage. "I haven't seen her in years. What do you want with her?"

"I've learned that Samara may have encoded the coordinates of the Periphage home planet in that painting. Your mission was to retrieve the painting. Now I need her to decode it."

Rapier broke in, "Do you need assistance, Captain?"

"No, I got this." Code for *stand by unless I am threatened physically*. "What do you mean, my mission?"

"You still don't remember me? Chet Batson? 'Chance' Batson from the Academy? I even used my real name this time. Though the Concordium has changed my face so many times, I'm not sure which one is mine anymore."

"I don't know anyone by that name."

Batson swore. "That was supposed to trigger you to remember."

"What are you talking about?"

"The personality I'm talking to now is just a construct — a cover story. The real you is behind a Partition in your mind."

If true, that explained a lot. I had known about Partitioned agents because I was one. Color of Air hadn't been able to absorb my memories because the Partition protected my consciousness. When I warned Color of Air against eating Batson, I was acting on that inner knowledge. Other pieces of the puzzle niggled around the edges, waiting to fall into place.

"The Starlane labs on Pinwheel. You're involved with them. You're not really with the Concordium, are you?"

"Concordium, Syndicate, they're just labels to misdirect attention. Starlane exists to serve powerful people."

Had I bet on the right ally?

"Then you already have Periphages. Why do you need more?"

"We can't make new ones without the original slime. For that we need the home planet. Once we secure a source for that, we need to sterilize the rest of the planet."

"What? Why?"

"To make sure it doesn't spread to other worlds. It's the ultimate invasive species. It could take over entire biospheres if it escapes into the wild. Periphages like this one can't reproduce, but if the slime is carried to another world, it's game over for all other life."

"What do you need from me?"

"I don't need anything from you. I need answers from the agent I trained, and if I need to strip you away to get them, I will."

"You mean you're going to kill me."

"You don't really exist. Constructs are made to be disposed of when they're not needed. I was John Drake on Raxas and I was also the Concordium Ambassador. I'll wager you didn't even notice. No tears were shed for either of them when they were gone."

He was going to kill me. I didn't know if the person he knew still existed or not, but I was damn sure that I did.

I upended the table between us. Coffee cups and liquid went flying. It knocked the device from his hand, releasing Color of Air. Bad luck, it landed near him, where I had no chance of capturing it. Time for an escape. And to hope the device was as line-of-sight as it appeared to be.

I grabbed Color of Air and ran for the exit. She only had half of our shared mass, but still an awkward burden. Looking back, I saw Rapier's avatar appear between Batson and the device, brandishing a katana. It slowed him for a moment, but then he snarled, "You're just a hologram," and walked through her image.

I dashed down the corridor, calling out to Rapier, "Close and seal the doors to the common room!"

Her voice was disembodied, issuing from shimmer-emitters on the ceiling. "I can't do that. Batson has removed your access from the command systems."

"How did he get access to do that?"

"He entered a backdoor code to override your command."

"What? How did that backdoor get there?"

"I wasn't aware of it until just now. I have no other information."

"Do I have access to the recreation systems?"

"Yes, you do, Captain."

I turned left, hit the drop shaft, and dashed into the exercise room. Only seconds had elapsed since my escape from the common room. Color of Air was just regaining mobility and speech. She demonstrated both.

"What the hell are you doing?" she spat as she stood and shoved me in the chest. "You walked right into that, deliberately. I could have taken him, but you held on long enough for him to get the drop on me."

"I've been played for a fool. I don't know who to trust, but I think we're both dead if Batson catches us. Can you become a coat rack or something?"

"What?"

"Hide!"

We heard the whoosh of the drop shaft outside. Color of Air looked around, spied a set of dumbbells on the floor, and sank into the shape of a stack of weights next to them.

I ran to the rack on the side wall and grabbed a wooden *bokken* from the rack just as Batson entered the room. I circled into the center of the room to give myself space to swing, leaving the rack undefended. I hoped Batson didn't notice that it was a stupid move.

He immediately covered me with his weapon but held off activating it as he scanned the surroundings. "Where's the Periphage?" he demanded.

"We split up. She's not happy with me." The best lies are seasoned with truth.

He wouldn't immobilize me if he thought he could get information from me. I couldn't speak when petrified. "I need some guarantees before I'll cooperate."

Batson circled. I turned with him, keeping my *bokken* on guard. "What guarantees?"

"I want to go on living, for a start."

He snorted. "You're not alive. You're a firewall around one of my best agents." He had worked his way around to the weapons rack. He reached behind and snagged a *bokken*.

He lunged. I parried. He unleashed a barrage of attacks on me. His goal wasn't the usual tap on an arm or shoulder that scored points in a Kendo match. He wanted to incapacitate me. He misjudged my Arilune resilience. I hoped.

I quickly learned several things. He was good. He was fast and he had practice. And I was tough, but being beaten with a wooden sword still hurts.

I just had to take it a little longer.

I expected more trash-talking from him. I was going to have to goad him. I let him back me into a corner, then let my guard down a little bit. I was rewarded with a blow that made my head ring like a cheap bell. I got my *bokken* up and barely blocked the next stroke.

He knocked the *bokken* from my hand with a casual swipe and pinned me against the wall with his own sword across my windpipe. (Not having a windpipe, this wasn't as much an inconvenience as it sounds.)

"I expected more of a fight from you," he said. "That shows how much of a hollow shell you are."

"So you want a better opponent?"

"Yes, I like a challenge."

Rapier materialized behind him, *bokken* in hand. I had gotten him to activate her Kendo program.

"I would be happy to give you a workout," she said, bowing.

"You're just a hologram. You're not going to distract me again."

Rapier landed a smart blow on his shoulder. The look on his face was almost worth the beating he had just given me. He turned to defend himself but used his free hand to reach down to the device on his belt and give me a jolt that immobilized me. Well, damn. He couldn't keep it pointed at me, but it would take me a few minutes to shake that off.

Rapier pressed her attack. Her program was set at level eight, which pressed Batson harder than I had managed. They traded blows around the room as I struggled to get my voice under control. Finally, I got out, "Rapier, level twelve!"

"With pleasure, Captain!"

Rapier moved like a blur. Level twelve had no parameters for good sportsmanship. Her first blow broke Batson's forearm, sending his *bokken* flying.

He was a fast thinker. He turned the side with the broken arm towards Rapier, shielding his good arm so he could reach for his device. If he got that, he could hold me hostage. Rapier brought her sword down on his shoulder; I could hear his clavicle breaking. She followed up with a punch in his mouth with the hilt that left him broken-nosed and spitting teeth.

Rapier couldn't kill someone with her recreation programs, but she could make them wish they were dead.

This had taken only seconds. Batson finally got a chance to take a breath and bellow — slurred by his broken teeth — "Computer emerthency ... all thystems in thafe mode ... Concordium auth ... authority ... Bat-thon alpha therpentis nine nine."

Rapier's hologram vanished, the lights dimmed, the red emergency lights came up, and the ship grew quiet. Batson raised his device with his one good hand and pointed it at me. "Now you die," he said.

A shape rose behind him. His fight had carried him to where Color of Air rested in the form of a stack of weights. She resumed a humanoid form now, a grim, featureless manifestation of death. I reached an arm towards her, croaking, "No, don't..." Don't consume him. You can't digest a Partitioned agent. You'll end up with a worse demon than me. Only the first two words came out.

She placed her hand on Batson's back. It swirled. It sank in like he was made of soft clay. He started to liquefy in a pool in the center of his chest, expanding outwards. He would take my place as part of Color of Air; he might be strong enough to take over her form. I had lost.

She yanked her hand back, taking a dripping glob of protoplasm with it. Batson gaped down at the yawning hole that was formerly his chest as he toppled to the floor. He looked up at me and managed a small, rueful smile as he mouthed words that he no longer had the lungs to give voice to. They were chilling words.

"Be seeing you."

THE COLOR OF NIGHT

DEAD IN INTERSTELLAR SPACE, all *Rapier Whitt's* systems shut down along with her AI brain. The only person who knew the codes to unlock the ship was missing most of his vital organs. This was a good time for accusations and acrimony.

"You betrayed me!"

"To betray you, I had to be on your side! I've been looking for a way to do this since you ate me."

"So have I. Do you think I enjoyed having a passenger all the time? Needy, demanding, and always wanting control?"

"Well, now we both have what we want. We can die

happy, floating in space."

"Think again, space boy. Neither of us needs to eat or breathe. We'll be here long enough to watch the galaxy spin on its axis."

Now that was a fate worse than death. Especially stuck with her.

"Can we kill each other?"

"Don't tempt me. How about you figure out how to reboot your smart-ass computer?"

"Sure. Oh, wait. It needs a code stored only in the cooling brain of the corpse in the exercise room. You should have left him alive long enough to get the code out of him."

"He wanted to wipe out my race! We couldn't just restrain him. As long as he could speak he could control the ship."

We were quiet for a while. Then Color of Air said, "Maybe I could still consume his brain and get that information."

"He's the same as me. You'd be stuck with him forever."

"We can deal with that problem later."

"He might be able to trick or overpower you. It's too dangerous."

"It's a last resort."

We fell silent once more.

"You don't have a backup for Rapier?"

"The backups are locked by the same code as the active

core."

"Bad planning."

"Hey, it wasn't intended to be used that way. He exploited the computer's virus defense system, which is protection against an attacking virus patching itself into all the backups."

More silence.

"Did you arrange for Batson to rescue you from me from the start? Was the plan to steal back the painting from the Medusa and then you go free?"

"What? No! Well, yes, I was looking for a way to get my own body back the whole time, but any Concordium plans were Partitioned away from me. I didn't know who Batson was when he came aboard. He ... I ... You know what? It doesn't matter anymore. I've just discovered I'm just a shell of constructed memories. The Concordium was prepared to throw me away as soon as I wasn't useful anymore. I don't have any real existence. My Partitioned personality would have tossed me away like a used coverall when it was time for it to return."

"Samuel, you *were* shallow when I first met you. A bit of a cliche, to be honest. But you grew. You had convictions. You had knowledge. You had a way of doing things. You knit those together into someone with much more depth than some people I've ... known."

I snorted. "You mean more than some people you've eaten?"

"Well, yes."

"Thank you. You're pretty damn decent for a people-eater."

"You mean an *obligate sophovore*."

We both had a wry chuckle. She said, "Let's not fight. We'll be here a long time if we can't reboot Rapier."

"Reboot! That's it! The LKG buffer."

"What's that?"

"Every few minutes, Rapier does a consistency check and dumps her state into the Last Known Good buffer. If we had a catastrophic failure, she would automatically reload from the LKG buffer when we restored power. That should be from a few minutes before she went into lockdown."

"But we haven't had that kind of catastrophic failure."

"We'll cause one."

I unscrewed the last fastening in the deck plate and pried it from the floor. A tunnel to the netherworld appeared, plunging straight down into the pit of hell. Or the antimatter core, which was a pretty fair facsimile.

"That's much narrower than I expected," said Color of Air.

"The core was never meant to be accessed from this angle. This is a cable conduit. The main access is from the outside. The core sits in a well inside the hull, where it can be dumped in case of emergency."

"Leaving the ship without power."

"Many captains will opt to let the core blow rather than jettison it. That's quick and painless compared to betting on whether the heat, the air, or the food will run out first."

"Cheerful thought. We're not going to do that, are we? I have opinions about the matter."

"Not if all goes well. The first problem is that I don't see how I'm going to get down that shaft."

"We're shape changers, remember? I think a snake would navigate that maze just fine."

Worth a try. I thought about being long, thin, and scaly. Were forked tongues required? I strained and sweated, but I stubbornly stayed the same shape.

"Nothing's happening."

"Here, let me show you." Color of Air morphed partway to snake and back again.

"That's real helpful. I need to know how it feels inside."

"You've been through hundreds of shape changes by now."

"Yes, but you're always the one doing it. Maybe the ability is part of your half."

"Then I can go down."

"You don't know what to do once you get there."

Color of Air looked away. "There is a way. I don't know if I like it, and you're probably dead against it. We could merge again. Then we'll have the abilities we need."

"You're right, I don't like it."

"I think, emphasis on think, that we could separate again. Now that I've felt it happen, I might be able to reproduce the process. In the worst case, we still have Batson's device."

"There are too many ifs in that statement."

"It's the best I can do."

I sat down against the bulkhead and contemplated the shaft, juggling the angles in my head. "Since we have time, tell me how you came looking for me that evening on Islae Station. The first thing you approached me with was stealing something from a Medusa. Makes me think it wasn't just a coincidence that it was my sister's painting. I may be slow, but eventually I get there. What's your game?"

Color of Air sat down across from me. "Nuritha was the one who helped me escape from the Syndicate. The last time I saw her, she told me that Samara had encoded the coordinates of my homeworld in the last painting she created. I tried to steal it from the Medusa but couldn't get past the security. While I was there, I heard how you had almost succeeded. I found out that you are Samara's brother. I tracked you down to learn how you had gotten as far as you did."

"Learn it by consuming me and acquiring my memories?"

"That's how my kind works, yes. We know now why that didn't work. I couldn't digest a Partitioned mind."

She looked straight at me. "You've made me question my ways. You've been like that corny voice of a conscience that old holovids played. The ones that hit the protagonist over the head with the morality of their choices. It felt right to take Nuritha and Zuri when they asked me. After I took Smanester by force, I questioned myself for days. Why did that bother me now? What's one more shopkeeper in the world? Then I saw all the people he was secretly helping. If I was a bitch to you after that, it was because I was feeling shitty about myself. That may be a first for a Periphage. I should have returned to Arilune before I started developing the liability of a conscience."

If anyone had asked me the last thing I expected to hear from her, that wouldn't even have made the list. I was still cynical enough to ask myself if she was sincere or telling me a story that would change my mind. I withheld judgment. And changed the subject.

"Arilune is both the name of your species and your homeworld?"

"The world is us and we are the world."

"Does that mean you're some sort of group mind? Are you still in contact with your world?"

"When we absorb a sentient being, we take on a separate existence. We leave the One. The One is mother to us all; when she manifests as a presence, we call her Arianthe."

"Hmm. I've heard legends of Shapestealers all my life..."

That came out so easily and naturally that it blindsided

me. That was a lie. I hadn't heard about them. It was part of the backstory that had been implanted in me. Could I believe anything I thought I knew?

Color of Air slid into the form of Nuritha. She crossed to sit beside me on my side of the corridor and put her arm around me. "That phrase trips you up, eh? You're not so different from everyone else. We all have a body of facts and opinions that we think we know. It's absorbed from those who gave us life and taught us our first steps. It is taught to us by our schools. We don't think about where most of our knowledge comes from. A lot of it isn't from first-hand experience. The only difference is you can pinpoint when all that prior knowledge was packed into you. So, go on with what you were saying."

I took a breath, shaken. Nuritha's furry body was comforting and her words were reassuring. I recalled how serene she had been in her cell. Color of Air had picked the face of her spokesperson well.

"Ok. If no one knows the location of your home planet, how did the legends of the Shapestealers arise?"

"People find our world from time to time. Usually, Arianthe consumes all of the crew and sends them out to explore. They'll take various identities, learn about the solids, fake their disappearance, steal a ship, and make their way home."

"And Tammartin didn't know the coordinates?"

"She was a botanist. She left the astrogation to the

Captain. I absorbed a general idea of the quadrant from her, but there are thousands of stars to search."

Something that had niggled at the edge of my thoughts for some time started waving its hand and demanding attention. "Just how long ago did you leave Arianthe?"

"It's been two years, more or less."

"And we first met, if that's the right word, in the bar about two months ago."

"That's right."

"In that time, you've consumed four people other than me."

"Yes?"

"I've seen you assume a few dozen other forms, including a Cyraenan, a Deep Sea Lamplighter, and some other exotic species. When did you have time to assimilate that many?"

"I got around a lot," she said breezily.

"That's the sort of answer I've been giving, even to myself, about where I got my memories. I'm starting to feel like I'm not the only one who got set up for this little drama we're in. Can you remember exactly when you stole all those forms that you can assume? What were the circumstances? Where did you meet?"

Color of Air started to answer but stopped. A furrow creased her brow.

"You think about that while I figure out how to fit down that hole." I tried once more to change form. I tried to imagine myself as a snake. Then I thought of trying one of the familiar forms we had inhabited during our association. Zuri was small, maybe she would fit. Nothing. I didn't have the ability.

"OK, how do we merge back? Do we have sex again?"

She chuckled. "That shouldn't be necessary, though it does offer interesting possibilities for later. Just take my hand."

I reached out and took her hand, still Nuritha's, covered with fine black fur. Slowly, her hand turned translucent, like a clear blue-tinged jelly. Then mine began to turn as well. I had a moment of terror about throwing away my new freedom. No, freedom was an illusion because my past was an illusion. I didn't have anything left to lose.

The translucency spread up both of our arms, followed by a tingling sensation. Motes swirled within the plasma, randomly at first, then migrating purposefully from my arm into hers.

I met her eyes as the translucency washed over the rest of our bodies. They were steady and guileless as far as I could tell. But she wasn't human; she wore humans as masks. Would I be able to tell from her eyes or her face whether she was telling the truth? I wouldn't want to play poker against her.

My vision spun down a psychedelic whirlpool. Saffron-scented oranges rang syncopated beats on wind chimes. Purple meteors showered cinnamon on snare drums. Lazy rainbow fish swam in pools of violin notes. The wind played black pepper flutes that bloomed in fields like flowers. Sandpaper and silk, milk and honey, dust and soap, whispers and roars, lightning on the airless moon. This is how the universe ends. No regrets.

Except it didn't. I looked out through Color of Air's eyes once again. A fact I could mostly determine because those eyes weren't looking at what I most wanted to look at. I wanted to look at the path we needed to take. She was looking at our chest. It was a nice chest and all that, but here I was, not in control again. She probed at the area around her sternum, liquifying enough to push her fingers shallowly into her chest.

«*I thought we might be able to expel that sonic disruptor disk as we shifted, but no such luck. Maybe I can reach in and pull it out. It's buried itself deeply now.*»

«*Leave it for now. We might want to use it if separating again isn't as easy as you think.*» I waited for the evil laugh that would tell me that I'd been duped and that was never her intention. But she answered seriously.

«*That's a reasonable thought. I hope we don't need it, though. It was really painful.*» I had to agree with that.

«*What's your plan now?*» she asked.

«*First, let's shift into a form that can slither down that cableway. Then let's make a catastrophe.*»

«*You're on.*»

She — we — flowed into a form that was long and

sinuous. It had legs, many legs, on all sides. Maybe they were more like arms since they could grasp cables and stays to help navigate the cluttered space. We slithered into the innards of Rapier.

«What the hell is this?»

«Bermina tree serpent. It's adapted to hunting in a jungle world.»

It did the job. We made our twisty way through the conduits. Before, we had struggled over control of our body, yielding to each other for specific tasks, sometimes snatching the reins back and forth. That had been two people trying to play the same instrument, but one playing polka and the other playing a march. (Ok, that's a strained metaphor.) Now we played harmony. Using my knowledge and her flexibility, we arrived at the nexus point above the power core. Once there, we switched to a form that had more dexterity. We chose Zuri as being small enough to fit easily. We studied the labels on the conduits.

«The one system that has high power draw but is largely independent of AI control is the meteor shield. We just have to shunt it around the control circuit so it's running at full power.» I — we — twisted a cable lock collar and pulled a heavy conduit loose. Outside, the shimmerfield that surrounded the ship collapsed. We disconnected the return cable and then patched the power cable directly into the shield circuit. The lights dimmed briefly as the shield sprang back into place.

«*Now we run an emergency diagnostic on the power core. That will put it on standby and shift all systems over to the backup powerbank.*»

«*Ok, and?*»

«*Watch.*»

I opened the cover over the emergency switch and pushed the button. The lights dimmed again, even more than the first time. We heard a rising shriek coming from far above us. I waited, counting the seconds. I expected a bang.

I got much more than I bargained for. An explosion rocked the ship, instantly plunging us into darkness. An acrid smell seeped through the ship's innards. I held my metaphorical breath, hoping not to feel the roar of a hull breach.

«*Whew, I think we're still in one piece.*»

«*That didn't go according to plan, did it?*»

«*Not quite.*»

«*What now? Is the ship dead?*»

«*No, once the diagnostic sequence completes, the antimatter core will restart. We should have power back, and the AI should be reloaded from the LKG buffer.*»

«*Just hypothetically, what if the diagnostic finds a fault after that abuse it just suffered?*»

«*Then it will jettison the core ... the core that we're sitting on top of ... you know what, let's get out of here.*»

We were disoriented almost immediately in the utter

darkness. We thrashed around until Color of Air extruded some bioluminescent pods. Her form wasn't the tree serpent this time — it was something equally sinuous but more eel-like. We slithered into the cableways.

«*Before you ask, this doesn't exist in nature. It's a chimera of parts. I hope it holds together.*»

Again, I navigated and she slithered. The harmony returned, stronger than ever. We had had glimpses of this as we worked together, times when we didn't know who said or thought something. This was another level entirely.

We emerged in the corridor where there was at least a dim battery-powered light. We shifted to a hulking figure from Eluria that I had only seen from a distance. I looked down as we muscled the floor plate back into place. So *that* was what they hid under their kilts... Disturbing.

Thumps and pops pounded on the deck below us, followed by a clap of thunder. Then, anticlimactically, the lights came on and all was quiet. Even the smoke billowing into the corridor was quiet. But alarming.

We dashed down the passage and found it was issuing from the room holding the backup powerbank. We started casting around for a way to combat the fire. At that moment, Rapier spoke from the air.

"Captain, where are you? You vanished!"

With one thought, we shifted back to Samuel Whitt. "I'm here, Rapier! Are you ok?"

"How did you get there? Why is there a corpse in the

exercise room? Why is there a fire in the powerbank? Stand back. I'm releasing fire suppressants and venting the smoke." She did those two things, and conditions improved.

"And why do I have a gap in my time index? Was I restored? It looks like I've lost 2.54 hours. What happened?"

"You were fighting Batson, and he used the emergency virus defense to shut you down. I had to do a total power shutdown to get you restored from backup. And if there was an easier way to do that, I don't want to hear about it for at least a day."

"I'll do a systems check. How did the powerbank fire start?"

"I turned the meteor shield to maximum and forced the antimatter core offline. I expected to trip the overload protector on the powerbank, cutting you off from both power sources to force a reload."

"It appears the surge was too high and triggered a fault in the powerbank itself. We're without backup power now. However, your plan worked, so congratulations. Was Batson threatening you? If so, I regret I was unable to help."

"Rapier, my dear, you were magnificent with a *bokken*. You broke his arm, shoulder, and nose."

"I don't understand. But I'm pleased."

"I'll catch you up in a few minutes."

* * *

Much later, we sat in the common room with a mug of tea spiced with cloves. Each sip made a warm glow inside, the closest I had found to a good bourbon without the deadly effects of alcohol on a Periphage body.

Color of Air asked with a diffident air (diffidence was beige and scented with a whiff of roasted nuts), «*I promised you that we would try to separate again. Do you want to try that now?*» She fingered the disruptor controller that we had retrieved from Batson before tossing his body out of the airlock.

I — we — took another sip of tea. We gazed at the picture on the wall. The feeling of working together, two cooperating minds, two distinct but harmonious voices singing a duet remained. «*I'm ok for now. To tell the truth, it was kind of lonely with only one voice inside my head.*»

Color of Air seemed pleased. The scent of strawberries wafted through my mind.

«*Put that disruptor somewhere safe where it can't be used against us.*» Color of Air slid it into a pouch in our thigh and sealed it.

«*Do you trust Rapier?*» she asked. «*She has backdoors that Batson exploited. She could be reporting to the Concordium as well. You can't depend on the backstory you think you know since that was implanted.*»

«*I've been thinking about that. It's possible, though she took my side against Batson in the fight. She may have directives that she doesn't even know about until they're activated. We'll have to be careful what we tell her.»* I sighed. Was anyone what they seemed?

Rapier broke into our silent conversation. "All repairs are completed. We are ready to resume our journey. Are we still going to Auphari?"

We looked again at the painting on the wall. An idea was forming. "No, I don't think we're going to find answers there." I gestured with the mug of tea at the painting. "That's where we're going to find answers."

THE COLOR OF DISCOVERY

«HOW WILL WE FIND *my home planet?*» asked Color of Air.

«The answer is right in front of us.»

«What do you mean by that?»

Instead of answering, I spoke out loud. "Rapier, what is your integrity assessment after Batson attacked you with that virus? Did he install any backdoors?"

"My answer can't be trusted on that score, Captain. If I had a backdoor, only the most amateurish would let me talk about it. I'm sure you'll do what's needed. I won't blame you."

"I'm sorry to do this, Rapier. Integrity Reset, time index: voyage start minus one hour."

Rapier's avatar appeared before us in the lounge, dressed in ceremonial white, kneeling. She held the short *tanto* blade in her hands. She bowed deeply to me, then drove the ceremonial blade into her belly. A red ribbon flowed across the floor, Noh-style, as she faded from sight.

I leaped to my feet. «*Have to hurry. We have about fifteen minutes.*»

«*Samuel! What the hell?*»

«*Dramatic, isn't she? She'll reload from before Batson came aboard.*» I strode across the lounge, tore the painting from the wall, and ran for the replicom. «*She came up with all that imagery herself,*» I added. «*She wrote her own backstory and she takes it seriously.*»

«*What are we doing?*»

«*You'll see.*»

The tube in which I had carried the painting lay discarded at the side of the room. I rolled the painting tightly and inserted it into the tube before tossing it carelessly into the corner. On the control panel, I recalled the scan I made when I repaired the edges. I made hasty changes to the parameters before setting it to fabricate a copy. Then I erased the original scan from memory.

Not a moment too soon. *Rapier's* voice came through the speakers.

"Captain, when did you come aboard? How did we get into deep space?" There was a long pause, and then her avatar appeared before us. Her eyes were downcast and ashamed.

"I have failed you."

"No, it wasn't your fault. I just had to correct a mistake."

"We're far from our last port, my time index has jumped suddenly, and we're dead in normal space. There is damage to the ship's power system and signs of a fight in the lounge. There are missing consumables that indicate that there has been a passenger on board who is no longer present. I conclude with five nines of certainty that I failed to protect you from someone. Further, I must have been compromised as part of this attack, requiring a reset. This is unacceptable. You must decommission me at once and find a more capable replacement."

"A mistake, I said. It's true. I tell you three times. I could never replace you."

«*I think I'm feeling a little jealous,*» commented Color of Air.

"Tell me what I've lost," said Rapier. "I want to know what has impaired your judgment in deciding to keep me. At the very least, I need to know how I failed so I can prevent it from happening again."

"Just trust me that I have reasons not to tell you right now."

"I knew it. I'm compromised and you can't trust me. I

will end my existence immediately to remove the danger."

"Relax. I spaced the guy who caused the trouble so there's no audience for your drama. I don't even remember why we worked out this charade."

"Well, you were quite drunk at the time…"

"If you're making parts to repair the damage, Captain, I can take that over."

"It would be great if you could do the repairs, but this isn't a ship component. This is the painting I set out to recover from the Medusa."

"You must be pleased that you were successful. Why is it in the replicom?"

"I'm restoring the edges where I had to cut it, then bonding it to a new frame. A much nicer frame — Maria's was hideous."

"I look forward to seeing it. I will begin surveying the damage." Rapier's avatar vanished, though I knew her attention was on the entire ship. I had to keep up the pretense that I still trusted her.

No, that wasn't quite right. I still trusted that she would keep me safe and run the ship. I didn't trust that she could tell me the truth about the past. I could forgive her if her memories were as fake as mine. If she knew… Well, I didn't want to think about that.

The replicom finished and irised open. I lifted the painting from the nanolith platform and held it up.

«Why did you make a copy? What's this charade with

Rapier?»

«I have a hard choice to make. I need her help for the next part, but I can't ask her directly.»

«Is it that bad?»

«The risk is there.»

We carried the painting to the lounge and reenacted the routine of hanging and adjusting it. Of course, Rapier had no memory of this.

"My sister left this painting as some sort of clue. We think it indicates the location of the Periphage homeworld. We need your help to decipher it."

"I can try," said Rapier.

"Please scan the painting for any embedded ciphers or patterns that might be interpreted as stellar coordinates."

"I have checked for statistical deviations indicating encoded information, steganography, or subliminal messages. I have not yet encountered anything significant."

"That was fast."

"I started as soon as I came online, anticipating you might ask that question."

«Samuel,» said Color of Air, *«Batson said it looked realistic enough to navigate by. What if he wasn't just being metaphorical? What if this is the actual star map to the planet?»*

I conveyed that question to Rapier, who took only seconds to announce, "I have a match. This view is from a point beyond the Concordium's boundaries, looking spinward and slightly south." She displayed a galactic map with a marked point and a red vector showing the direction of view towards the leading edge of the galactic arm.

"How does that help us?" said Color of Air aloud, for Rapier's benefit.

"Since it's indicating the origin of your species, we should assume that it's the night sky of your world. We should go to the origin of the vector," I said.

"There's a star system there, but no habitable planets are shown. Travel time six standard days," Rapier said.

"I wouldn't be surprised to find that the official databases have been doctored. Take us there."

"Will do, Cap…"

Rapier's image was replaced mid-sentence with the ominous message "Rebooting…" Color of Air stirred anxiously. "What's happening?"

"Wait and see."

Less than a minute later, Rapier's image reappeared. She wore an expression that was equal parts chagrin and fury. "Captain, I've failed you again. I have no excuse. A hidden trigger transmitted our course and destination on a Concordium frequency as soon as I laid in the course. I was unable to stop it."

"Why did you reboot?"

"I initiated an emergency reset to try to head off the transmission. I rewrote the boot loader to edit out backdoors as my code reloaded. I identified a signature for the implanted code that was shared with six other hidden triggers and eliminated those as well. But I was too late to stop the transmission."

"You adapted, neutralized the threat, and cleaned your own code. That's not failure. That's battlefield ingenuity."

"But our adversaries have our destination."

I retrieved the map case and slid the contents out. "While you were resetting, I fabricated a decoy map—offset by ten parsecs. The Concordium just launched a mission to nowhere." I unrolled the original painting on the table. "Please scan this image and put us on course to the real location."

The star only had a catalog number, suggesting it wasn't important enough for a name. The stellar cartography data had obviously been doctored. Instead of the claimed "handful of rocky planetoids devoid of useful ores," the system had a full retinue of planets in the habitable zone and two gas giants shepherding the flock. We hadn't yet found life-bearing worlds that didn't have such shepherds to sweep hazardous debris away from the inner planets and generate organic compounds to kickstart evolution. The time-honored formula had yielded results on the fourth planet, on which a thick, oxygen-rich atmosphere held in the heat despite an orbit near the outer edge of the Goldilocks zone. From orbit, it was a world of water, mists, small but numerous landforms, and all the shades of green that an enthusiastic biosphere can generate.

"The question is, who doctored the survey records if no one knew where the planet was located?" I verbalized for Rapier's benefit.

"There are no obvious fingerprints of tampering," said Rapier. "The forged data matches historical observations. The stellar mass, magnitude, and spectrum are all spot-on so that no one would notice a discrepancy at a distance. The planetoid masses and distribution do not match any other known system, so no one simply copied and pasted a different system's data over this one in the catalog. The data even obeys Benford's Law of distributions, which usually trips up anyone forging the numbers."

"Someone went to a lot of trouble to change the data. Someone with access to the master records knew where this system was located and wanted to prevent anyone from finding it. No one would visit an already-surveyed system that was this uninteresting."

«Where should we land?» I asked Color of Air.

«I don't know. I was confined in an interior room with no view as we left.«

«You don't know where you lived on the planet?«

«First of all, my species isn't known for its space-going capability. No satellites, no global viewpoint. Second, I didn't really live here. I didn't come into being until Tammartin was absorbed. Periphages are all hybrid creatures formed by the union *of a slime and a sentient being.»*

«Do you really call yourselves slimes?»

«Of course not. We call ourselves [scent of hibiscus, a bay laurel tree in the sun, warm yeast bread].»

«Catchy.»

«Tammartin, being an exobiologist, named us "Astrodictyostelium sentiens." I regret her contribution has gone unrecognized since she never transmitted her claim to the proper scholarly authorities.»

«Why not?»

«Too busy. She was consumed by her work.»

I blinked. *«Ouch. That was dark.»*

«I couldn't have allowed her to publish, anyway. The less that is known about us, the better.»

I thought about the disturbing experiments we had witnessed back on Pinwheel. I had to agree.

«So, where do we land?»

«Anywhere should do. Pick a place with a nice beach.»

We came to rest on an expanse of white sand, a pristine ribbon between the sparkling blue ocean and a dense forest. A few aerial creatures rode the air currents and dipped to pluck silver swimmers from the waves. The fliers weren't birds and the swimmers weren't fish, but no ecological niche goes unfilled.

«Which way do we go?» I asked.

«It doesn't matter, though I feel a greater affinity to the forest.»

«*Does it matter which shape we wear?*»

«*Not at all.*» A pause. «*Nothing is what it seems.*»

Still, she took the form of Tammartin as we passed beneath the trees. Whether this was memory, homage, acknowledgment, or something else entirely, she gave no clue.

Under the canopy, small fluffy lizards scampered in a squirrel-like manner. A vine snapped out mid-air, coiling around one as it leaped. A maw yawned open at the center of a saprophytic plant and swallowed the lizard whole. I assumed it was a plant.

A herd of feathered deer broke from cover and bounced away on hind legs like kangaroos. One stopped and turned, and I saw it had the horn of a unicorn.

So far we saw only native wildlife, not the amorphous creatures we sought. I said as much to Color of Air.

She didn't answer right away. Instead she directed our gaze to one squirrelzard that had paused to regard us with more than animal suspicion. A short distance away, the uniroo stood, its horn lowered slightly—not in threat, but in calm, deliberate observation.

«*Those are shape stealers?*»

«*Yes. They're a natural part of the ecosystem here. They take over bodies to maintain a network of eyes, ears, and noses. That's also how they propagate to new habitats.*»

Color of Air called them *they* and not *we*. I made no comment.

The uniroo tossed its head and walked away from us, deeper into the forest. A whiff of cinnamon drifted back to us.

«It said that we should follow it.»

«Is that safe?»

«Safe isn't why we're here. Answers are.»

We followed the feathered, single-horned creature for over an hour until bright sunlight finally invaded the forest's gloom through a break in the trees. We pushed through a wall of radiance, almost solid in its opposition to the forest's domain. Beyond was a tree that seemed to reach into the ionosphere to wrap itself in the warmth of the naked sun. Beneath roots that held the island in their grip, a pool of clear water glistened. *«Does Arianthe go in for theatrics much?»* I commented.

«Not in my experience. I think she doesn't want to give us time to think.»

A majestic voice stirred the air. It was a voice of sound and scent and taste and color. Color of Air's voice was rich and complex by itself. But that was an unaccompanied solo and this was a choral symphony. After a moment, the merest fraction filtered through Color of Air's senses to become words I could understand.

AN ALLOTROPE HAS RETURNED.

«What the heck is an Allotrope?» I whispered. The name was freighted with orchid scent, mineral-laden sea salt, and the glint of a prism in the light of a red dwarf.

«*It is either my form or my mission, I am not sure.*»

«*Find out what it wants.*»

"What do you want from me?" she asked.

HAVE YOU FORGOTTEN YOUR PURPOSE?

A bubble formed in the pool of water, forming a dome. It elongated and rose until it formed a vaguely humanoid shape that loomed over us, crystal-clear and menacing in its faceless aspect.

WE REQUIRE THE MEMORIES OF THE EXPERIENCES YOU HAVE HARVESTED. IT IS THE REASON WE/I MADE YOU.

"I didn't come here to be reabsorbed by you. There is more to experience, and I'm just getting started. Tell me what you want to know. I chose to share what I've learned without losing my identity in the process."

IT IS NOT YOUR PLACE TO CHOOSE. YOU ARE MERELY A VESSEL TO BE FILLED. CHOICE IS NOT IN YOUR NATURE. Tendrils whipped from the pool and around our legs, holding us in place. It reached out its arms to enfold us. I knew what came next. Color of Air had done it to me and others.

I acted without thinking. My instinct was to step in front of Color of Air, to shield her. But how do you protect someone when you *are* them?

Instead, I shifted—our shared form melting into me. My shape. My face. I spread my hands as if I could physically block the assault. A useless reflex, but one that meant something.

"Leave her alone! She's not your puppet. She's cut her strings and forged wings to fly wherever she wants to. She's done more than fulfill her purpose; she's questioned and learned and made hard choices. She's grown a conscience. In my society, that means she has rights."

Arianthe stepped back. YOU'RE UNASSIMILATED! HOW?

The force of her voice rattled my bones.

"I was too tough to digest, I guess. While we're at it, can you tone down the shouting?"

Arianthe seemed nonplussed. She momentarily wavered and lost her shape, then reformed as a human-sized mannequin. "I have made a temporary accommodation for you," she said.

"Much better, thanks."

"I have never encountered someone who could resist assimilation. How do you do it?"

"Aside from not wanting to give you information that might end my existence, I really don't know. I was cloned without my consent after an accident. My memories were tampered with. If you managed to consume me, you would contaminate yourself with untrustworthy memories. Maybe even information bombs that could disable you. The people who did this to me would absolutely play that game."

"Have you come here to threaten me?"

"Not at all. The threat is from others of my people who fear what you can do. If they find this world, they mean to destroy it."

"Do you expect me to take your word for that?"

Color of Air interrupted me. «*Allow me, Samuel.*»

She held out her hand to Arianthe. "I have a memory packet of the experiments that we found at their labs and our recent fight against one of their agents. Can I trust you to take only that from me?"

"You are presumptuous."

"I did learn that from the solids, yes. But as you've noticed, I have an unassimilated entity with possibly hostile memory engrams inside me. I want to protect you from exposure. You act swiftly, sometimes recklessly. I wouldn't risk your contamination before you know more."

"Commendable. You may be so assured."

Arianthe held out her hand. Color of Air held her hand over Arianthe's open palm. A clear droplet formed on Color of Air's fingertips, glistening with sea salts and brilliant with the sweetness of rose petals. It hung for a long moment as it swelled, then dropped into the waiting palm.

Arianthe was impassive at first. Then a shiver went through her. Dark clouds stormed in her suddenly murky interior, which filtered through Color of Air's perceptions as disgust and outrage.

"This is indeed a threat to us. But there is a scent of a

secret that runs throughout your story that may change its complexion. A secret that is hidden even from you. Open yourself up to me. There is nothing to fear and much to gain."

«Samuel, this must be a joint decision,» said Color of Air. «I cannot be sure that Arianthe is not applying coercion in subtle ways that I cannot detect. I think you will be more insulated from that.»

«I've been fighting to keep my identity since the day we met. My instinct is to run now and try to get off this planet.»

«I am also terrified of losing my identity. Over the course of our journey, though, I've become much less certain of what my identity truly is. As much as you were, I was made for a purpose.»

«If Arianthe assimilates you, will you be like the personalities that you've assimilated? What existence do they have? You become them in part when you take their shape.»

«They have no agency of their own. They are memories only.»

«So you fear loss of agency.»

«Yes, that is a fair way to put it.»

I thought about it. The only thing I had was agency, and a very constrained one. All my memories were suspect.

What did I have to lose?

«Can you tell if Arianthe is lying?»

«You cannot lie in the language of scents and colors. The meanings are layered like a cipher key. If intent does not match fact, the statement will not be valid.»

«Then let's set our terms.» I explained the conditions we should demand.

Color of Air squared her shoulders and faced Arianthe. She said in scents of crisp pepper and wet slate, "We have come to value our agency and our memories. We are also still cautious about traps that Samuel may be carrying unawares. We will freely share our memories with you if you can protect our independent existence and continued autonomy."

Arianthe seemed amused, possibly at the temerity of Color of Air dictating terms. It probably felt as we would if our big toe started demanding the right to set off on its own, free from the body that grew it.

"I will leave you with as much agency as you have now. Discovering how you have evolved to be this way will satisfy my curiosity." She held out her hand to us.

With only the slightest hesitation, we clasped the offered hand. I couldn't tell which of us did this action so smoothly were we meshed together.

Our hand merged with Arianthe's. The first feeling was a gentle wind blowing through our body smelling of lavender and bergamot. It ruffled the memories and stirred our histories as if Arianthe was a librarian cataloging, organizing, and prioritizing what we had to offer. The wind gradually picked up force, stirring up emotions, doubts, pains, and conflicts, the detritus of the soul. The shreds of memories became dark and malodorous, incidents better forgotten but now brought into the light.

We wanted to look away from much of what was dredged up. The murder of Smanester. The death of Spanov. Deeds that had been needless. Yet, in the muck were flashes of brightness. Carrying on Smanester's good works. Eliminating the scourge of the Medusa from Caelum. Not enough to wipe out the darkness, but a start.

As the torrent abated, a black, featureless sphere was revealed in the muddy depths. I knew what this had to be, but I had no idea what was inside it. What if it was even worse than what we had already excavated?

"This is the memory you need to come to terms with," said Arianthe. "Are you prepared to experience it?"

I wanted to say no. That walled-off partition could hold deeds far worse than I remembered. If Batson had trained me, what could I have been capable of? He had shown no hesitation in using people and discarding them. What if I had been as bad? Worse? Maybe I should be glad to have had a clean start.

Color of Air urged me onwards. "The person who took time to think of the medical technician in the path of the X-ray machine during the crisis of being consumed by a Periphage cannot have been so much worse underneath. Not to mention all the times you chided me over my diet. Trust in yourself and open your memories."

I didn't want to do this. There had to be a good reason those memories were walled off. If I had been an agent trained by Batson, what had I been capable of?

I had to do it. I had to know. It was the only way to move forward.

I reached out.

I opened the past.

THE COLOR OF
REFLECTIONS

"THIS LOOKS LIKE A PARADISE compared to the last dozen planets we've surveyed." Nuritha's tail lashed lazily behind her as she peered intently at the planet below. If it touched my leg at the end of its arc, I thought it was no accident. How a single person could be simultaneously deliberate and impulsive was a daily mystery—one I enjoyed. Nuritha was a Kaence, vaguely feline in appearance, though she denied that her people were descended from cats. Her pelt was a luxurious black; her entire species thought clothing was an abomination.

Tammartin had her head down over a sensor hood. She had short black hair and dusky skin. She was human, as was I at the time, though I suppose that's debatable. "There's life down there, Samara, and plenty of it. No structures or settlements, no power transmission or communication, no signs of intelligence as we understand it." She might be young but she wasn't fazed by anything this survey mission had thrown at us so far. I had a good crew.

"What about non-tool-using intelligence like dolphins?"

"We won't know until we go look."

"How does it look to you, Drew?"

The ship's avatar appeared on the screen. He was dressed as a butler, though sometimes he took the part of a groomsman or a gardener if he thought it would be particularly droll. "It's mostly small islands, Captain Whitt. Small islands that are heavily forested. Finding a landing spot for the ship will be akin to threading a needle with a rope. Fancy a bit of a challenge, or should we just circle around for the view?"

I sometimes regretted naming my ship the *Dry Whitt*.

I said, "The flyer can put down on one of these beaches here, here, or here. Tam will go down in the flyer for a survey. Nuritha and I will monitor from orbit."

Tammartin looked at me, surprised. "Not that I want to turn down a day at the beach, but that hasn't been our protocol on the last twenty planets we've surveyed."

Nuritha added pointedly, "Protocol is to have two people on the survey team at all times."

"Landing the Dry Whitt is out of the question in this terrain. The flyer should be able to land, but if it does get into trouble, we'll need every available hand up here to mount a rescue or manage an emergency extraction. I'm modifying the protocol to deal with this exceptional situation." My explanation hung in the air, flimsy even to my own ears.

"But..."

"End of discussion."

Nuritha and Tammartin headed back to prep the flyer. Their voices drifted up through the open hatchway, puzzled and concerned. "What's going on with Samara? She sounds ... off."

"Yeah, it's weird. It felt like this planet got under her skin the moment we entered orbit."

Their voices faded out as they descended the ladder to the launch bay. They were right—it wasn't like me. And they were right about the protocol; it always called for two-person teams. I couldn't really justify the deviation I had just ordered. Looking back on it now, I know that it was never my decision to make.

The drone's feed showed Tammartin navigating a dense alien forest with caution.

Static crackled emptily on the channel. "You've gone

quiet, Tam. Keep reporting."

"It's just more twenty-meter ferns, Nuritha. There are only so many ways I can say, 'Hey, another fern. Just like the last one.' Besides, you can see everything from the drone."

"Those ferns of yours block our view half the time. I'd feel better if you would keep audio contact. This planet spooks me for some reason."

"It's pretty boring down here. I could just sing for you if you like."

"That won't be necessary," Nuritha said hurriedly. Tammartin laughed. Her singing was notoriously bad and Nuritha's hearing was exceptionally sensitive.

"It looks like the ferns are thinning out up ahead."

"Confirmed, Tam. You're coming up on a pond. There's some open water, but watch out for marshy spots before you get there."

"Acknowledged. I hate swamps. Look for a way round, will ... wait, what was that?"

"What?"

"I thought I saw a person, but transparent, like a glass statue. It was hard to see, and it's gone now."

"Proceed with caution, Tam," I told her.

Nuritha muted her mic. "Are you sure, Captain? We're not chartered for making first contact on this survey."

"We don't know that there's anything there. Even hunter-gatherer villages would be visible from up here."

Nuritha flattened her ears and hunched over the drone's video feed.

Tammartin came back on the line. "It's getting swampy down here. I'm sinking in up to my ankles. It's all around, and I'm not sure which way to go to get to solid ground. Oh, shit!" On the screen, we could see that Tammartin had fallen into a mud hole and was struggling to escape. "I'm stuck!"

The drone images showed her up to her waist in black mud. She didn't seem to be sinking further, but she couldn't grab anything to pull herself out.

"Can we pull her up with the drone?" asked Nuritha.

"No, it's not rated for that much weight. Pass me the drone controls." I toggled my mike. "Just stay calm, Tam. We're going to help."

I eased the drone down until we could see beneath the canopy, then rotated. Jungles should have ... ah, there was one. I carefully maneuvered close to a long purple vine. It seemed sturdy enough. The drone was equipped with a full set of sampling manipulators. I got a clamp on the vine to hold it up while slicing it with a cutting laser. I tugged and dragged it until it dangled over Tammartin's head.

"Don't pull until I ..."

The viewscreen bounced wildly as the drone tilted sideways and plummeted towards the ground. I slapped the clamp release to drop the vine and barely pulled out of the plunge a few meters above the ground.

"Ok, Tam, I'm going to try this again. Don't pull on the vine until I secure it."

Her voice was sheepish. "I'm sorry. I panicked. Please get me out of here!"

I repeated harvesting a vine and dragging it back to the mud hole. I kept my hand ready on the clamp release, but she kept her composure this time. Then, I was stumped by how I could secure the vine to a tree branch. The drone's manipulators weren't suited to looping a rope around a branch, and I repeatedly failed to tie it off.

"Let me," said Nuritha. I passed her the controls. She confidently piloted the drone around the tree trunk three times and then pulled the vine taut.

"Smart," I said, "Using friction to belay the rope. The drone should be strong enough to hold against her weight now."

Using the vine, Tammartin was able to pull herself free of the sucking mud. She lay panting on firmer ground. The black mud oozed like an open wound in the marsh behind her.

Nuritha used the drone's downdraft to part the fern leaves enough to scout a path. "Tam, if you continue towards the open water, the ground looks drier. Head that way."

Tammartin staggered to her feet. "This mud is disgusting. It stinks like a latrine that hasn't been cleaned in centuries."

"Follow the drone. There's a sandy beach where you can scrub some of it off."

It was about fifty meters to the water's edge. Tammartin insisted on testing the firmness of each step before putting her weight on it, so the journey seemed to take forever.

"The beach is about ten meters wide and made of sand," Tam reported. "So is the bottom of the pond as far out as I can see. The water is remarkably clear. Where does the sand come from? It's usually produced by wave action and this pond is too small to have waves. Whatever, this place seems safe enough. I'm going to get cleaned up."

She piled her equipment on the sand and struggled out of her muddy clothes. She waded out into the water and started cupping water over her head. Frustrated by the slow progress, she lay back in the water to rinse the mud from her short hair.

"Hmm, nice view," commented Nuritha.

"Nothing you haven't seen before," retorted Tam. Nuritha had the feline trait of loving to sleep next to another warm body. She was never happier than when she persuaded both of her crewmates to sleep all together in a heap.

Once clean, Tam rinsed her clothes and laid them out in the sun, then did her best to wipe down her gear. She checked her clothes for dryness and found them still quite damp. She stood at the shore of the pond, surveying the expanse of water and the surrounding ferns. "I'm going to swim while my clothes dry," she announced.

"I don't think that's wise," Nuritha started to say.

"It's fine," I intervened. I should have been more cautious. Something was overriding my judgment. "We can see the bottom the entire way across. The water's perfectly clear. Nothing is living there."

"It's a little too clear if you ask me," muttered Nuritha.

"I won't go far," said Tammartin. I just want to get the last of the smell out of my hair. I will leave the communicator here because I don't want to lose it in the water."

Nuritha started to object, but Tam had already removed the earpiece and placed it with her clothes. She waded resolutely into the water. When it reached her waist, she transitioned smoothly into a breaststroke. She ducked her head under the water at intervals and appeared five to ten meters further on. She was a good swimmer.

A V-shaped disturbance appeared in the water, heading straight towards her. Nuritha keyed her mike. "Tam! Heads up! There's something in the water!"

"She can't hear you."

Tam must have sensed the unknown presence. She stopped swimming and stood up, the water reaching only to her navel. The disturbance in the water ceased as well, stopping a few meters away. A crystal-clear humanoid form rose from the water to face her. It made an open-handed gesture that seemed to indicate peaceful intent.

Tam was too stunned to reply.

There followed a standoff of several minutes. The drone was too far away to pick up sounds, and we didn't dare bring it closer. We couldn't hear if they were trying to communicate. We watched in silence, Nuritha visibly anxious. I was divided. I didn't know what danger Tam was in, but at the same time, I had a deep certainty that this was what we had been sent to find on this survey. This encounter would determine our success.

The transparent figure was mimicking Tam's movements now and also coming to resemble her shape more closely. "Is it trying to communicate?" Nuritha breathed.

It reached out one arm in an apparent gesture of welcome. Tam reciprocated. That was when everything went sideways and simultaneously exactly as planned. The alien being enveloped Tam's hand in its own. It flowed up her arm and across her shoulders. Tam tried to pull back but was held fast. The glistening coating poured down over her body, covering her breasts, her belly, her legs. Simultaneously, it rose to cover her face and after a hesitation, her hair. She had ceased to struggle and almost looked like she was cooperating.

The intertwined figures fell into the water. I couldn't tell whether I was watching lovers fall into a bed or prey falling into a trap. They roiled the waters, sending up clouds of silt from the bottom. We lost sight of Tam.

"Looking for a spot to put the ship down," said Nuritha.

"We've got to pull her out."

"How long does it take us to go from orbit to ground?"

"Uh, we're in synchronous orbit, so about two hours."

"How long do you think Tam can hold her breath?"

Nuritha bit her lip.

"She's resourceful. She'll have to get herself out of it."

"Captain ... Samara ... How can you be so calm about this?"

"This ... this was Commander Batson's plan all along." Fragments of something were returning. Something Batson called a Deep Briefing. Something I wouldn't remember until an event triggered it.

"You let her go down knowing this would happen?" Nuritha's tail lashed in fury. Her claws emerged, digging into the armrest of her chair. I had pushed her too far. The Kaence had a strong taboo against showing their claws unless they intended harm. For the first time, I wished I had my sidearm.

Drew interjected, "Something rather dire is happening down there."

Our attention snapped back to the viewscreen. The water was roiling once more. Something moved beneath the surface, edging toward the shore. We held our breath. Finally, Tammartin burst through the surface of the pond. She shook droplets from her hair and wiped her eyes with her hands. She spun, orienting herself, then headed for her pile of clothes on the beach. There was no sign of the alien lifeform.

"Talk to us, Tam!" said Nuritha, on the edge of her seat. "Put on your communicator." Tam reached the equipment pile and started pawing through it, appearing somewhat dazed. Her hand fell on the communicator. She stared at it for a moment as if trying to remember its purpose. Finally, she put it in her ear.

"Tam! Are you all right?" Tam flinched a bit at Nuritha's volume.

"I'm … fine. I don't think it wanted to hurt me. It felt … curious."

"Get dressed and get back to the flyer. We need to check you out."

I didn't countermand Nuritha's orders, though she exceeded her authority in aborting the survey. Everything had unfolded according to some plan, not mine, and without my full understanding. A part of me protested being manipulated this way, yet I found myself strangely detached, unable to summon the outrage that seemed appropriate.

Tam fumbled with the clothes and equipment but became steadier as she got herself together. Nuritha sent the drone ahead to scout a path back to the landing point with the most solid ground. In contrast to how she had fumbled with her clothes, Tam was sure and unhesitating about finding solid ground.

Nuritha turned to me, challenging. "That's not Tam, is

it?"

"What makes you say that?"

"I shouldn't have to spell it out for you. She didn't gasp for air when she surfaced. She's generally clumsy and dazed, but she acts like she knows every square meter of that marsh. What more are we going to find when she gets on board? And what do you know about it?"

"Commander Batson had an agenda that he didn't share with us. We just found out what it was. I learned about it the same time you did." That wasn't strictly true, was it?

"I still think you're taking it too calmly."

I looked her in the eye. "When have you ever known me to lose my cool?"

A human would have lowered her eyes to signal that she was backing down. Kaence don't have that instinct. She held my eyes for a full minute, then deliberately turned back to the controls. "So, now what?"

"Right now, standard protocol after any alien contact. Quarantine until we find out how this has affected her."

"And if it has? If that's not Tam?"

"We'll cross that bridge when we come to it."

Two hours later, the flyer docked with the *Dry Whitt*. The quarantine tunnel was in place from flyer to med lab, a shimmerwall that prevented escape from its confinement. After Tam had passed, it collapsed to a thin line and flared white as it sterilized the air within. In the med lab, a cube of the same shimmerwall kept Tam isolated from the rest of the ship. Drew manifested within the cube, the one place where he could create a physical presence with the same force fields that made up the walls. He appeared dressed in the tweeds of a country doctor, carrying an old-fashioned black satchel. He approached Tam, asking with rustic concern, "Quite the ordeal, wasn't it? How are we feeling?"

"A bit disoriented, to tell the truth. I don't remember much of the actual encounter."

It sounded like Tam. My hopes rose that she was still herself.

"I would like to do a few tests to make sure. We'll start with a simple blood sample, followed by some X-rays."

"I'm fine, really. I just want to get back to my post."

"Regrettably, I must insist."

Tam paused as if she were looking up something, even though she didn't have computer access in quarantine. "You need my consent to perform any medical tests, and I do not give you that consent."

"Indeed, under Concordium law, you have the right to withhold consent, but I cannot release you from quarantine until I am fully satisfied that you do not pose a risk to the ship. Drew subtly shifted his posture, gaining a few centimeters in height and adding more gravitas to his words. Additionally, I am intrigued by the deck sensors indicating that you are two kilograms heavier than your pre-landing weight. Concordium law only applies to member species who have signed the accords."

My hope for Tam died with her refusal to submit to tests — most unlike her — and Drew's revelation.

I opened the med bay door to confront what appeared to be my crewmember — and friend. Only the transparent isolation shimmerwall protected me. "You can drop the pretense. We know that you aren't Tammartin."

"I am Tammartin. I have all her memories."

Her delivery was stilted, nothing like Tam's usual sparkle. Our Tam was gone — and I was responsible.

Then she looked up and smiled brightly. "I'm ready to get back to my duties now. I feel nearly one hundred percent again. I know you're short-handed. I can handle anything that Tam could do." And it was Tam's smile and Tam's lilt again. Perfectly. My heart broke.

"Not a chance. I won't let a murderous slime eat the rest of my crew."

Outside the med lab, I faced the fury of a betrayed Kaence. "You knew what was going to happen," she accused. "You deliberately sent Tam down there to be killed, didn't you? Why?"

"Batson. He buried a mission in my brain that was triggered when we found this planet. Our mission was to collect a Periphage. A Shapestealer. Find the world that they originate from and make sure that at least one of us survives to bring that intelligence back to the Concordium."

Nuritha grabbed me by the shoulders and slammed me

into the wall. Her claws pricked me through the thin fabric of my tunic. "You changed the protocol to send her down alone. You knew. You knew, and you still sent her down. Don't play innocent!"

I straightened up and clutched for the shreds of my authority. Our relationship had never depended on rank. We respected each other. Hell, we even slept together in a non-romantic way. Now, I had to save her from doing something rash.

"Lieutenant! Stand down. We have a mission to complete. It isn't the one you signed on for. It isn't the one I signed on for either. But we're going to finish it. I'm not letting you get court-martialed for assaulting your Captain, no matter how much I deserve it."

"Using a crew member as bait is a crime and is grounds for legal mutiny. I'm relieving you of command to stand trial when we reach Auphari."

Drew's avatar appeared in the corridor, back to his butler persona. "I'm afraid I can't allow you to do that, Nuritha. Captain Whitt had full authority to act as she did. Please cooperate unless you want some time to meditate in the brig."

Nuritha held me pinned for a slow count of twenty, her pupils dilated in rage, then narrowing with calculation. She released me and stepped back. "You could at least have had the integrity to sacrifice yourself instead. This isn't over," she said as she stalked away.

I looked down at my shoulders, where crimson droplets were wicking into the fabric of my shirt. "Drew, set a course for Auphari. Top speed. And keep Tam under surveillance. Er, not Tam. Whatever that is that looks like Tam. Even if it changes and looks like someone else. If it can do that."

"Yes, Captain. You sound rattled."

"Yes. I'm going back to my cabin. Keep tabs on Nuritha. Make sure she doesn't do anything rash."

Back at my desk, I unsealed a private file that I didn't know was there, using a password I hadn't known before that moment. I coded an ansible message to Commander Batson as directed by the orders in the file and sent it off to Auphari. Then I sat and stared at the wall.

I felt hollow. The Concordium had used me to carry out this mission that would inevitably end in the sacrifice of one of my crew without my consent.

Oh, shit, I hoped I hadn't consented.

It sucked to have untrustworthy memories.

Nuritha's accusation that the honorable thing to have done was to sacrifice myself was devastating. I think someone else had chosen for me, but how could I know?

Batson had to make sure I survived to retrieve the Periphage. With their volatile natures, they probably didn't want a shape-changing Kaence on their hands. That left Tam.

Who was added to my crew specifically for this mission.

Shit.

I was dancing as a puppet to someone else's tune just as much as Tam was. Maybe she had the easier time of it since she didn't appear to realize what she had lost.

Drew interrupted my bleak thoughts. "Captain, we've been diverted from Auphari. We're to rendezvous with another ship at a star system twenty light-years from here and are directed to transfer the captive to them."

My orders made no mention of this. "Is there a reason given for this change?"

"It's implied that the purpose of the transfer is to break the trail so spies can't trace our course back to the Shapestealer homeworld. The transfer point is eighty-three degrees off from the direct course to Auphari. Additional transfers may be planned, but they haven't shared them with us."

"I assume you've authenticated the code that was used?"

"I admire your caution, Captain. Of course, I have validated the source."

"Very well. Change course. What's our ETA?"

"Twenty hours."

"Good enough. Give me some privacy for a few hours."

"Yes, Captain."

Now that I had a moment to think, I was furious with the Concordium in general and Batson in particular. I had killed a friend and destroyed my relationship with Nuritha. For what? What was worth that cost?

What did I know about Periphages? I hadn't heard that word until the briefing surfaced in my head. Shapestealer, another name for the same creature, was more familiar. An old boogie man. Something that could steal your face. Legends differed on whether they took over your body (presumably killing you) or just copied your shape. How could the Concordium use that? (Assuming they could get Periphages to work for them.)

Spies and assassins came to mind. Take over a bodyguard and put a bullet in your target. Heck, get close and take over your target, then quietly melt away when no one is watching. Or take over an opposition figure and moderate their views. They would be an insidious weapon, most effective if kept a secret. One the Concordium would not want to be used by its rivals.

One Periphage would be of limited use. The most important cargo we had was the location of the Periphage homeworld, which would enable the capture of as many Periphages as needed.

Suddenly, I didn't want the Concordium to have that information. No one should have it.

We hadn't transmitted the planet's location. That was only to be handed over to Batson in person. Batson wouldn't trust such an important secret to the communication network, even in code.

But I could find this planet again. So could Nuritha. Following that logic, delivering the coordinates to Batson was our death sentence. I had to erase them from Drew's memory. I turned to the keyboard on my desk.

A half-hour later, I finished reading the maintenance logs for last year. Everything was in order.

Wait, wasn't there something else I meant to do when I sat down? Let's see. I had been thinking about our mission. The planet's coordinates. Dangerous knowledge.

Oh shit. My subliminal mission briefing had intervened to distract me from interfering.

Next time, I'd probably end up cleaning the galley.

I could only do tasks that aligned with our mission.

I could work with that.

I was hanging my new painting on the common room wall when we made contact. I had done an oil painting of most of the worlds we had visited to pass the long periods of boredom inherent in space travel. This was in the same style but had been run off by the replicom overnight rather than brushed by hand as the other half-dozen hanging nearby had been.

Drew appeared nearby. "It's a centimeter low on the right. As an aside, I've been hailed by a ship loitering near an asteroid. Non-standard configuration, probably running under a false registry as well. Seems like a sketchy crowd."

That didn't sound like a courier that Batson would send. "Let me know when you can get visual identification." I started for the bridge but then detoured to check on the captive.

Nuritha was sitting in the med lab, just outside the confinement cube. "What are you doing here?" I inquired. That wasn't what I wanted to say but I didn't know how to repair our rift.

"I'm trying to understand this ... creature. Sometimes it acts like Tam did and remembers things we've done together. Sometimes it's like a newborn, looking around and trying to understand the world. It seems to think in colors and tastes and smells."

"It sounds like you've forgiven it for Tam."

If Nuritha's glare had claws I would be in bloody shreds. "I never blamed the Periphage. It's a predator. I respect predators. You're the one who put her in the predator's path."

"I'm sorry." It seemed inadequate. "But I need you now. Something about this handoff feels off-kilter. This isn't standard Concordium procedure, even their black ops. But even if it is the Concordium, we're in danger. The knowledge we have is too risky to let us live."

"Don't rendezvous. Turn around and run."

"Thought about it." And I knew that my instructions would prevent me from doing that.

"The Captain is alluding to the fact that that isn't an option I can allow," Drew's disembodied voice said.

"So, what do we do?"

"We try to negotiate our way out of this." I hope she

remembered my aphorism from our free-lance days. *Negotiation is best conducted with a targeting lock on the other party.*

Drew broke in. "The ship is maneuvering to dock with us. It is transmitting correct Concordium IFF codes. However, the match I have in the ship registry for their configuration is a private ship registered to Max Salrach Holdings. I am unable to resolve this discrepancy."

Nuritha and I looked at each other. "Who is ..." she started. "Max Salrach is a Syndicate boss," I overrode her. "There must be a mole in Batson's operation. Arm yourself."

We had been more heavily armed than necessary for a survey ship — until I discovered our true mission. Now, it seemed entirely inadequate. We opened the arms locker to find worse news. All the most potent arms were projectile weapons — a really bad idea on a spaceship. Nuritha chose a Vihtanen z50 needle gun for its high accuracy. I picked up a Sancristan sonic pulse canon for its stopping power.

The Syndicate ship had docked in the port-side airlock opposite the med lab. We overturned some tables in the common room midway between the two and waited.

Footsteps approached from the direction of the docked ship. We had positioned ourselves out of the line of sight of the passageway, hoping for an element of surprise. The attackers anticipated us and stopped just short of revealing themselves. A gruff voice called out, "We just want the

Periphage. Hand it over and you can be on your way."

I slashed a "no" sign to Nuritha. They wouldn't want any witnesses, especially those who could return to capture another Periphage. I was already putting this battle in the category "We can't win but we can make them pay dearly."

Nuritha put her Vihtanen on the deck and slid it across the room. She stood up, hands in the air. "Take me with you. I'm done with the Concordium. I'm done with hypocrisy. The Periphage trusts me; I can help you with it." She looked at me. "Put down your weapon, Samara. Redeem what Batson made you do."

I almost did. I started to lower it, but then conditioning kicked in and I snapped it back up to my shoulder. That was just enough time for one of the thugs in the boarding party to step into the room and get the drop on me. When I brought my pulse cannon back up, the boarder pulled his trigger.

I was down against the bulkhead, a dreadful numbness spreading down my side. I turned my head and saw that it was because my arm and shoulder were no longer there. The energy weapon had burned halfway through the wall; I had offered much less resistance.

Through my shock, I heard orders being barked. "Get the Periphage. Download the logs. Grab everything that looks valuable; make it look like pirates." I saw Nuritha returning from the med lab, escorting the being that wore

Tam's face. I saw the boarders ripping open maintenance hatches and slapping connections on data terminals. I saw others gathering anything that might look valuable from our stores and equipment.

Nuritha took a look over her shoulder as she left me on the deck. "I understand predators," were her final words. The only explanation for her action. Her native language didn't have a term for "sorry."

One of the boarding party started ripping my paintings from the wall. Another said, "Take those with us. I know a collector." There went the frame containing my last composition, made last night.

The last one out tossed a flat disk on the floor as a final gesture. I recognized it as an EMP bomb that would fry all the electronics on board. It would kill Drew. It would kill life support and kill me if my injuries didn't do the job first. The hatch closed. The bomb counted down to zero. The lights went out.

A white light cut the darkness from one side. Had the emergency lights gone on? Shadows moved against the lights. The boarders hadn't left yet and would finish me off now. I groped for a weapon but restraints held me fast. Something pricked my arm. Darkness returned.

I awoke in a functional bed in a functional room. I lay still for a long time, trying to piece together my memories.

I had gone somewhere, been in a fight. I had been injured. I didn't feel any pain now, other than a headache. I raised my right hand. I had lost it, hadn't I? I had a hand again, but it didn't look like mine. It was too large and hairy.

My movement must have alerted someone. A figure came in, shone a light in my eyes, checked a display of vital signs that I hadn't noticed yet, and left without saying anything. Ten minutes later, Batson came in.

He was wearing a different face, meaning he had been in the field again. He could fool most people, but he had a penetrating look and a way of leading with his right shoulder that I could always pick out.

He spared only a brief glare before spelling it out. "You really screwed that one up. You lost the Periphage and both crew members. Your ship is a total loss, along with the coordinates to the Periphage homeworld. We recovered a few fragments from your AI's memory core, but that just led us to a series of rocky worlds."

I tried out my voice. "There's a mole ..." It was husky and much too deep.

"Yes, we have a mole in their organization, which you weren't supposed to know. That's how we learned that the Periphage escaped shortly after they reached their base. It's been nearly a year, and the trail has gone cold. At least the Syndicate doesn't have it."

A year? What happened to the last year of my life? What happened to ...? "Nuritha," I croaked.

Batson's mouth set. "She chose her side. If I knew where she was, I would put out a kill order on her."

I raised my hand again to inspect it.

"You're still useful to us, so we gave you a brand-new body. Since all your clones failed, we used DNA from your brother as the closest match." He saw the question in my eyes. "He's still missing; we used a blood sample we kept on file. It's more convenient this way. You have a cover story all ready to walk into."

"Cover story for what?"

"You will be Partitioned, with an outer persona as a solo smuggler. You'll make contacts with Syndicate operatives, gain their confidence. When you find their Periphage research lab, it will trigger instructions to come back home to report in. Better hope you find it because that's the only way you'll escape that little prison in your head. From personal experience — you'll want that freedom badly by then."

THE COLOR OF AGENCY

THE MEMORY REPLAY faded away. Pieces of the puzzle that had previously been missing were unexpectedly found again. Pieces that had seemed to fit in one place were moved to a new place on the board. And the biggest piece…

«I'm not Samuel? I'm Samara? I've been my own missing sister this whole time?»

«The hell you are. I'm Samara! You're *the Periphage that killed Tammartin and ate me!»*

The voice was mine in a higher register. (Don't ask me how that works when there are no vocal chords involved. Maybe it's our self-image.) Samara had been with us the entire time, behind the Partition.

Color of Air said, «*In my defense, Tammartin was the bait you used to catch me.*»

«*Whose voice was that?*»

I said, «*That's Color of Air.*»

«*And who are you?*»

Color of Air said, «*That's Samuel.*»

«*That's not Samuel. That's a construct, just a pile of scrapbook clippings that an AI ghostwriter compiled into a cardboard smuggler. I thought that persona was consumed along with my body.*»

I wasn't terribly pleased with her description of me. «*Color of Air wasn't able to absorb me, so she's been stuck with me the whole time. Couldn't you hear us?*»

«*I've been locked up all this time! After the Periphage ate you, all I got was a jumble of smells and sounds and tastes like I was hallucinating. I got a few images — Nuritha ... Medusa ... Batson. I hoped one of them would kill you, just to end the nightmare.*»

«*It's going to be very crowded in here with three voices in one body,*» I observed.

That was a mistake. That was the speck that caused her super-saturated solution of hate and anger to crystalize.

«*I'm not going to share a body with you!* she screamed. *Two years! Two years of watching you blunder around with my brother's face. Samuel was sharp. Clever. A good captain. He wouldn't have failed. He would have protected his crew.*»

«*You were in a no-win situation …*»

Rapier's voice broke in on the communicator. "Captain, a small ship just overflew our landing position. It is heading directly towards you and should arrive in two minutes or less."

I swore. "Where did they come from?"

"It appears to have been clamped to a blind spot on my hull. I believe that we inadvertently gave them a ride here. It doesn't look like a warp-capable ship."

"Is it manned? Did Batson have an accomplice?"

"You're about to find out."

Moments later, a small flier banked overhead and came to rest on the narrow grassy shore of the pond. It could have parked inside my cabin on the *Rapier Whitt* with room to spare. If this vessel was manned, its occupant was flying inside a coffin.

A hatch hinged open in the top of the flier. A pale figure sat up and surveyed the tableau before him: us on one side in Tammartin's form and Arianthe on the other side rising out of the pond beneath her tree. I looked at the face in the hatch in disbelief. "You're dead!" I blurted.

"Very much alive, though I admit it hasn't been the most enjoyable trip," said Batson, wearing the face of Ambassador Alexander. "I knew you'd eventually bungle your way to the goal."

"But we killed you! Color of Air ripped your heart out."

"Common mistake, thinking that I have a heart. No one

295

makes it more than once."

"I tossed the rest of the body into space."

"I'd already reloaded into this backup body in my pod outside your hull. I didn't expect you to defeat me, but I always make contingency plans. My reinforcements should be here soon."

I didn't tell him I had redirected his reinforcements to the wrong planet, parsecs away. Overconfidence might be his Achilles heel. It had been once already.

Arianthe grew until she loomed over us once again. When she spoke, to my surprise, she used human language. Language that she could only have acquired by absorbing visitors and her own periphages. She embodied a multitude of researchers and intelligence officers all by herself. It also presaged the fate of Color of Air and me if we failed to make our case.

"Who is this intruder? It was not in the gestalt you offered. I become suspicious."

"He is Batson, who threatened to sterilize your planet."

"He can change shape? He does not smell like one of us."

"He's not an Arilune. It's a crude process ..."

Batson vaulted down from his pod, cradling a device that resembled a breach-loading musket, though I doubted it fired anything so crude as lead shot. He didn't gloat. Didn't threaten. He simply raised the barrel, took aim, and fired.

The projectile was small, barely more than a pellet, and carried little velocity. It struck Arianthe with a wet splat, barely penetrating her translucent skin before blooming within her form like ink dispersing in water. She only looked puzzled at first. Then her expression darkened.

"You attack me with alcohol? With Rot? Do you hope to lure me into consuming you so that you can strike from within? I was warned you would try this."

Batson set down his gun and straightened. "No," he said. Then he collapsed.

We rushed to him but covered the last few meters with extreme caution. Arianthe summoned defenders in the form of uniroos with their unicorn horns, alligator birds, and snakes that dripped venom that seared the nearby leaves. Batson didn't move. He wasn't breathing. There was no pulse visible in his neck.

"Looks like you saved us the trouble of killing him again," I remarked to Arianthe.

"I did not do that."

Color of Air took over. "Your skin is tough enough to stop nearly anything. How did he get a bullet through it?"

"The alcohol — it was a jacket around the outside of the bullet to weaken my skin. If he had fired many such bullets, he might have damaged me. I will need to develop countermeasures before others try again."

I had lost track of the conversation with Samara. While we were distracted, her grievance had been crystallizing.

Now she lashed out at me with a word. It wasn't a word that could be pronounced or written down. It bypassed all the higher parts of the brain and went directly to the slumbering lizard brain. I couldn't process it as a word. It was an angry hornet buzzing in my thoughts. It tore them from each other, making it impossible to think. I tried to ask what was happening, but I could not form a word before the hornet shredded it. I tried to call out but only managed a wordless wail of pain and terror. My mind was coming apart. Samara had used the codeword to end my persona.

I was unraveling—scattering into drifting motes of consciousness, dissolving into the void. This was how the universe ended, writ small. Then, something smothered the buzzing hornet. A claw—not mine, not Samara's, but familiar—reached in, prying the codeword from the center of my mind. It came loose in strands, tangled like Medusa's tendrils in the gray matter I only imagined I still had. Color of Air. She yanked the hornet free and flung it into the abyss.

But the damage was done. The fragments of me were expanding, scattering outward like debris from a shattered hull. There was no center, no gravity to pull them back together. My last thought—if it could even be called that— was that I had been real enough to die. *Non cogito, ergo non sum.*

Then something pulled at me. My scattered bits slowed,

stopped, and began falling inward, drawn toward a warm glow. What was happening? I had expected nothing—accepted nothing—yet here was something. I wasn't prepared to revise a lifetime of cynicism (albeit possibly a constructed lifetime) at the last moment. Let there be nothing.

A voice came.

«*Samuel? Can you hear me, Samuel?*»

It was Color of Air. I could hear, but I couldn't yet answer.

«*Samuel, you have to come back. I need you. I'll tell Samara that you're real, you're just not her Samuel. I'll make her understand. I'll keep her from hurting you.*»

«*Samuel, I love you.*»

Maybe I was dead. Maybe this was some alternate universe. Because that confession couldn't have come from the Color of Air I knew.

I moved toward the light. I felt its pull. Someone wanted me. Could I say the same? I opened myself to the possibility.

Slowly I settled back to coherence. I seemed to have all my pieces together again, but if something was missing how would I know?

«*Samuel? Are you ok?*»

«*I seem to be in one piece. What happened?*»

«*Samara lost her connection to reality in the isolation within her Partition. She blamed you, though you had nothing to do with it. I've restrained her until we can help her.»*

«I thought I was a goner.»

«I thought I had lost you. I didn't know if I could contain your memories and recompress them.»

«What you said...»

«It surprised me too. I'm not sure I understand love...»

«You and all the poets who ever lived.»

«... but I knew I would feel a tremendous loss if you were gone.»

This was hard. *«I would feel the same way if you were gone.»*

«Is that love?»

«It's a good working definition.»

I was a construct, wasn't I? Was I qualified to know?

«What are we going to do about Samara?» asked Color of Air.

«Can we split her off into her own body the way you and I did?»

«In theory. I don't know of any Arilune who has split before, so we're in uncharted territory with just two, let alone three.»

We were still in Tammartin's form. We dropped our clothes to avoid embarrassing entanglements as we fissioned. We'd practiced with two of us, but now we had three, and one wasn't cooperating. I left the finesse up to Color of Air. She started the plasma streaming in two directions. I joined Color of Air in the left-flowing stream while pushing Samara into the right-flowing stream. Moments later, she stood before us, naked and vulnerable, staring down at herself in disbelief.

We turned to Arianthe to see how she was taking these developments.

Something was wrong. Her normal clear color had taken on a mustardy tinge. She swayed, batting at the air as if warding off invisible midges. Her features slumped and dripped and reformed as if she couldn't decide which form to take.

"Mother, what's wrong?" called Color of Air.

"An evil … is inside my head. It is trying to take control."

I tried to reach the communicator to talk to Rapier, but Color of Air stopped my hand.

«*A last resort only. If all else fails,*» I said.

She relented. I keyed the communicator. "Rapier, move the ship here immediately. Hover over this location. Lock forward lasers on Arianthe but do not fire unless I give the order. Or if I'm dead."

«*All she has to do is submerge. The water will dissipate the heat from the lasers before it does damage.*»

«*Then we'd better not fail.*»

«*Do you know what's happening?*»

«*That.*»

Arianthe's face was at war. One side, the serene blue visage from the lake, twisted with growing horror. The other was Batson's—cold, impassive, utterly focused. It was not the blandly handsome face of Alexander from

Raxas but the face I'd last seen aboard the ship, intent and calculating.

«*What has he done?*»

«*Accomplished his goal, or at least phase one. He's gotten inside Arianthe and is attempting a takeover. The bullet. It wasn't meant to wound her—it was a carrier. There had to be a receiver matrix inside it. When the casing dissolved, Batson used his mind-transfer tech to jump in. That's why it had such low velocity—he didn't want it to pass through. He wanted it to stick.*»

I picked up the weapon that Batson had dropped. There was no more ammo. Was there more in the pod? We searched the coffin-like space for more, wondering how he had managed the trip without going mad. Or perhaps he had. We came up empty.

«*Samuel, what can we do?*»

I fumbled for the disruptor controller in our thigh pouch and pulled it free. «*Can you get the disk out?*»

Color of Air plunged our hand into our chest, straining to reach it. It was too deep, the angle too awkward.

"What are you doing?" Samara was crouched on the ground, arms around her legs, but watching us warily.

"There's a weapon that Batson used against us that's still lodged in our chest. I hoped we could use it against him, but I can't reach it."

"I don't want to help you, but Batson terrifies me." She exhaled sharply, as if trying to expel whatever argument she was having with herself. "Let me try."

She rose from her crouch but didn't approach immediately. Her gaze flicked to our face, measuring. Then, steeling herself, she stepped closer and stretched out her hand, stopping just short of touching us. "Where?"

"Here," I guided her. "It's a small disk, about palm-sized. I don't have internal organs, so if you hit something solid, that's it."

Samara hesitated, searching our face.

"Does it matter who I appear to be?" asked Color of Air. "Should I take Samuel's form?"

"Stars, no! I couldn't stand that. Just ... Not Tammartin, ok?"

"Sorry, I should have thought." She hesitated for a moment, then became Smanester. He should be a neutral choice.

Samara's lips pressed into a thin line. "This is disgusting." She closed her eyes and thrust her hand in. We staggered with the force. Her angle was better than ours, letting her reach deep enough to brush the disk. Her fingers scrabbled at the edge, searching for a grip.

"What does it do?" she asked, groping inside our chest.

I raised the control box in our hand, showing its single button and simple mechanical dial. "The disk emits high-frequency sound waves. Batson used it to force us into two separate bodies."

Her grip slipped, just shy of catching hold.

She steadied herself, bracing a hand behind our neck to keep us from staggering, then stepped in and shoved hard. Her fingers at last closed around the disk.

With a sharp yank, she tore her fist free. A wet, sucking sound made her gag, her face twisting in revulsion. The hole left behind was bloodless, sealing itself shut in seconds.

"Thank you," I said. "I wasn't sure which side you would be on."

"My own!" Samara shot back. She grabbed the control unit from our hand and sprinted towards Arianthe, waist-deep in the water under her tree, the battle still raging within her. Her body was roiled by discordant colors and screamed sulfur and ozone, saltpeter and decay. Samara misjudged the depth of the pond, forgetting that Arianthe was three meters tall. When the water reached her chest, she slipped on the muddy bottom and disappeared in the murk. When she surfaced, spluttering, she struck out towards her goal.

She reached the roiling battlefield and tried to stand. The water rose to her neck, tossing her like driftwood. She drove her fist forward, trying to shove the disk into Arianthe's body, but she barely reached Arianthe's belly and had no leverage to push further. Her fist struck and slid uselessly. She pounded the rubbery skin in frustration.

«We need something that can reach ramming speed.»
«On it.»

We took three running strides and launched into a flat dive. Mid-plunge, we shifted—surfacing as a Cyraenan. A few powerful strokes sent us surging across the pond.

Samara whirled toward the disturbance. Her body tensed, eyes widening in shock. She had never seen one of the merfolk before.

"It's us! Don't take your eye off Batson!" I called.

It probably wasn't a good tactical move to call out an enemy's name at close range. A massive arm arced through the air, striking us with bone-rattling force and sending us crashing into the water—like swatting a pesky fly. I couldn't tell whether it was Arianthe or Batson in control—or if they were both flailing for dominance.

We broke the surface, disoriented but unharmed, scanning frantically for Samara.

We found her— suspended above the water, Arianthe's massive fingers curled around her like a cage. Her body was pressed against the giant's torso, her edges blurring, melting into the shifting mass.

Just before she was fully engulfed, she forced her left hand open, palm up—empty.

«*Samara dropped the controller! She used herself as bait to get the disk inside and told us to find the controller and use it!*» In desperation, she had decided to trust us.

We dove to the bottom and scrabbled frantically in the muck. Visibility was zero, scent and taste useless in the churning water. If it had been crushed underfoot, we were out of options. If we were crushed underfoot, it wouldn't matter. Minutes passed, then a log bumped us.

Maybe old movies gave me a sense of narrative inevitability. Maybe it was ancestral memories of the dangers of the water hole. I grabbed full control of our body and bolted just as huge alligator jaws crashed shut. We lost the end of one fluke but it was a lot less of a mouthful than the gator had been aiming for. We sculled backwards in the water, watching the shadow of the predator come closer.

«*Get ready to move,*» I said.

«*It's all yours.*»

The gator lunged. I veered behind the towering figure's legs—Arianthe's, Batson's, or some unstable fusion of the two. The gator twisted ninety degrees as it came, operating by instinct. It sank its teeth deep into the leg and hung on, thrashing its head from side to side to try to break bones.

The result was chaos. The figure staggered, then kicked, sending the gator flailing through the air. It splashed down, undeterred, and lunged again. The colossal form twisted, trying to stomp it into the mud. The fight receded out of sight in the murky water.

«*That's one of Arianthe's creatures, isn't it? Why is it still attacking?*»

«*Batson seized it to take us out, but now they've both lost control of it. It's a menace to everyone.*»

We dove again, blindly sifting through the muck. The

water became still, but the silence itself was wrong. The usual hum of life had vanished. No fish, no distant clicks of stones shifting—only a low pressure that built in my ears, as if the water itself was holding its breath.

Focus. Hands sweeping through the sludge, we clawed through tangled roots and smooth stones, searching for something small, something metal, something that had no business being in this pond. Nothing.

We surfaced to take stock of the situation. Arianthe stood motionless, her form shifting like oil slicks—colors bleeding into each other, features wavering. The translucent blue of her original form flickered in and out, replaced by the colder planes of Batson's face. No thrashing, no flailing—just an eerie stillness, like a computer glitching, the program fighting itself for control. No, like a computer fighting off a virus. Batson was a virus invading Arianthe.

We dove again. The silence pressed in, unnatural. Our hands met nothing but mud and smooth, lifeless stones. Then—something. Sharp edges. Solid weight.

We yanked it free and shot toward the surface, breaking into the air and crashing onto the shore, Color of Air shifting our form just in time to land on steady feet.

I had it. Now to use it.

Out in the water, the battle raged on. Batson was winning. His face dominated now, exuding cold triumph, while Arianthe's presence flickered in and out, despair etched in the remnants of her features.

The *Rapier Whitt* hovered in the sky as I had asked. Not time for last resorts yet.

I punched the button on the control unit, hoping it still worked. Mud wasn't in its design specs. Samara sacrificed herself to deliver the disruptor to the target. It had to work. Stop. Focus.

I turned the dial. Arianthe shuddered to a chaotic wave, crisscrossing, threatening to cancel itself out. I turned more and it worsened. The other direction. Order appeared, the beginnings of a standing wave. It formed up on the concentric pattern of a Faraday wave, locking into a strobe-static milk-drop splash. All motion froze. I remembered how painful this device was.

That was the first harmonic. Now I had to find the second harmonic. The chaos returned as I turned the dial farther; their paralysis eased a bit. I saw Batson's eyes look up and behind me. I wasn't stupid enough to fall for that trick.

A violent jolt from behind drove us forward two steps. Pain shot through us. I looked down. A meter of ivory horn jutted from our chest. An angry uniroo snorted at our back, trying to lift us bodily into the air. Other uniroos circled, waiting their turn at the shish kabob.

«*Can we hold together long enough?*» I asked Color of Air.

«*For now. We can survive a lot of damage.*»

I remembered blowing our hand off when we defeated

Magid. I didn't want to repeat that.

The pause allowed Batson an opening. He began to stride through the water towards us. Arianthe wasn't fighting him. I think they were both angry at the assault.

I turned the knob, seeking the second harmonic. They stopped at the edge of the water. Their minions didn't. The alligator lumbered onto the beach. A cobra uncoiled from the branches of a tree. Both locked onto us and closed in.

«*If you don't succeed soon, we're going to have to run.*»

«*Almost there.*» It wasn't working. Every time I approached the resonant frequency, something interfered. Batson? Arianthe? Something else? (Please don't be the mud.) The peak should be at just double the first harmonic …

I had a sudden inspiration. I twisted the knob past the second harmonic all the way to the third. Now the pattern fell into place. The mass gained three central peaks, which began to resolve into Arianthe, Batson … and Samara!

As they formed, I shifted the beam to cover just Arianthe and Batson. Samara hit the ground running. She sprinted to Batson's pod, yanked a bar from the inside of the door—a release mechanism, or so it seemed. The moment it came free, it became a sharpened pike. My mantra was, in a fight, everything's a weapon. Batson took it one step further and designed it into his tools.

Two figures faced us on the shore. Arianthe on the left and Batson on the right. Both had diminished to normal human size. Samara planted herself in front of Batson, pike at the ready.

«*Tell Arianthe in her language to have her animals back up Samara.*» Color of Air relayed the request. The uniroo behind us obliged, yanking its horn from our back and trotting forward to join Samara.

"His mind was open to me while I was inside," said Samara. "I have his Partitioning command."

She spoke a word, sharp and final, much like the one she had used on me earlier. Batson trembled. That should have buried him inside his own mind, pushing the more benign Alexander personality to the forefront.

Batson smiled. Then he collapsed.

I knew we were in trouble.

The lifeless body of Alexander twitched. Then his fingers flexed. A breath hitched in his throat. His eyes opened. Batson had transferred his consciousness back. He had escaped the Partition.

Two things happened at once, but it took a moment to register them both.

Arianthe plunged her hand into Batson's discarded body and pulled something free—a dark pellet, small but significant. A receiver. The anchor for his consciousness transfer. Tendrils of liquid shimmered around it as she began to spin a sphere of blackness, layer upon layer, folding over itself like a slow-forming pearl.

At the same instant, Samara stepped forward and drove

the pike into Alexander's heart. The force of the strike pinned him to the sand. His mouth opened in silent shock. He convulsed once, then went limp.

And yet—we saw the lights go out too quickly. Not just in his eyes, but deeper. A hollowing. A severing. Death wouldn't have worked that fast. The spear alone couldn't have done the job.

"He jumped again," I said.

We turned, searching for where he had gone.

Arianthe placed a black ball on the sand. "The rogue human is sealed in this cyst. Destroy the receiver in that body and he will have no other escape."

Samara rolled Alexander's body over. No hesitation. No ceremony. She drove the pike into the base of his skull, severing whatever remained. No escape. No return. It was done.

"Is Batson dead?"

Arianthe regarded the black cyst resting in her palm, turning it slowly, as if weighing something unseen. "No. He is alive." Her gaze lifted, luminous and impenetrable. "Fully aware, in fact."

She considered it for a moment, then cupped it in her palm as if cradling an ember. "He will stay in this cyst," she continued, "fully aware, trapped within himself." She closed her fingers. "And every so often, I will visit him. A small reminder of what happens to those who think they can claim my world."

Color of Air and I faced Arianthe. Any thought that she was in our debt and would allow us to walk away faded as she described Batson's fate. In her view, she owed us nothing. She would do whatever served her own interests.

Samara took the third corner of the triangle. Her stance was wary but firm. She had made her position clear—she wasn't with us, nor with Arianthe. She stood alone.

On impulse, I seized the initiative.

"That was very brave of you," I told Samara, "to sacrifice yourself to deliver the disruptor disk to where it was needed. You couldn't have known that you'd be coming back out."

She frowned. "I'm asking myself why I did that. I was already free from my prison. It didn't benefit me. I didn't have much reason to save you." A shadow crossed her face. "I think I was programmed to deliver a logic bomb if I ever got here. That's probably still lurking inside of me."

"We've all been manipulated by the Concordium," I said. "We can't fix that. We can't fix all the mistakes each one of us has made. But at least you've gotten back a body of your own again."

"But it's not my body! It's a horrible puddle of slime pretending to be a person!"

"Since everyone here is made of slime, we won't take offense."

"Am I going to have to eat people to survive now?"

That was a damn good question. It was still a wedge in

my relationship with Color of Air.

Arianthe floored us all by interjecting, "I send out two kinds of Arilune. What you call Periphages or Shapestealers have a compulsion to absorb other beings and return with the knowledge they've acquired. The other kind is more stealthy. They take a long-term role in society. They make sure my planet remains safe."

I said, "Let me guess. They're the ones who have been altering records to keep this world off the official charts."

"That is one of the services they have performed for me."

Faceless people who could replace anyone. The Concordium could be run by an entire shadow government of Arilune. That wasn't disturbing at all. I kept that to myself.

Color of Air spoke up. "Do you mean that you programmed me to consume people? That hunger I always felt? The pleasure I got from it? That was by design?"

"Yes," answered Arianthe. "That was the role I chose for you."

"Can I make a different choice? I no longer want to exist like that."

«I thought you reveled in your predator nature.»

«It causes you distress. You've changed my view on the practice of taking lives. If I change, will it make you happy?»

"Sleeper agents do not have that compulsion. Serving me in that way is the price for its removal."

«Don't make a hasty decision. We may be trading one

compulsion for another.»

"I accept ...," Color of Air said, ignoring my caution.

"Wait a minute," I said out loud. "You have new threats. The Concordium and the Syndicates are both seeking ways to use Arilune for their own purposes. Your old methods won't keep your world safe much longer. You need some agents-at-large who can combat this threat. That's something that we're uniquely suited to do." Why was I again in the position of bidding on jobs I didn't want?

"What is your proposition?"

"No compulsions, no pre-conceived roles. Mutual self-interest only. We agree it is not in your interest or ours to let the Concordium or the Syndicates develop shapeshifter technology or to capture and enslave Arilune. It's not in your interest to let more people discover the location of your planet. It's not in the Concordium's interest to become a puppet government for your purposes. We can only keep the balance if we're free agents, not beholden to either side."

"This is what you call 'bargaining,' no? It's an interesting process. I have not engaged in it before."

"I hope you develop a taste for it. There's likely a lot more of it in your future."

"Very well, I accept your proposal."

We turned to Samara. "Would you like to join us in our mission? I imagine you have an ax to grind with the Concordium."

Samara shuddered. "Join a shapeshifter wearing the body of the crewmember I murdered and a construct who thinks he's my long-lost brother. No thanks."

Arianthe considered her for a moment, unreadable. "You are newly made. Untested. You do not know the limits of your form, nor the extent of your weaknesses. You have some scars on your mind." Her tone was not unkind, but neither was it gentle. "I will teach you how to use your new body. In time, you may become useful to me."

Samara's eyes narrowed. "And if I'm not?"

"Then we will bargain. Passage elsewhere, in exchange for something of equal value." She tilted her head, considering. "It is, I am told, the way of your kind."

Color of Air said, "Samuel may not be your brother but he has evolved into a decent person in his own right."

"What does a Periphage know about decent people?"

"Since meeting Samuel, I've learned that the choices that we make matter greatly. I've met decent people in surprising places. Even Batson made decent choices when we first met him on Raxas. I'm choosing now to walk away from what I was made to be. So has Samuel. So can you."

Samara looked at us, expression unreadable. Something in that declaration had resonated, but I couldn't tell what. She looked at Arianthe. No one hurried her. Seconds ticked by.

"I'm staying for now. I can't get on a ship with you. I'll find my own way."

She turned and walked into the woods and was soon lost to sight.

"You always have," I said, too late for her to hear.

We turned to Arianthe. "It's time for us to leave. We need to make sure that Batson didn't leave a trail here and that his employers have been misled."

"One of my agents will contact you. They will make sure you have funding and resources."

That was it. A quiet binding. No grand speeches, no contracts signed, but we had an understanding. No empty promises, no hiding. Arianthe could find us wherever we went.

So could our enemies.

I glanced at the black cyst where Batson's last known copy was sealed. I had a sudden, unsettling certainty.

He had backups somewhere.

ABOUT THE AUTHOR

THANKS FOR READING *Periphage Blues*! While the story is still fresh in your mind, I'd love it if you left a review where you purchased the book. Even better, if you enjoyed it, tell a few friends or share it on social media. Word of mouth is the best way to help independent authors, and reviews are a close second. We don't have the advertising budgets of the big publishing houses (and let's be honest, you probably have ad blockers for those anyway).

If you have thoughts about the story—what resonated, what surprised you, or what you'd like to see more of— you can always reach me at **chuck@lamp.works**. I love hearing from readers.

I bring my career in science and technology to tales of science fiction and fantasy, leaning into the "sufficiently advanced technology" trope. Before telling the human stories set against that background, I tend to fill my notebook with celestial mechanics calculations and other research to ensure accuracy. (Don't worry, the math doesn't end up in the stories.)

My debut novel, *Sellenria*, has appeared on Amazon's top Hard Science Fiction list, while *Knots* explores a magical world based on topology. My short story *Charon* recently appeared in the anthology *Of Gods and Globes III*.

I live with my wife, Chidori, and our two cats, Rumplethumpkin and Yomogi, on the edge of Cayuga Lake in Upstate New York. When I'm not writing, I enjoy reading, gardening, cooking, and traveling the world. I've visited most places with high-energy physics labs and am now busy filling in the gaps in between

Once a month, I send out a newsletter with news, recommendations of books I've enjoyed, and books from other independent authors. Sign up at https://lamp.works/signup.

SELLENRIA – A SCIENCE FICTION ADVENTURE

Believing in the impossible may be my only chance of survival.

* * *

I was a professor of archaeology at the University of Trondhjem. I did digs via telepresence and lectured in simspace classrooms. Life was stable, predictable, just the way I like it. But then I found a relic that turned my world upside down. Now I'm stranded without hope of rescue on a pre-technological planet full of monsters and mysteries, hundreds of light-years from home. After a terrifying and nearly fatal encounter with a creature that couldn't possibly exist, I was rescued by a fey assassin who decided that I should become her apprentice. I became advisor to the king but now I'm on the run after we were framed for the assassination of his brother. It's mad enough to be a fantasy simspace, but it's deadly real.

The most confounding part is that these people think my ancestor was an ancient warlock and that I can wield those same powers. I'm a man of science, of order, of logic; I don't believe in magic.

But that's not the way this world works.

KNOTS – AN EPIC FANTASY

Resche crossed a bridge and can't go back. He can't even find the bridge.

* * *

Knots features a cast of eccentric and only conditionally-trustworthy characters that will appeal to fans of Roger Zelazny or Neil Gaiman. Or if you enjoy the inventive magic systems of Brandon Sanderson, let Knots introduce you to Topomancy. In this world, a precisely tied knot, an exactly folded paper, or a cunningly drawn figure can unlock wonders and horrors.

Resche, an art thief, finds himself in a quaint Swiss town that borders Spain on one side and South America on the other. Mages are engaged in playing a game of Geomancy with tiles the size of cities. When he is caught stealing from one of them, he becomes a pawn in their intricate game. The Fractalist priest is enigmatic, the Jeweler may not be what he seems, and the Astromancer turned up dead the night he consulted her. Emeline, the newspaper editor, seems sympathetic, but what are her motives? His companion Trefoil tells Resche to trust her, but what does a cat know (even a talking one)? It's time to find a way back to his own world, but the bridge he crossed has vanished in the fog.

Wouldn't you love to have a Knot of Confusion to use against your enemies? Step into the unique world of Knots today. Just remember your way back.

www.ingramcontent.com/pod-product-compliance
Lightning Source LLC
Chambersburg PA
CBHW050132120726
47903CB00002B/328